WHITEY'S KID

WHITEY'S KID

Hal Glickman

Copyright © 2000 by Hal Glickman.

ISBN #:   Softcover   0-7388-2809-2

All rights reserved. No part of this book may be reproduced or transmitted in any form or by any means, electronic or mechanical, including photocopying, recording, or by any information storage and retrieval system, without permission in writing from the copyright owner.

This is a work of fiction. Names, characters, places and incidents either are the product of the author's imagination or are used fictitiously, and any resemblance to any actual persons, living or dead, events, or locales is entirely coincidental.

This book was printed in the United States of America.

To order additional copies of this book, contact:
Xlibris Corporation
1-888-7-XLIBRIS
www.Xlibris.com
Orders@Xlibris.com

CONTENTS

PROLOGUE 9

CHAPTER 1 13
CHAPTER 2 24
CHAPTER 3 33
CHAPTER 4 38
CHAPTER 5 49
CHAPTER 6 57
CHAPTER 7 69
CHAPTER 8 73
CHAPTER 9 83
CHAPTER 10 93
CHAPTER 11 99
CHAPTER 12 105
CHAPTER 13 117
CHAPTER 14 129
CHAPTER 15 139
CHAPTER 16 148
CHAPTER 17 154
CHAPTER 18 160
CHAPTER 19 170
CHAPTER 20 177
CHAPTER 21 179
CHAPTER 22 184
CHAPTER 23 198
CHAPTER 24 207
CHAPTER 25 211
CHAPTER 26 219

CHAPTER 27	224
CHAPTER 28	237
CHAPTER 29	242
CHAPTER 30	247
CHAPTER 31	251
CHAPTER 32	268

*Dedicated to my wife,
Beatrice Marden Glickman,
who has enhanced my literary career
with her own unique psychological insights,
demonstrated in her poetry and early childhood
education literary accomplishments.*

PROLOGUE

September 1918.

The air that blanketed Triton Avenue was heavy with the sour smell of mudflats at low tide, and insufferably warm. All day a naked sun had generated columns of warm air over the village perched on a cliff overlooking the blue Atlantic. Now, as deep night began, unseen by the slumbering people, a dark island of cumulus clouds crept into the scene and anchored overhead. A cat on the prowl saw the thunderhead boiling up and wailed a warning to its mate.

An infant in its crib stirred uneasily and uttered a brief cry of protest.

However, it was a man, not nature, whose tension-laden presence threatened the peace of the frame dwelling—a broad-framed man whose close blond hair contrasted with the glorious chestnut waves of the woman sleeping alongside.

Even in repose the flesh around the man's chin was sucked tight to the bone. The squarely hewn fingers of an outstretched arm hooked the corner of the bedspread in a grip of steel. He slept in a state of perfect unrest, the inheritance of an imperfect waking existence, an existence that engendered more restraint than was good for him, more violence than was good for those about him.

Now the mild perturbation of baby thunder came on stage, waking the woman with chestnut hair. She rose to quiet the low whimper of her infant. Her husband slept on. He was the kind of man for whom neither the rustle of dry leaves before the wind nor the Titan symphony of thunderclouds could be said to have an audience. On the other hand, the keen upper register of his responsive self was entwined, chapter and verse, with the utterances of humans. He first lay impervious to the advancing storm, then sat upright when his child screamed in fright.

"Godammit to hell!" he exploded. "Can't you keep the little bastard quiet?"

The woman rushed to her son. Aided by a lull in the storm, her cooing and cradling finally took effect. The infant's crying subsided.

There was guarded peace for a time. Then the main event of the day, the year, the lifetime began to evolve. Within the turbulent cloud mass suspended close to the rooftops, infinite splittings of raindrops accumulated great charges of electricity. Suddenly a stroke of white lightning poured millions of volts into a tree not fifty feet from the front door of the dwelling. For a brief second, the faces inside were illumined, chalk white, marbleized. But only the sleepless, terror-filled eyes of the woman saw the hammer of Thor before it struck.

Thunder cracked directly overhead. The infant shrieked loudly, waking the father, who cursed the woman and her son. When the baby's crescendos showed no sign of coming under control, the man flung aside the bedclothes and got to his feet. Violence showed in his face when the woman screamed a protest.

"No, no! He's crying because he's wet. I'll change him!"

A fresh peal of thunder spurred the crying to still greater heights. The man wrested the child roughly from the mother, cursing all the while.

"He's a sonofabitch. I'll change him, all right!"

The child on his knee, the man's heavy hand fell on its backside. At first the blows came slowly, then, when the child's screams did not subside, the hand fell faster and faster.

The mother's attempts to rescue her child were brushed aside by a powerful forearm that hurled her to the floor. The man deposited the infant in his crib and laid stroke after stroke of a heavy leather belt against the tiny bared body. Now and then, between bouts of painful sobbing, the baby gazed upward at its tormentor.

But soon the eyes opened less often, the baby's face became a mask, the sobbing retreated and became a fitful whimpering that filled the room and spilled down a hallway to a small alcove where a brother buried his head under the pillow and wept quietly.

Three thousand miles eastward, a lean mustached man with the stripes of an army sergeant on his shoulder, pointed at distant puffs of gray smoke over the bridge at Chateau Thierry. He spoke quietly:

"I tell you, Dennis, where there's smoke, there's sure to be a fire fight and soon."

His companion, an undersized runt of a man, nodded and smiled, the smile deepening the creases around his mouth and eyes.

"You're right, Alex. It's time to bring up the reserves-Barney and Lester."

A low chuckle from the sergeant:

"I really don't like this bridge—let's do something about it."

CHAPTER 1

April 23, 1936. Dreamland Ballroom smelled of dried sweat, a bequest from the dancers who had swung and swayed the night before. To Herbie Roberts, coming into the day-dark caverns from the fresh April sunshine, the smell was an unpleasant shock. He half-held his breath and accelerated his pace across the expanse of glistening hardwood towards the distant bandstand.

A dozen musicians were cooperating in the final bars of what to Herbie's ears was a big band version of "Moon Over Miami". To the ears of bandleader Jack Charles, his sound was "off" because his regular pianist had quit at the close of the Friday night session. The ratatat of Herbie Roberts' leather heels on the waxed floors, far from being a distraction, represented a possible valuable replacement. Roberts was one of three candidates sent by union headquarters in response to Charles' call for help.

So it was with a pleasant wave of his baton that Charles acknowledged the bespectacled, sturdily built youth.

"You Roberts? Get your ass in gear—you're up."

Herbie thought these words lacked a certain warmth that he craved. But the challenge was here and now, and he was ready to convert five years of on-again, off-again interest in jazz piano into a steady weekend job. Now, a mustached fellow with slick black hair slid off the piano bench as Herbie approached. He evidently doubled on piano since he immediately picked up a saxophone and blew a few reedy notes.

Herbie crouched over the keys, sweaty fingers rippling off a difficult progression, a flashy effect he had practiced often.

"I'm ready. What do you want?" His voice, he hoped, reflected more self-assurance than he felt.

"We'll test your sight reading first, then we'll fake two choruses of "Night And Day" in the key of A, then we'll drop out and hear you play for Claire Strong in one chorus of "Tea For Two" in the key of G. You'll solo the transitions."

For the first time, Herbie saw the singer, a bosomy blonde in her mid-twenties dragging on a cigarette from a seat in front of the brass section. One hand went up as she heard her name, brightly painted nails twinkling hello in the glare of ceiling floods.

The score of a recent Broadway musical, "Anything Goes", was on the rack before Herbie.

Herbie's eyes were glued on the leader's baton. An almost inaudible "one-and-a-two-a" preceded the dip of the baton. Herbie strained to pick up the beat. The band made it through the reprise into the lively melody of the title song. The score would have been easier to handle if Herbie were playing on his mother's Steinway. The action was stiffer on the Baldwin. Halfway through "You're The Top" the leader left his out—front spot for a listening post within arm's length of Herbie' flying fingers. Drops of sweat rolled down Herbie's fingers and made the keys slippery under the triple strain of the leader's close attention, the task of reading the score cold, and the need to anticipate the conclusion of the final number in the show score when he was expected to create an appropriate modulation from the key of C to the key of A.

The emergence of Herbie's razzle-dazzle solo transition was greeted with respectful silence from the rest of the band. A half glance at the slim figure of Charles caught the barest glimmer of a smile. Herbie usually played "Night And Day" in E flat as originally written. The requirement to transpose into A major put him at special pains to play mostly chords on beat, eliminating the showy fill—in stuff played with the right hand. Herbie's fingers plucked a strong series of triads and sevenths out of A major, G minor and then D major, slowing enough to give Claire an easy entry into "Tea For Two." A nod in Herbie's direction thanked him as she launched into lusty singing of a tune that Herbie believed should be sung with lightness and reserve. Herbie was careful to support the singer with simple chords, filling in, when Claire took a breath, with arpeggios and broken chords with the right hand. Gradually Claire worked her way over to the piano for the cozy effect this would create with dancing couples who get close to the performers, seeking to transfer the verve and syncopation felt at close range to their own bodies.

Herbie had never before worked with a singer whose principal attribute was the way she used her body to accent the words of a song. Claire's swaying breasts, cleverly outlined under a silky black sweater, cut low to show cleavage, captured the young pianist's timid glance so completely that he found himself creating fantasies as well as music. He had struggled through adolescence with a burden of fears about contact with girls that grew right along with his developing sexuality. Parental education in this, as well as in other areas important to a healthy normalcy, was non-existent. As a result, experimenting with girls was unknown. His virginity, he thought, must surely be evident to one so sexually exuberant as Claire Strong, so he attempted to show appreciation for her bouncy style, responding when she touched his shoulder with her breast by sliding closer along the piano bench. This move unfortunately placed him at a disadvantage when it came to playing chords in the lower register, a difficulty he was certain Charles would notice. His prodigious effort to play wide-stretching chords with his left hand from his off-center location resulted in dissonances that would have ended the tryout abruptly had he not covered up with right hand improvisations whenever Claire took a breath, which her lusty style required frequently.

Nearing the end of the set, Claire flexed her breasts for the concluding bars with so much vehemence that Herbie's right hand fluttered weakly in mid-air when he should have synchronized with progressions by the left hand. Still, all was not lost. An appreciative kiss on the cheek and a whispered "Let's get together at my place" was a promissory that demanded collection in the near future.

Breathing heavily, Herbie turned toward Charles with what he knew, and tried vainly to suppress, was a look of prayerful expectancy.

"Okay, Roberts. That's enough. We're set for tonight. We'll call you if we need you."

So that was that. Show 'em the old fight, Roberts. He flashed an expansive grin, waved a nonchalant adieu that trailed off towards Claire, and made for the reviving salt air that encapsulated the ancient wood structure perched close to the Atlantic.

The disappointment that grabbed at him for the failed audition was quickly replaced by a familiar panicky sensation as he looked at his watch. Quarter to five. Must pick up Whitey and Myrtle at a quarter after. No ifs, ands or buts.

"I want to see you in front of the clubhouse at five fifteen, immediately after the eighth race. If you're late, it's the last time you will be."

His father's words and the blue-steel look reinforcing them were a pinprick, a goad, thunder from Jehovah, and a time bomb resident in Herbie's breast. Orders from Whitey Roberts had almost 18 years of stimulus-response conditioning behind them.

The sleek black Chrysler flowed easily through traffic, pausing only for lights between Dreamland Ballroom and Atlantic Downs, home of the sport of kings for Whitey Roberts and many thousands more devotees of horseracing. Coming in sight of the row of flags atop the blocks-long grandstand, Herbie relaxed. It was only five o'clock and a parking attendant obsequiously waved the imposing car into a space in front of the clubhouse entrance.

"Plenty of time to make the eighth," said the attendant, a red-faced man in a green monkey suit.

Herbie considered. He had dropped his parents off at the track on prior Saturdays, using the interval between drop-off and pickup to visit his cousin, Rob Romanoff, in Beachtown next to the track. But he had never been invited inside the Downs. And not to be invited meant to keep out. But still—why not take a quick look around to see what took so much of the time and money of the group of cronies Whitey referred to as Satcor—his "Saturday Corporation". There was no admission charge after the seventh race, and Herbie carried his brother Larry's I.D., which would get him past any guard questioning his age. Helping to resolve his uncertainty, the track announcer's voice boomed across the concrete apron before the neat white clubhouse:

"It is now twelve minutes to post time."

Stop the baby stuff, Herbie. You can have a look around and be out before Whitey shows his face. You've got to see what grabs Whitey every weekend, occasions to be thankful for if you asked the Roberts kids: Herbie, his brother Larry, three years older, and their sister Reggie, two years younger than Herbie.

As a vendor to Atlantic Downs—his company supplied meats for the clubhouse restaurant—Whitey got season passes for the Paddock Club. He would be there today, so the prospect of Herbie running into his father was unlikely.

The pleasant buzzing of the crowd, visible through the exit doors opened for bettors taking advantage of free admission for the eighth race, teased Herbie out of the car and into the clubhouse, past uniformed guards, past hawkers of performance sheets.

Those inside the Downs immersed in research and betting, were immune to Herbie's arrival. Their faces were buried in the Morning Telegraph, a past performance newspaper Herbie had seen frequently in his mother's possession. She was charged with its purchase early Saturday mornings so Whitey could browse through it over coffee and popovers. The Daily Racing Form, a competitive sheet, was in lesser evidence. Other bettors, having completed their preliminary studies, were queuing up at ticket windows or betraying uncertainty by seeking the counsel of others.

Over the roar of thousands talking at once came a trumpet call. The horses were leaving the paddock for the post parade. This caused a sudden rush in the direction of the track itself. A shapely brunette in a tight-fitting sweater winked at Herbie as she leaned back in her canvas chair. She was possibly the only bored person in the entire chaotic scene. Herbie figured her for a high-class prostitute looking for a client and retreated into the crowd.

A hollow-eyed wreck of a man tugged at Herbie's sleeve. "Go a buck with me on number three!" Herbie shook his head and pulled away.

A grimy, well-thumbed program thrust into Herbie's hands by a departing patron who barely looked at him was the only other testimony to the fact that he, Herbie Roberts, second son of the great Whitey Roberts, had penetrated the Saturday retreat of the horse-mad.

Now the lines of bettors became unruly with the approach of post time.

Well-dressed businessmen, dignified ladies, doctors and dentists, soldiers and sailors surged up to the windows demanding pasteboards in exchange for handfuls of cash.

"Five minutes to post time—hurry to avoid being shut out!" The voice was full of authority, causing a renewed rush to the ticket sellers whose faces became instantly grayer, grimmer and more exhausted, like the faces of whores who slumped into the South End nightclub at three in the morning, where Herbie took an occasional fill-in job at piano.

Herbie prodded himself. His Cinderella time was running out. Now he hastened to see the track itself, dimly glimpsed between bobbing heads as a thin brown ellipse rimming the vast jeweled carpet of the infield.

Vroom! There it was, the great wall of the totalizator board, looming up before the startled youth like an apparition from childhood stories about ancient walled cities of the Bible. No music was playing for anyone else, but the Beethoven Fifth played for Herbie, filling the empty places in his chest and stomach and swelling his head until he felt it would burst with joy.

It was more than simply a gigantic odds board. Herbie imagined it to be the home of the great god Baal, mountain deity of the ancient Phoenicians, fleshed out in shining, yellow-orange numbers four feet high. Instead of being a golden calf, like the idol worshiped by the Israelites on their march through the desert from Egypt, it was a golden wall, worshiped by the Hopefulites. Now Herbie became aware of a distant thunder. With an effort, he extracted himself from his biblical reverie. The distant thunder became peoples' voices responding to the shifting odds on the great board. The board was painted black and stretched several hundred yards from a point well before the finish line almost to the end of the clubhouse. The giant overhangs of the upper level of both grandstand and clubhouse were matched foot for foot in height by the huge tote board.

"Look at number five—down to three to one from twenty to one. Somebody's pulling a fast one!"

"Go a fin with me on number four-I've got it from the trainer. They're going with him today!"

"Screw the four-he's burned me for the last time!"

One by one, every number on the board got attention. Herbie had a sudden sense of loss. He wished he had a number to cheer for, a number he would bring across the finish line in front. Perhaps to give him, Herbie Roberts, great wealth. Or, still better, the unqualified admiration of Whitey Roberts The new thought slid smoothly across his mind: why not add this jewel to the others he had earned over the years: Herbie the dandy home gardener, Herbie the straight A student, Herbie the piano player Could this be the catalyst that would unlock the main riddle of his life—how to get his father to love him?

Herbie shook the stardust that had momentarily blinded him. Now he looked at the wicked witch of the infield through narrowed slits of eyes. His gaze traveled absently from number one through ten. Ten sets of shimmering, pale orange digits.

Which number would win? He glanced at his gift program. This was the feature at six furlongs for horses three years old and up. The names were dazzling: Frontier Sue was number one, Ajax The Magnificent number two. And so on down to Kansas City Sam, number ten. Herbie found himself liking some names, disliking others. No good. Better look at Baal again. Maybe Baal would give up its golden secret to him.

Once more his gaze flickered over the odds, pausing in astonishment: was his vision playing tricks? The numbers flashing 15-1 on number 7 were definitely brighter, a deeper orange color. His whole being felt at acute attention, as though a current flowed from the ancient god of the mountain to him.

He shut his eyes tightly. If it were a mirage, it would be gone when he re-opened them. He looked again—the odds on number 7 were still shimmering brightest of all, only now they had shot up to 20-1.

"They're in the gate—it is now post time!"

The announcement sent a chill through the crowds. Herbie felt his throat tighten, his mouth go dry. At last he was not alone—he had number 7 with him. Number 7's name was Red Crab.

A jangling bell sounded from the distant starting gate across the infield. Herbie's goose pimples rose with the cavalry charge of the horses sprinting out of the gate.

' "At the quarter pole it's Frontier Sue by a length. On the outside Red Crab is second by a head over Ajax The Magnificent. Herbie admired the evenhandedness of the announcer, who called off the position of each horse.

"Around the turn, Frontier Sue has it by three lengths, Ajax The Magnificent has moved up to be second. Red Crab is third along the rail!"

Ajax The Magnificent was the 8-5 favorite, so this call brought roars of encouragement from the crowd and stirred terror in Herbie.

"Come on, number 7, Baal is with you!" Herbie found the sound of his own voice reassuring.

"At the head of the stretch, Frontier Sue is in front by half a length, Ajax The Magnificent is coming on. Red Crab is third along the rail!

Did Herbie detect a bias in the announcer's voice for Ajax The Magnificent? Or was it really the end for Frontier Sue and Red Crab? How could this be when it appeared to Herbie that the big chestnut horse with number 7 on his saddlecloth was moving right with Ajax The Magnificent?

"Near the finish it's Ajax with Red Crab on the inside. Ajax and Red Crab. Red Crab by a neck!"

Herbie did not hear the groans and curses around him. Baal had listened. Baal was with him.

A heavy hand on his shoulder interrupted his bliss, powerful fingers grasping the suit cloth hard enough to pinch flesh.

"Do you think you could tear yourself away from all of this?" The voice was low-pitched, deceptively calm.

Herbie stiffened and the hand released him. He turned to face Whitey Roberts. Myrtle stood next to her husband's powerful figure, a frightened smile on still-pretty features.

Echoes of a previous time when Whitey Roberts had surprised his son reawaked in Herbie. Once, when Herbie was five and Larry was eight, they slipped away from their Beachtown apartment to go fishing off the town pier half a mile distant. It had been a hard-won junket, paid for with a few pennies lifted from Whitey's clothes to purchase two hooks and hanks of fishing line. They told their mother they were going to play at cousin Romanoff's house. Whitey had gone into the city to see a customer. His departure was the signal for this fishing escapade to commence.

The two young fishermen dropped their lines over the edge of the pier, hooks baited with worms donated by a friendly youth. They dangled their feet happily over the green Atlantic waters below. Into this blissful scene after half an hour had gone by without a bite, entered a furious Whitey Roberts. The barrel-chested Whitey easily hoisted a boy with each fist and hauled them off for punishment. Once home, they were stripped naked on the back porch, then strapped with a heavy leather belt until their screams aroused neighbors. Only a threat from an aroused Celia Tamkin to call the police ended the thrashing.

Now the cold blue eyes fastened on Herbie's anxious green-blue eyes. The thin lips tightened.

"Well? I'm waiting for your answer?"

Herbie flushed as though he had been struck.

"I got here early." Herbie tried to be casual.

"Never mind. Where's the car? Did you get the job? How much does it pay?" This was the start of a typical Whitey Roberts inquisition, at which he had proved himself as skilled as any prosecuting attorney.

"Hey Whitey, what time do we get together tonight? I'm going to skin your hide this time." The friendly question, from a strongly built man with thick black eyebrows peering out over heavy eyeglass frames, brought an abrupt change in Whitey's mood, and an unspoken sigh of relief from Herbie.

"Why you sonofabitch, any time I can't take you in pinochle, I'll kiss your grandmother's ass." Whitey's tone was jovial, accompanied by a hearty laugh, softening the curse for anyone listening.

"Eight o'clock all right?"

"Perfect, Frank. Bring a full wallet. I've got to make up for today's nonsense."

Frank Bannerman, Whitey's insurance broker, was one of a quintet of cronies who assembled each Saturday from April to October under Whitey's leadership to do battle with the pari-mutuel machines at Atlantic Downs in Boston, Rockingham Park in Salem, New Hampshire and Narragansett Park at Pawtucket, Rhode Island. They were Whitey's Saturday Corporation, or Satcor, as they referred to themselves. The business of Satcor was gambling. Evenings they continued their fellowship at Wonderland Dog Track or at the Roberts house in Brookline to play cards for high stakes. When he didn't have a job playing piano, Herbie was expected to play for Whitey's guests during the break for snacks, elaborately prepared by Myrtle Roberts.

"Herbie, it's good to see you, but I want you to know that I don't approve of children at a racetrack, especially this crooked track." Frank smiled genuinely at Herbie,

Frank then scowled a question:

"'How could a dog like Red Crab win that race if it weren't crooked?"

Whitey agreed.

Herbie smiled inside and stole a sidelong glance at the huge odds board. Baal knew.

"Let's get moving. I hope we don't have to walk half a mile to the car."

"You won't. I've got a surprise for you." More than one, said Herbie to himself.

CHAPTER 2

When they left the track, the Roberts family detoured to Warner Sarnow's house in Point Of Pines, a cluster of small homes on a spit of land thrusting into the Atlantic. Whitey had business with Warner who, besides being a friend, was Whitey's bookie.

"I'll be twenty minutes. Come in and say hello," ordered Whitey.

While Myrtle chatted with Warner's wife, Nancy, Herbie allowed Lenore Sarnow to fetch him a lemonade. Lenore was a precocious fifteen-year old with whom Herbie had kept up a kissing acquaintance over the two years Whitey had been doing business with Warner.

Lenore had ideas for the lean-waisted, slope-shouldered youth that went beyond kissing. Herbie, she had decided, was the logical person to introduce her to the world of grown-up lovemaking. He was good-looking, with a slow, shy smile and thoughtful, green-blue eyes.

"Gee, Herbie, you're going to be a Harvard man. That's what Dad says." Her high-pitched, whiney voice had always annoyed Herbie. Which was why, when they were alone together, Herbie was just as well pleased to pass the time with soul kisses. A long, narrow face, chinless like her father's face, disqualified Lenore from first choice in Herbie's sexual fantasies. He was quite willing, however, to share in Lenore's awareness of her developing breasts. Before he could get to this stage, he would have to answer her about Harvard.

"I haven't heard, yet," he said, without enthusiasm. He was shaky about his performance in the college boards. And even if he did get in, there was no guarantee that Whitey would pay his tuition. Despite Whitey's standing as a hot-shot beef wholesaler, it was apparent to Herbie that his father's growing preoccupation with gambling owed as much to a real need for money as to any desire to impress his friends.

Herbie was ready for serious necking, but Lenore preferred to talk about how wonderful it would be to go to football games and dances with a Harvard man. Her prattle went on against a background of muffled telephone rings from the basement below the room in which they sat. On a prior visit, Herbie had seen the battery of phones downstairs, manned by sharp-eyed characters taking bets on horseracing all over the country. Now, at six o'clock eastern time, the phones were ringing from people placing bets at tracks in Illinois and California.

"Let's go." Whitey's terse command got Herbie a hurried kiss and an entreaty to call Lenore when Herbie heard from Harvard.

Back in the car, Herbie was cross-examined about his audition with Jack Charles. Whitey then fell into a grim silence that lasted until they pulled into their driveway. Something must have been unsatisfactory at Sarnow's. It would take a lot more that a failed audition to shut his father up when he had two slaves captive for the forty-five minute run from Beachtown to Brookline. In the mailbox there was a letter for Herbie from Harvard. Myrtle, worried, gave Herbie the letter, saying, "If it's not good, dear, please don't tell me." Myrtle never did enter into the spirit of things very well when events had dire outcomes. She was in Florida when her father died and did not hurry home for the funeral. When her oldest, Larry, flunked out of Southern California in his freshman year, it ended her dream of seeing her blond Adonis break into motion pictures. The news caused her to crack up the expensive LaSalle that she had driven cross-country to deliver Larry to the gates of Hollywood the previous year.

Myrtle explained to Herbie, who knew her best, that she didn't like bad news because, she said," You know, dear, I feel too much."

So, with the letter in his hand, Herbie went to the bedroom he shared with Larry. He stared at the envelope a long minute, then a secret smile, starting in his stomach, crept upward to the hairs behind his neck and showed at the corners of his mouth, drawing a puzzled query from his brother, who had followed him into the room.

"What are you so happy about? I heard you didn't get the job."

Herbie handed him the envelope. "Go ahead, open it," he said.

"No guts, huh?" Larry slit open the envelope, still wondering about Herbie's good mood.

"Wow," he exploded, eyes traversing the contents, "looks like you're in." Then, fixing Herbie with a suspicious stare, he said, "But you knew it."

The glow that Herbie had felt before Larry opened the letter showed in a broad grin. Yes, he had sensed the content without reading the letter. It was the second time that day that something extraordinary had occurred.

Whitey reacted as expected, with a double-edged congratulation. "I'll have to call you big shot from now on," he said, adding cynically, "I hope you'll be able to afford it."

Nonetheless, Herbie knew that Whitey would drop the news to his cronies. Having a son at Harvard would enhance his stature as leader of the pack.

Although they had all lost at the horse track, the Satcor bunch arrived for pinochle in a typical roistering mood.

Jake Michaels, who sold liquor for a bootlegger turned "legit", was a big, bluff man with raw tastes in language and, very likely, in women as well, Herbie observed to himself, when Jake bussed Myrtle and slapped her on the flanks.

"You're drivn' me crazy. When you gonna ditch this guy for me?" He nodded at Whitey, who was setting out cards and cigarettes.

"Maybe never," said Myrtle with a girlish giggle

. Frank Bannerman arrived with Sam Dana, still talking about the unexpected victory of Red Crab." That dog wasn't in the money in twenty races. There wasn't a handicapper gave him a rec.".

Herbie, thinking he'd better start his campaign to get invited to the track, said quietly, "I thought he'd win."

Whitey aimed cold blue darts over smoked glasses in Herbie's direction, but said nothing.

Thick black brows knotted over Frank Bannerman's dark brown eyes as he stared at Herbie."You had a bet on Red Crab?" His tone was disbelieving.

"Just in my mind," said Herbie lamely. He hadn't wanted to attract so much attention. Herbie's role, when he was at home during Whitey's pinochle evenings, was to stay out of sight until the players broke for snacks about ten o'clock, and then entertain them at the Steinway until they resumed play.

Sam Dana, a stubby little man with heavy circles of flesh under his eyes that made him look as though he had been crying, spoke up, not unkindly,

"We've got a rule, Herbie. If you don't put your money where your mouth is, you don't say anything."

"All right, let's cut the crap, guys." The speaker was Mitch Weller, a blue-joweled giant who sold advertising space for the Boston Herald. Entering, he sensed that Herbie was uncomfortable with the attention,

"We've got some serious work to do and I suggest we get right to it," he said with a wink that took in both the admiring Myrtle and grateful Herbie.

As the players seated themselves around the green felt pads covering the big dining table, Herbie figured that only tiny Sam Dana would have been comfortable at one of Myrtle's card tables. The others, all big men needed the elbowroom afforded by the spacious dining area.

The players cut cards for partners, then took several minutes to discuss rules for tonight's bout. Because five were present, one would sit out every fourth hand.

Herbie watched with a show of interest. If he seemed a good sport, maybe they would insist on his presence at Atlantic Downs next Saturday.

Whitey was in his best mood in this setting. To Herbie's surprise, conditioned to Whitey's short fuse with his own family, the more intricate the rules discussion, the more Whitey enjoyed himself, displaying good-humored patience with the pickiness of Sam Dana who argued that the first card of the widow should be exposed when the bidding reached 250 rather than 300 as was the custom.

"Let's play it Sammy's way," he said, in his most reasonable tone. The others assented.

He's acting, thought Herbie, covering up so that he can take advantage during the play. Herbie was familiar with his father's chameleon-like qualities. Yielding to his son's entreaty on Herbie's eleventh birthday, he took Herbie with him on his Connecticut trip. Herbie was forced to sit and watch painfully as Whitey delivered appropriate belly laughs during Walker Wilson's jokes about Negroes and

Jews. Wilson, who owned the leading hotel in Hartford, didn't know that the blond beef salesman with classic Nordic features was Jewish.

"What's important is getting the order," Whitey explained later.

This incident, while not forgotten, had failed to blunt the keen edge of Herbie's need to be loved by his father. Even now, seven years later, Herbie was trying to close the gap that yawned as big as ever.

"Misdeal." The slap of Frank Bannerman's cards on the felt pad brought Herbie back to the pinochle game.

"For what? The protest came from Mitch Weller, whose disappointment indicated that he was holding a king's ransom in valuable cards.

"There are three heart queens in this deck." Bannerman pointed to the cards lying face up.

"Geez, we've played three hands with a bad deck," growled Weller.

"All points stand except this hand," said Sam Dana, who was keeping score.

Whitey brought out a new deck, stripped the protective foil, shuffled the cards expertly, laid them face up for all to count Herbie found himself watching the swift, precise motions of his father's hands, the broad, powerful fingers, reddened and calloused by years of exposure to icy temperatures in beef coolers, stained yellow by nicotine. Those hands, untaught, guided only by an ear for music, had pounded the keys of a movie house piano in Whitey's youth. When their owner was still in his teens, those hands had bounced stew bums from the New Brunswick bar owned by his father. Herbie faintly recalled his grandfather Roberts, a dour man who kept a bottle of whisky under his bed on infrequent visits to the Roberts home in Brookline. In contrast with the roughness of the skin on his hands, Whitey's cuticles and nails were meticulous, carefully manicured weekly for his business trips. Whitey's hands had never touched Herbie except in anger.

Studying the other men, Herbie couldn't believe they were as rough on their families as was his father. Frank Bannerman had always spoken kindly to Herbie; his two children were in private school. Sam Dana, glum and unsmiling on most occasions, had revealed his true self during the High Holy Days, when the Roberts kids, in company with their parents, met the Danas exiting from Beth Elohim. "Mazeltov, Happy New Year," Sam Dana had said, arms around his two children, a warm smile wreathing his face. Jake Michaels, Whitey's buddy at their Masonic lodge, had been thumping Herbie on the back affectionately for most of Herbie's life.

"You've got great kids," Jake often said to Whitey, in Herbie's presence. "And you've got a great dad," he would say to Herbie. Jake and his wife, Sandy, had no kids of their own and spent their affection on the children of their friends. Mitch Weller, also childless, had taken an interest in Herbie's future. "Think about the newspaper business," he advised. "There's good money in it if you get with the right outfit."

It was difficult for Herbie to look directly at his father. But now, safe from a jolting return glance while Whitey concentrated on his cards, Herbie searched his father's face for clues that might explain why he seemed to treat strangers more kindly than he did his own children. Just now, Whitey scowled as he took several consecutive tricks. On the surface, Whitey appeared to be an average, workaday businessman enjoying an average, workaday card game. But Herbie believed that Whitey's passions, Whitey's appetites, Whitey's prejudices and hates, were far from average. Right now, Herbie knew that Whitey was memorizing every card exposed, counting every trump card buried, anticipating feeble-minded mistakes by his opponents that he could pounce on. Card play meant more than sociability, more than money won or lost. It meant an opportunity for Whitey to show that he was a superior man.

Whatever it took for Whitey to gain an edge, whether practicing card memory or bribing chefs to favor his beef cuts, Whitey did it. About once a month, Whitey would bring a chef back with him from Connecticut for a two-day holiday. The chef was put up in the guest room, with Myrtle and Delia to wait on every beck and call. "If Jim Curley can buy votes and get elected, I can buy chefs and get my beef on their want lists," he said to Larry, Herbie's brother. At twenty-one, Larry seemed to have a liking for his father's business. Herbie was certain his brother would be Whitey's willing slave.

"Who am I to call my brother "slave"? Herbie reminded himself that for as long as he could remember, he had run to get his father's slippers after he returned from his weekly business trips. And not only did he bring the slippers, but he removed his father's shoes and gently worked the slippers into place.

The rattle of glasses and tinkling of ice cubes brought Herbie back to the present. The players were taking a break and being revived for another session with Myrtle's sandwiches, cookies, and lemonade laced with gin.

"How about a number, Herbie." It was not a suggestion, but a command. "Or perhaps I should call you big shot, now that you're going to Harvard." Whitey paused, measuring the effect of his announcement.

"Congratulations. I knew you could do it!" Jake said. "Mazeltovs" were heaped on by the others, all except Whitey, who was busy counting the hosannas, all of which he credited to his own account.

A small pool of grateful warmth flickered in and out of Herbie's throat, smothering whatever thanks he might have spoken. Then he got down to business on the Steinway, serenading the guests with a full portfolio of classics and jazz tidbits. Because he believed he was playing for his life, he really put out, concluding with a flashy presentation of Rachmaninoff's Prelude in C Sharp Minor. Herbie then sat back and waited for a reward.

Sam picked up the cue. "What are we going to do for Herbie in recognition of his admission to Harvard?"

"What would you like, Herbie?" reluctantly, from Whitey.

With Whitey under pressure, it was unlikely his request would be denied.

"How about a trip to the Downs with you next Saturday?"

"That could be a horse of a different color," quipped Jake slyly. "We could be corrupting the lad."

"Bullshit. He's entitled," said Sam Dana. Myrtle, embroidering nearby, put her hands over her ears.

Thank you, Sam Dana. Herbie looked at his father, who was testing which way the wind was blowing. In the face of apparent indecision, Herbie played his ace card: "It's my birthday a week from Monday."

"That settles it," said Jake. "Do the members of the Saturday Corporation say with me that Herbie goes to the races?" He made a mock count of upraised hands.

"How about you?" Jake aimed his huge forearm at Whitey, who sighed, "Oh Christ, the kid can go."

Thank you, Baal. Of course it was Baal who somehow made it happen. With the help of Sam and the others.

It was all wonderful, the meeting with Baal, the humanity of the Satcor guys, and the new feeling, however threatened by his father's iron mastery over his emotions, that he had a destiny. Yes, April 23rd, 1936, would be a day to remember.

CHAPTER 3

So Whitey Roberts played the chameleon to achieve status as a hotshot beef man and leader of the Satcor pack. But what kind of a father?

No spoiled kids for Whitey! Larry and Herbie had their behavior corrected often with heavy strappings until well in their teens. He also gave them the back of his hand for minor infractions like rattling the newspaper when he expected peace and quiet. Verbal lashings were routine.

Having thus reduced his boys to quivering jellyfish, he was faced with the task of equipping them with the tools to make their way in the real world.

Whitey made sure his boys understood how tough things could become. For example take the Saturday of Herbie's Bar Mitzvah ceremony. After the ancient rites performed at Ohabei Shalom, Rabbi Shulman presiding, Herbie and Larry naturally expected Herbie would at least fall heir to a superb repast and celebration at the Prime, a favorite restaurant and a customer of M. Roberts & Company. After all, Larry had been so honored three years earlier on his transition from boyhood to ritual adulthood. But Whitey had special plans for Herbie.

Myrtle and Reggie were dropped off at the Roberts's mansion and Whitey, his stern features nursing a secret smile, headed downtown in the direction of Charlestown. Herbie and Larry exchanged knowing looks—Whitey had rumored recently that his boys would get a close look at Bunker Hill monument, a mandatory visit to this symbol of the Revolution that had somehow been omitted from their early education.

They got a look at the famous monument and that was all. Whitey made a right turn from the monument up the ramp and over the rail yards connecting Charlestown to Cambridge. In a few minutes the huge black Chrysler was nosing into a public parking space in front of the massive gray concrete structure notorious as Charlestown State Prison.

Herbie had a sudden choking sensation. He looked at Larry. His brother was grimly silent. Only their father evidenced anticipation.

"Let's go, boys. We're going to get a look at the chair that burned Sacco and Vanzetti." Herbie was dimly aware of the infamous pair whose final appeal for conversion of their death sentence had been denied by Governor Alvan T. Fuller. He and Larry trudged behind their father to the visitors' lobby, then up two flights of stone steps to the execution chamber.

"Come on, I want you to get a taste of what happens to wrongdoers", said Whitey with a smile, forced for the benefit of their uniformed guide. Whitey took the guide aside for a private conversation. The result: Larry and Herbie took turns sitting in the electric chair that had killed convicted persons in Massachusetts like Sacco and Vanzetti. Herbie was certain his father slipped a bribe to the guide to permit the special privilege accorded the youths.

Larry affected a blasé, unconcerned expression as he submitted being strapped into the massive electrified chair. "Nothing to it," he imparted breezily when he was unbelted from the chair." Your turn, kid. It doesn't hurt, really."

Herbie was not reassured by his brother's phony confidence. He knew that Larry, like he, was smothering feelings of revulsion at being subjected to the experience. Seated in the chair, he closed his eyes as the restraining straps were belted around him. "Oh God," he said to himself, "what did I do to deserve this? Did I not perform the ancient ritual of bar mitzvah in accord with the precepts of my faith? Did I not honor thee in my reading from the Torah? Did I not study for many weeks with Rabbi Shulman in order to fulfill my obligation to thee, my Lord? How can thee suffer the insult, coming from the temple to this house of horrors?" He had always felt close to God, a feeling nourished by his grandfather Nattelson, who provided Herbie with the hugs and kisses that were never forthcoming from his father. His grandfather, aware of the unnatural chasm between Whitey and his sons, often told both Larry and Herbie that they were "God's children." Although his eyesight was so poor that he was considered legally blind, grandfather Nattelson took the boys on lengthy walks around Franklin Park, near his home. When he would take long walks by himself, he overruled their voiced cautions with comments like:" Do you think that God is only in my living room?"

There was no divine intervention, no rolling thunder, as the result of Herbie's questioning of his God, but he felt suddenly relaxed and even wore a smile when he was unhooked from the chair.

"What was so funny?" Whitey was determined to make a huge impact with this Bar Mitzvah "treat".

Herbie did not reply. What kind of a monster father did God present him with? His father's sarcasm was expected. And Herbie's silence was his way of replying to the riposte. He knew this infuriated Whitey.

Needless to say, Larry and Herbie got the message: their father was out to instill them with fear of retribution for any transgressions of the rules laid down, either by the state or Whitey Roberts.

Another Whitey Roberts answer was as close as the mansion across the street from the Roberts home where Doctor William Loyola Railey plied his trade. Railey's College Of The Spoken Word had achieved notoriety for grooming James Michael Curley as a public speaker who became mayor of Boston. This success brought politicians, embryonic as well as those stuck in their careers, into Railey's classes. Nor did it hurt when another pupil, Warner Oland, made it big as Charlie Chan in a popular movie series.

So Whitey herded his boys across the street into a session with Railey. Large and pontifical, Railey directed a kindly smile at the two boys shuffling nervously in their chairs.

"What do we have here, future stars of motion pictures? Or dynamic leaders of the business community?" Railey was aware of Whitey's star status in the beef business, indeed, had been well prepared for this meeting with gifts of meats from the Roberts coolers.

No sound from Herbie and Larry, just nervous scuffling.

"See, I told you. They're absolutely tongue-tied. And they can't even look you in the eye. I'm afraid they'll end up bums on Boston Common. "

Railey got impressively to his feet, adjusted gold-framed pince nez on a Roman nose, and appraised Herbie and Larry. Their anxious faces told him that here was prime raw material ready for molding.

"Mr. Roberts, I believe you've underestimated these young men. I can see substantial possibilities." Thankful grins told him he had made his case. They enrolled for classes in public speaking and drama two nights a week for three months.

So Herbie and Larry declaimed, elocuted, recited and debated. They also learned to walk. That is, they were taught to walk in a straight line, from chest to target, admirably and elegantly demonstrated by Railey.

Would this extra schooling give Herbie and Larry what was needed to talk a winning game in the world of business? Time would tell. Now, having done everything in his power to try to beat them into a pulp, Whitey took the next illogical step: he brought in Joe Rocco to teach Herbie and Larry the art of self-defense.

Joe Rocco, with flattened nose and ears pounded into knob-like projections, came every Wednesday night from East Boston, Orient Heights to be exact, to impart basic boxing skills. The boys were impressed. Rocco had once fought for the lightweight title, though a loser. Now, his voice reduced to a hoarse whisper, Rocco coached the Roberts boys to stick, feint, jab, uppercut and cover up in two-hour sessions in the cellar of the Roberts house.

It went like this: first, Rocco would put on the gloves with Herbie or Larry. Then Herbie and Larry would go at it, unlocking the dormant hiding place of Herbie's lifelong hatred of his father. He took it out on Larry, cuffing and punching his more muscular brother into a near helpless state, when Rocco would step between them.

"What's got into you?? Larry gasped in protest.

"I don't know, Larry. Excuse it—I just lost it." Herbie's reply wasn't the truth. He knew he had substituted the face of his brother for Whitey, but he couldn't unwrap his feelings without confessing his plan to someday do their father in. And that would have been too frightening for Larry who, although punished frequently by his father, had not been imprinted with his rage as an infant in his crib—and that made a difference.

CHAPTER 4

It was a week of feverish anticipation. Would he be able to connect again with Baal? What famous teachers would he have at Harvard? As a prospective English major, Herbie had hoped that Lyman Kittredge, the world's top Shakespearean scholar, would be his teacher. But the Globe carried a story that Kittredge was retiring in June. Herbie's disappointment was partly abated by his Wednesday night dream. A woman with a scarf hiding her face came up to Herbie in Harvard Square and asked him to go home with her. As they walked to her apartment, she shed her garments. Once inside her apartment, she took Herbie's hands in her own and brushed his fingers over her magnificent body. She then removed the scarf from her face—it was Claire Strong, the singer from the Jack Charles band.

Images of the singer made additional appearances Thursday and Friday. In French class, she sat on the corner of his desk, winked at him from the entrance to the men's toilet. In his physics exam, she handed him his test paper Her influence, aided no little by the fact that she always appeared in the nude, extended even to the tennis court and Herbie's Friday afternoon date with Lenny Atlas. The match proved wholly unequal, because the bosomy Claire played alongside Lenny.

"For Chris sakes," Lenny exploded, after a series of weird misses by Herbie. "What's got into you?"

Of course Herbie could not explain that he was up in the clouds over being permitted to accompany his father to Atlantic Downs the next day. Lenny would have replied, "What's so great about that?" In Lenny's experience, for a son to be close with his father was as natural as ice cream with apple pie.

When he returned Friday afternoon from a lengthy Connecticut trip, Whitey Roberts was as depressed as Herbie was sky-high. Herbie was aware of his call from New Haven to Myrtle at suppertime on Thursday, and her subsequent call to Warner Sarnow with a bet at Santa Anita.

After supper, Frank Bannerman phoned to confirm the Satcor plans to meet at Atlantic Downs the next day. A mask of coarse congeniality canceled out the dark mood that had gripped Whitey.

"Frank, let's meet in the restaurant at one-thirty. Bring your balls with you and I'll do the same. We'll show those cheating bastards who's boss."

The Roberts household arose shortly after dawn the next morning. When Herbie awoke after a restless night, the smell of his mother's freshly baked popovers was in his nostrils. Early breakfast attracted only Herbie. To avoid their father, Reggie and Larry slept through breakfast on the weekend. Delia Delancey, who had suffered through more than a few Roberts family crises in her four years as Myrtle's housekeeper, was busy in the pantry. After Herbie seated himself, Whitey looked up from his newspaper, impaling Herbie with those soulless blue eyes that always seemed to be measuring Herbie's worth.

"We're leaving for the office in half an hour. From there we'll go to the track. I've got a schedule, so please be ready."

"Please" was hardly in keeping with his usual style. Whitey's forebears came from Austro-Hungary. In Herbie's point of view, this origin had to account for his father's near-militaristic approach to being head of the family. Despite the fact that Herbie figured his father a "natural": for military duty, he had managed to avoid military service in the Great War because he had fathered two children by the time the United States entered the conflict.

"I'll be ready," said Herbie, attacking the bowl of cereal Delia had placed before him. It seemed to Herbie that his father was operating under unusually tight inner control. Probably had to do with Warner Sarnow. . Or maybe there was a Mr. Big in the picture. Somebody to pay off with cash or free meats. Whitey spent time at his office Saturday mornings to pay for favors received the preceding week.

It was ten o'clock when the black Chrysler wiggled through the swarms of Saturday shoppers and fruit peddlers in the Haymarket area. Whitey sounded the horn in long blasts to clear the way to the storefront on North Street over which a sign read, "M. Roberts & Co, Provisioners."

Half a dozen Roberts employees were on hand, busy making up packages for persons who came to receive largesse for services rendered to Whitey Roberts. While Herbie waited in the car with his mother, he made a game of identifying those who entered empty-handed and departed with hefty bundles. Herbie recognized two men departing with their loot as policemen dressed in civvies. One was a motorcycle cop who gave Whitey escort service, especially on holidays, making it easy for Whitey to reach his office in double quick time. The other cop directed traffic on Commonwealth Avenue, stopping oncoming traffic to allow Whitey to make a turn across Cottage Farm Bridge to the Cambridge side of the Charles River, from where it was a fast run downtown.

Herbie said to himself that the meats given to the policemen comprised an inflated price for the small favors given. Of course Herbie knew that Whitey wouldn't agree-those small favors made him feel very big indeed.

Four or five of the visitors were probably chefs at various hotels, figured Herbie. He recognized several who had been honored guests in the Roberts home. They would get envelopes containing cash as well as parcels of prime meats. The ruddy-faced man in the green uniform who had waved Herbie to a favored parking space at Atlantic Downs the previous Saturday was among those arriving for a handout. He looked furtively up and down the street before he went in. A few minutes later, he came out carrying a sizable parchment-wrapped package under one arm. He waved the other arm in Myrtle's direction. She waved back and smiled happily.

At eleven o'clock, Nick Civitello came to the car to say that Whitey would like sandwiches and coffee and would Myrtle please get them. Nick, a black-haired, heavy-shouldered man in a white butcher's coat, was Whitey's foreman.

While Myrtle ran the errand, Herbie speculated that an important visitor was due soon and would get a special welcome.

Shortly after Myrtle brought the refreshments inside, a thickset man with swarthy features, wearing a broad-brimmed hat, got out of a long green Cadillac that parked in front of Whitey's Chrysler. Through the rear window, Herbie saw that the man at the wheel wore a dark suit and chauffeur's cap.

The swarthy visitor looked sharply at Herbie then went into M. Roberts. In the next hour, a dozen persons exited M. Roberts. The man in the wide-brimmed hat was not among them. This meant his business with Whitey was talk, not meat.

Connecting the steady betting with Warner Sarnow during the past week with Whitey's dark mood, Herbie thought it possible the unknown visitor was associated with Sarnow. Until his own brief excursion to the racetrack the previous Saturday, Herbie had never given more than passing thought to his father's interest in horseracing. To Herbie, his father's attendance at the races with Satcor and the occasional telephone betting with the bookie amounted to just another aspect of Whitey's high-flying style. It was in accord with his playing cards for big stakes, his winter luxury cruises, his months-long stays in Florida, his taste for expensive clothes and, if his mother were correct, expensive women as well.

Since he was ten years old, Herbie had been his mother's confidantes about Whitey's supposed escapades Reggie and Larry had also witnessed Myrtle's accusations of infidelity, but only Herbie had earned his mother's confidences, though admittedly by default. Reggie and Larry wanted no part of any more unpleasantness with their father than was already theirs by birthright.

Herbie did not share his mother's belief that Whitey played around. He had never seen any evidence that this was so. Myrtle's tearful confidences never contained anything more than references to suspicious absences, mysterious phone calls that Myrtle was never quick enough to intercept, or traces of lipstick on shirt collars that somehow weren't present when Herbie asked to see the evidence.

Perhaps it was wifely insight that caused her occasional outbursts at Whitey. Or perhaps, as Whitey said more than once, it indicated a delicate balance between reason and fantasy. This was Whitey's way of saying that Myrtle had a crazy streak like her mother. This red-haired harrigan, now deceased, had constantly barbered her husband about supposed infidelities. And everyone, especially Herbie, knew that Lewine Nattelson was one of God's best people.

At twelve o'clock, Myrtle came out of the office. The swarthy visitor held the door and tipped his hat as they said goodbye. Whitey followed the stranger to the Cadillac. He wore an expression of deference Herbie had seen only when the Roberts family listened to Rabbi Shulman deliver a stern talk during the Days Of Penitence.

On the way to the track, there was no reference to the stranger. But Whitey crawled out enough from tight-lipped silence to lay down a code of conduct for Herbie.

"Find yourself a place and stay there. I don't want you wandering around where I can't find you. If you see me talking with people, don't interrupt. If we decide to leave early, I don't want any sulking." He concluded by pointing his finger at Herbie's face in the rear view mirror and admonishing, "No betting. If I hear you've been betting, you'll never go again."

"Fine with me," said Herbie with a show of cheerfulness. His father certainly had a way of taking the bloom off the rose.

Arrived at the track, Whitey and Myrtle went into the restaurant for lunch. Free from Whitey's scrutiny, Herbie roamed around, directing his interest to those places where fans gather at a racetrack between races-the saddling paddock, bulletin boards announcing jockey changes and overweights, groups where retired jockeys and trainers spread the word on "hot horses." He found a knot of horseplayers with serious faces busily noting on their programs information posted on a large chalkboard. The words "scratches", "jockey changes" and "overweights" found their way into his memory bank under the heading of "important." Crowds were beginning to gather in the clubhouses. Herbie noted they were well dressed and had pleasant faces. He was glad to be wearing the new saddle shoes he had purchased with his piano-playing earnings at Hibernian Manor. A smudge on one shoe caught his attention. He would attend to that on his next visit to the men's restroom.

Asking his way to the paddock, Herbie was passed through to the grandstand, a vast concrete canyon gradually filling with tourists looking for a pot of gold. The only persons who shared the rail with Herbie at the empty saddling paddock were a trio of ossifications wearing neat shirts and ties knotted loosely around scrawny throats. Their conversations—about Man O'War, Regret and a fantastic Kentucky Derby Day long ago—had the flavor of mint juleps and soft southern climes. Herbie took them for sons of Confederate soldiers if not indeed original followers of Robert E. Lee.

Herbie counted sixteen stalls, which puzzled him, until he reasoned that for some special races, more than a dozen horses might be entered.

He turned to go, but a light tug on his coat sleeve stopped him.

"They're a comin' if you're a goin' to look 'em over." The pale blue eyes of the speaker smiled distantly from fleshless sockets. The old man must be ninety, thought Herbie.

A horse surely was coming, being led at a leisurely walk by a hard-faced girl wearing riding pants and a man's shirt open at the throat. Her blond hair was funneled into a pert tail resembling the silky, swishing tail of the chestnut mare she led into the paddock area.

Now a strange thing happened. Strange and a bit frightening. Herbie's instincts, unused to the ways of confirmed racetrack followers, had taken little note of what appeared to be lumps and bumps along the walls and roof pillars. Cued by the quiet approach of the chestnut mare, the lumps and bumps turned suddenly into live human beings. In seconds they were shoulder to shoulder along the paddock rail, pushing Herbie to one side.

Herbie would have stayed to study the horses now moving into their stalls to be saddled and mounted, but a glance at his watch told him to do otherwise. It was one-thirty, and in a few minutes his father would be looking for him.

In his haste to respond to the stress occasioned by the thought of his father, he bumped into a tall, square-shouldered man in a neat gray suit holding a position near the fifty-dollar window.

"Sorry," muttered Herbie, and would have hurried on, but a firm grip on his elbow detained him.

"Are you eighteen, son?" The steady blue eyes seemed friendly, so Herbie told his jumping pulses to relax.

"I'll be eighteen in a week," he answered, fishing for his wallet.

"Okay, I believe you." said the man, steady blue eyes not leaving Herbie's green blue eyes for an instant.

"Can I go?" Herbie figured the man was a Pinkerton, part of track security.

"Of course. Enjoy yourself."

My enjoyment, Herbie said to himself as he dug his clubhouse pass out of a pocket to show at the pass gate, will be many years in the future if I don't make the right moves today.

First, find Whitey. He'll be with Bannerman and the others. Whitey proved easy to spot. His hatless, well-shaped blond head, hair brushed close to the scalp, was in close formation with the heads of the other four members of Satcor. "Glad you made it," said Herbie breezily. He was determined to keep his welcome in top repair. A show of good spirits would help.

"You're aces with us, Herbie," said Mitch Weller. The others said, "Hi 'ya, Herbie," and returned to serious discussion about the first race. Whitey caught Herbie's eye with a finger wag, and pointed in the direction of the rail at trackside. Herbie had been given the word—find a spot and stay there.

It was now fifteen minutes to post time. The outriders in fiery red coats sat on their mounts within a few feet of Herbie. He thought them very handsome, with their ramrod carriage, white waistcoats; scarves knotted at the throat and polished dark boots.

The concrete apron in front of the clubhouse was well filled with groups of horseplayers, a-buzz with hope and good humor. Here and there Herbie saw a lone player in close harmony with his racing paper, a studious frown on his face. These loners, he thought, had the best chance of going home winners because others wouldn't sway them. On the other hand, he could understand why most fans stuck together in small bands of two and three. If they won, the giver of good advice would have a forum in which to boast. If they lost, the burden of misery would be lighter because it would be shared.

Near Herbie, a garrulous fat man wearing checks was making a case for a horse named River Bend. His companion, a lean man with a brush mustache, shabbily dressed, listened patiently, though apparently unconvinced.

"I tell you, Alex, I won big on this horse at Hialeah, and he looks fit to me."

The lean one said, "He's overweight in this company. That's the best advice I can give you." He left the other's side, walking with a limp, evidently catching sight of another whose fellowship he preferred, figured Herbie.

"It is now ten minutes to post time!" The track announcer's voice reminded Herbie why he was there.

He turned his attention to the odds board for the first time since Baal had sent him the message about Red Crab a week earlier. Since then, he had tortured himself with the worry that it was all a mirage, an optical illusion caused by temporary weather conditions that had deceived him into seeing the odds opposite one number displayed brighter than all the rest.

At this stage in the betting, the shimmering, pale orange odds were changing frequently on the ten horses in the race, interrupting Herbie's concentration just enough so that he was unable to capture the odds on all the horses at once with a single scan. Just then the bugle sounded "Boots and Saddles" heralding the post parade. The sight of the splendid animals mincing along just in front of him further distracted Herbie's attention, their riders reining in tightly to keep their mounts from breaking into a gallop.

"Please, Baal," he said silently. Once more his eyes traversed the three rows of flashing figures. The digits were all the same hue of pale orange in the first row. The same in the second row Herbie shut his eyes, hoping for a message when he opened them on the third row, showing the odds on numbers nine and ten.

There it was! The 8-1 odds for number ten were a rich, blazing orange color. Thank you, Baal. Tears welled up so that he could no longer see the odds board. No matter—Baal had kept faith with him.

"It is now one minute to post time!" The warning from the public address horns told Herbie he had better do something quickly with his golden message. Whirling around, he saw Whitey in conversation with a man wearing a large gray Stetson. Although the face was turned away, he recognized the massive shoulders and the squat frame. They belonged to the stranger who had visited M. Roberts & Company that morning. No Herbie—don't risk it. Whitey said no interruptions when he was with somebody. And, from his observations of the stranger's morning visit, this man was important in his father's life.

"Herbie, old chap!" The speaker was Jake Michaels, who followed his greeting with his usual friendly thump on the shoulder that had told Herbie for years Jake could be a friend if things got too rough.

"Hello Jake," he said, minus some of the enthusiasm he had shown earlier.

Jake moved to sweeten Herbie a bit.

"Here, take my program, I'll get another," he said putting his program in Herbie's hands.

"Look at it and tell me who's going to win", he said.

"Number ten," said Herbie, realizing the importance of going on the record before the race began.

"It is now post time!"

The announcement told Herbie it was too late for Satcor to make a beet on number ten. Besides, his opinion was received with disbelief.

"Number ten? Mahogany Tim?" Jake shook his head. What Jake knew and Herbie did not was that Mahogany Time had broken down a year earlier and had not raced since then.

Herbie looked at the program. Yes, Mahogany Tim was number ten.

"That's the one. Mahogany Tim," he said, just as the announcer's voice boomed across the clubhouse apron. "They're off!" This triggered a great roar from 20,000 fans that drowned out Jake's negative response.

"River Bend goes out in front, with Violetta second, and Vanish Me third on the outside!" The staccato calls omitted no one. The trailer was Mahogany Tim.

Herbie was hopeful there would be a change at the next call, and fixed his gaze on the last horse, telegraphing his urgency to fast-pounding legs: "Move up, move up!"

It was working. Mahogany Tim was moving up around the turn and passed two horses. This didn't get public recognition, however, because River Bend, the horse marked for defeat by the lean man with the mustache, was in front by three lengths at the head of the stretch.

"Here they come down the stretch, with River Bend holding the lead by a length, Vanish Me is second on the outside, and Handsome Does is closing on the rail!"

Where was Mahogany Tim? Did Herbie see a dark bay animal moving swiftly on the extreme outside?

"At the sixteenth pole, Handsome Does has taken the lead, River Bend is stopping! The caller hesitated, and Herbie held his breath. There certainly was a horse closing strongly, coming right at Herbie.

Herbie's spirits soared with next call.

"It's Mahogany Tim coming fast as a ball on the outside. At the finish, Mahogany Tim wins it by a neck, Handsome Does is second, Vanish Me third!"

"Sonovagun!" Jake clapped Herbie on the shoulder and winged it for his clubmates. Herbie knew the message would be about his brilliant prophecy, just as he knew that the credit was due to the great god Baal of the odds board.

CHAPTER 5

Despite his inexperience, Herbie knew that the payoff of $29.60 for a two-dollar win ticket on Mahogany Tim had a chance of being as important to his future as a full scholarship to Harvard College. Whitey and the others in Satcor should be impressed enough to want to see if he were the real thing.

Herbie thought his father would want to see him, but Frank Bannerman, accompanied by a stranger who walked with a limp, came up to Herbie.

"Herbie, I'd like you to meet Alex Goodman," said Bannerman.

"Howja-do," said Herbie. Goodman's handshake was on the tepid side, thought Herbie. And there was something familiar about him. Of course, he was the man who had punctured the fat man's hopes for River Bend by saying he was over his head against the competition.

"Glad to know you, Herbie." Herbie detected a flavor of Brooklyn in the way Goodman said "Hoibie."

Herbie speculated that the conversation would be directed to his opinion on the second race. Instead, Bannerman and Goodman talked about the poor ride by the jockey on the horse that finished second, Handsome Does. They discussed weight allotments for the featured seventh race. And talked about the merits of Discovery against Time Supply, two champions expected to compete against each other in races coming up at New England tracks.

"Dammit," Herbie said to himself, "What do I have to do to get noticed? Wasn't my pick of Mahogany Tim a world-beater?" Minus the immediate recognition he expected, Herbie concentrated on Goodman. Goodman had an air that reminded Herbie of Rabbi Shulman, who had instructed Herbie five years earlier to achieve Bar Mitzvah. The major similarity between Goodman and Shulman, speculated Herbie, was that when stumped for something to say, Goodman consulted the racing form tucked in his pocket, much as Shulman kept his prayer book handy for reference when confronted with scriptural questions. As Herbie came to really know Goodman, there was nothing incongruous about his frequent consultations with the Morning Telegraph. Alex Goodman was a racetrack tout.

At the age of 40, Goodman counted as his chief asset, other than his files of racing data covering major tracks around the country, a selected clientele of well-heeled bettors. They stuck to him like glue in his hot streaks and shunned him like a leper when the numerous forces controlling his racing fortunes became ungovernable, which was fairly often. Now, two weeks after the opening of the Atlantic Downs spring meeting, the hollows in his cheeks were flabbier than ever, theorized Herbie, doubtless due as much to a diet of watery coffee and stale donuts consumed in daily ruminations over racing charts as to the sunless gray tunnels of the racetracks where he plied his trade.

The first week of the Atlantic Downs meeting actually began well for Goodman, with a sprinkling of winners, most well scouted at the Florida tracks where he had spent the winter. But for the prior week, he had gone winless, and the half-dozen big bettors he had accompanied to New England were giving him the silent treatment and getting their wisdom from other touts or from Jack's Green Card that sold for fifty cents at the track entrance. In the present slump, as in prior down times, he could usually count on Whitey Roberts to put a ten spot on his selections. This made a difference in Goodman's ability to rebound from misfortune, as well as reviving his hopes for mankind.

"You beat me a neck in the first," said Alex to Herbie. "But my choice was not well ridden. The jockey stopped whipping 70 yards from the finish."

This was spoken without rancor. But Herbie detected an undertone of sadness. Whether the sadness was because his choice had lost, or because he was unhappy about his life, Herbie did not know. Nor did this line of speculation seem as important as the fact that the conversation now took a turn in the direction Herbie wanted.

"I was lucky," said Herbie.

"Let's have another piece of that luck in this race," said Bannerman, hopefully. "Who's the winner, Herbie?"

Of course Herbie was not prepared. Bannerman had come on the scene before Herbie had a chance to connect with Baal.

"Give me a few minutes. I'll come over to see you." Herbie made it sound matter of fact, like Max Levine, the druggist, when Max took an order for a prescription that would be made up and delivered promptly to the Roberts home.

He sensed that Bannerman was impressed with this show of confidence Goodman, however, looked skeptical, as he sauntered off with Bannerman in Whitey's direction. Herbie noted that the man in the gray Stetson was no longer with his father. He turned his attention to the odds board.

"It is now six minutes to post time." The announcement pushed Herbie to act.

Herbie's program told him there were twelve horses entered in the second race for maiden two-year olds at four and a half furlongs. He understood that "maiden" meant non-winner of a race. This thought gave Herbie special incentive to acquire the brilliant orange signal he had experienced twice previously. Herbie felt a kinship for all twelve horses entered—he, too, was a "maiden". He had yet to win any recognition from his father.

He scanned the board quickly. There it was! A vivid orange 30-1 opposite number three, Vita Yellow. Herbie thought he was mistaken. 30-1 horses got little believability from experienced bettors. So he scanned the board three more times. He received the desired bright orange signal from Baal each time.

Herbie was right about the reception to expect from this prediction.

"What the hell, Herbie. Don't go nuts on us," said Sam Dana, often cynical in his observations about people and events.

"I don't know, Herbie—looks like a high flyer to me," said Mitch Weller.

Bannerman spoke for the Satcor guys, with Whitey nodding agreement. "Let's put a kicker on number four, just in case."

Herbie didn't know what a "kicker" was, but he quickly found out.

"Myrtle, put ten on number four," Whitey ordered. Ten dollars was a measly bet for Satcor. . Herbie had overheard Myrtle making bets of fifty to two hundred dollars on the phone to Warner Sarnow. So a "kicker" must be simply a ticket nobody expected to cash unless the roof fell in on every other horse in the race.

Herbie was not surprised that his mother was the designated bettor. She was accustomed to carrying out Whitey's orders, to the detriment of her children, especially her daughter Reggie.

The abuses suffered by his sister, now sixteen, often gave Herbie thought about the bad luck of the Roberts kids when lots were drawn for parents. If Reggie, now nearly sixteen—tall, blond, and beautiful—asked for the privileges of her peers, like the use of lipstick, Myrtle said no, echoing Whitey. Whitey did not trust his children. He especially had little faith in Reggie, who he felt was born to sin, even though Herbie was absolutely certain Reggie had never given cause to deserve this judgment. On one recent occasion, after Reggie went to a movie with Herbie's friend, Seymour Barnofsky, there had been a scene of violent accusation and tearful denial between father and daughter. Whitey accused Reggie of necking with Seymour. Needless to say, Myrtle saw to it that Reggie operated under Whitey's strict curfew instructions following this contretemps. In addition, she was not allowed to bring friends to the Roberts home in the evening, a restriction applying also to Herbie and Larry.

What happened with the "kicker" horse—Vita Yellow? Unlike Mahogany Tim, Vita Yellow was unwilling to wait for the stretch drive to put on his best performance. Number Four went to the front right after the start and stretched his lead until he went by the finish line seven lengths in front. As astounding the margin of victory, the payoff of $66 for two dollars was more so. Their ten-dollar bet earned $330 for Satcor

Despite Herbie's role in salvaging something for Satcor, which had a thousand on the horse that ran third, he heard nothing directly from his father. Myrtle brought Herbie a hotdog. And Jake Michaels showed up to act as courier for Herbie's next prophecy.

"You made me look good, Herbie. Thanks. If that plug was out of the money, your father would never believe I hadn't shilled for you on the first race."

"It's okay, Jake. Anytime," grinned Herbie. He wondered what it would be like to be Jake's son. Or Frank Bannerman's. Or Mitch Weller's. Or even the son of a man with as dour an exterior as Sam Dana, who walked with his arms around his children during the High Holy Days.

Herbie now looked at Whitey, hoping to catch a benevolent glance tossed in his direction. But the huge-shouldered man in the Stetson hat was huddled with Whitey once more.

"Who's that with my father?"

Jake paused, answering slowly. "His name is Louie Septimo. He's called the 'Senator'."

"Who calls him "Senator'?" "I never heard of a Septimo in office."

"He's not a public man. In fact, he's very private." Jake shook his head. "I don't like to see your father with him."

"Why not? Because Septimo is Mafia?"

Jake became very serious, almost whispering his answer, inches from Herbie's ear.

"You're bright, Herbie. You see a lot you can figure out yourself. Septimo is Warner Sarnow's boss. Septimo bosses quite a few people in the rackets. That's all I know. That's why I don't like to see your father with him."

"Five minutes to post time!" blared the public address horns, changing the subject for both Jake and Herbie.

"Give me three minutes, Jake. I'll try to keep my streak going."

The revelation about Septimo's identity had planted a seed of uneasiness. He fought the urge to learn more about his father's liaisons with Septimo by studying the huge odds board thirstily for the deviant digits that were now a covenant between him and Baal.

Something was wrong. The odds opposite both Number 1 and Number 8 were the same vivid orange. Herbie shut his eyes then looked again. 1 and 8 were still on the same wavelength. Two sets of bright orange digits, seven sets of dull orange digits.

"It is now two minutes to post time!"

This call brought Jake immediately to Herbie.

"Anything, Herbie?"

Herbie shrugged. "Two horses. Numbers one and eight. Sorry, I can't separate them." He realized that Whitey would think he was just guessing, protecting himself by asking Satcor to bet two horses.

Puzzled, Jake trotted off to see Whitey and the others. Septimo had disappeared.

Number 1 was Bright Star. Number 8 was Rameses. Herbie didn't know who to cheer for. How could he, in good conscience, urge them both to win? If Bright Star won, now held at even money, Satcor wouldn't win or lose. If Rameses won, at 10 to 1 odds, everything would be fine.

As the starter raised his red flag across the infield at the six-furlong starting gate, Herbie stole another glance at the odds board. Numbers 1 and 8 were still equal selections from Baal.

"They're off!"

At the start, Bright Star and Rameses were both off the pace. Around the far turn, Bright Star moved up to third. Rameses was far back.

"Now, at the head of the stretch, Bright Star is moving to take the lead from Melissa May!"

"Near the finish, they're neck and neck, Bright Star and Melissa May." The voice of the announcer paused.

"Coming on the outside is Rameses! At the finish Bright Star with Rameses, Melissa May is third!" A long pause. ". Win position is too close to call. Wait for the judges call."

The roar of the crowd ebbed, waiting for the placing judges' verdict.

"The judges have ruled a photo finish. Please be patient until the camera decides the winner" The announcer's tone was precise, slightly pedantic, a parent telling a child to be patient for his goodies.

"What's likely to happen, Jake?" Herbie's question asked for a detailed explanation.

"Herbie, this is the first season when close finishes are decided by a new high-speed camera installed at the finish line. Maybe you've read about it—the Eye in the Sky?"

"I think I saw it mentioned in the Globe recently, but I didn't pay much attention."

"It's a good thing, Herbie. Absolutely impartial. The human eye can't be as reliable as science," said Jake.

Herbie had only one thought, a thought he could not share with Jake or anyone else: Baal had been straight with him. Even if Bright Star were decided the winner and his father came away totally frustrated, Herbie would always believe this race proved the ultimate truth—Baal loved him.

Sometimes an entire race meeting would go by without a single dead heat. Now it happened, with the announcement from the public address:

"Bright Star and Rameses have finished in a dead heat for first place! Wait for the deciding photo to be posted!"

There was, of course, an uproar from the supporters of Bright Star, who collected just $3 for each two-dollar win ticket. They would never be fully satisfied with the verdict of the camera, even though the prints showing the noses of the two horses together at the finish line were posted in minutes at a dozen locations around the track.

"I'll bet the judges fooled around with the photos!"

"Who's to say the people who made the prints are on the up and up?"

On the other hand, the supporters of Rameses were content with the $17 payoff for two dollars. Even though they knew it would have been much greater if the photo had favored his nose. The rancor and complaints subsided to a low buzz after a few minutes bickering over the honesty of judges, camera crew and photo lab.

In the fourth race, Herbie got a signal from Baal on Number 3. Unfortunately, Number 3 broke through the gate before the start of the race and ran away for half a mile. The announcement of the scratch came just seconds from the start of the race, too brief an interval for Herbie to reset himself for a magic message.

Still, Herbie was making history of a sort. The results of the next four races gave Herbie the most triumphant day in his 18-year relationship with his father. All four of his choices won. With six winners for the day, the men of Satcor went home happy. How happy Herbie did not care. All that was important was that on their departure after the last race, Whitey said to his son, in earshot of his cronies, "Not a bad day, big shot."

CHAPTER 6

Claire Strong was one of those fortunates who are untroubled by the status quo. In a century when taking a stand against injustice was praised in the pulpit and on the political podium, Claire relied on her most elemental instinct, not to fight, but to yield with charming goodwill, and by so yielding, gain her ends. Did a bandleader find her sassy, body-shaking style capturing too much audience attention; she became a shrinking violet. Did the man who presently held the baton in her life require more from Claire behind the scene than in front of the orchestra, Claire often submitted. Not that Claire was undiscriminating on whom she bestowed her favors. Her clear, open face and guileless brown eyes clouded with disappointment when she was treated like a whore. A man who would want her to be receptive must first offer consideration and respect. And Claire prided herself on her ability to recognize these qualities.

The well-built teenager who had accompanied Claire in his tryout for Jack Charles seemed to possess a special sweetness. She had found his nervous appreciation of her closeness intriguing—one innocent recognizes another. And so, a few days after she obtained his phone number from the musicians' union, Claire did something rare for her: she phoned a man.

"Herbie, it's Claire. Remember, we did a number for Jack Charles at the Dreamland?" The voice of Claire Strong, the person, was modulated and quiet, in contrast with the often-tigerish wail of Claire Strong the singer.

"Claire... Strong?" The undertone of excitement in Herbie's response did not escape Claire. She had made an impression on the youth. How else would he have recalled her full name three weeks after their brief teamwork in Beachtown?

It was difficult to keep a note of triumph from her reply.

"I didn't think you'd remember, really."

"Why shouldn't I? You're a fine performer." This was a fat lie. Herbie had been impressed with her body, not her singing.

"Herbie. I'd like to ask your help on a professional problem." This arrow struck dead center on Sir Galahad.

"Sure, whatever I can do."

"There's a new club opening on Faneuil Street downtown. The Golden Bull. I've got a spot there if I can work up a new routine. I don't know if piano is open there, but I'd be grateful if you'd rehearse me." She paused, reaching for heavier artillery. "There's a good Steinert at home. Just been tuned."

Now, Herbie, now. The watershed in your life. Move out, child, move in, destiny. She had said all the key words you'd ever want to hear: "grateful", "rehearse me", "at home". Claire was inviting him to shed his virginity. Or was she? Maybe he had misread her? His uncertainty showed in his reply.

"I don't know how much help I'd be. I haven't worked with many singers." This was true. But one of his strong points was his ability to transpose at sight from the key printed on the score to any other key. This talent had kept his jazz teacher interested in him even when Herbie shirked his practice schedule. No, there was no reason why he would not be able to accompany Claire. And Claire, for her part, had heard enough quality in the youth's playing at the Dreamland tryout to pursue her quarry.

"You don't know how really good you are, Herbie. Or how good you can be with more experience." She softly underscored "experience." but the emphasis was unnecessary. Open sesame! Herbie believed he was at the gates and the magic words had been spoken. All he had to do was stride in.

He thought quickly. Tomorrow was Saturday, his fourth day at the track with Whitey. Tomorrow night he'd be at Hibernian Manor with Ken Riley's band. Sunday morning cut the grass. He had looked forward to a few sets of tennis with Lenny Atlas. But first things first. It wasn't every day that a Venus like Claire invited you to have "experience." He dared not let himself think what that experience might include, lest it creep into his voice and frighten away this budding miracle.

"Let's see. Hmm. My Sunday afternoon is open after three. How's your schedule?" Whitey would be gone on his Connecticut trip by one-thirty at the latest. That would give him an hour to complete preparations for his maiden voyage down the Nile with Cleopatra, half an hour to hop the bus to a stop near Claire's house.

"We're in tune, Herbie. Perfect. I'll expect you by three-thirty."

When he hung up, thankful that Myrtle had not answered Claire's ring,

Herbie wondered if his encounter with the first woman in his life would be as memorable as his first meeting with Baal. Then a sudden thought struck home: he had read Baal's first signal on the day that he met Claire at the Dreamland. What could it mean? Coincidence? Or was Claire a Jezebel sent by Baal to entrap him in a life from which he might never escape? Ridiculous. The full-breasted woman who had tantalized him at the Dreamland was very real. On with the show!

The ride to the track the next day was loaded with small and large fears for Herbie. From the back seat, Herbie was aware of piercing glances aimed at him, reflected in the rear view mirror. As he had done all his life, Herbie looked away. This had always infuriated his father.

"When someone looks you in the eye, look back. That's how you know you're a man."

Herbie had grown up with this admonition. He felt himself a failure because he was never able to make another man's eyes a place of meeting. He concluded that this inability pointed to a serious defect in his personality. His father, who told him frequently, "If you can't look the other fellow in the eye, you'll never amount to anything", reinforced this self-judgment.

When the letter admitting him to Harvard in the Class of 1940 had been passed between his parents, what his teachers at

Brookline High would regard as a significant achievement had been downplayed by Whitey.

"All right, big shot. You passed a test on paper. Now let's see if you can be a man." Little question that "big shot" was the highest accolade ever received from his father. But Herbie knew that it fell below what his classmates must be hearing from their parents.

Truthfully, Herbie felt guilty about his intentions towards Claire. His do-good side, nourished by four years as a boy scout and a lifetime of commitment to his Bible, had interfered on prior occasions when there was a chance to go all the way with a girl .He admitted to himself that he was afraid he'd get a venereal disease. Afraid of getting the girl pregnant. Afraid of being neutralized by premature ejaculation or impotency. And there was always the possibility that Whitey, the omnipresent assassin of joy, would appear on the scene. As he did when Herbie discovered the delights of masturbation.

"The next time I'll cut your hands off!" Whitey's roar on this occasion, accompanied by a heavy strapping of the 13-year old, had pretty well brought Herbie's natural impulses under control and might carry over into the scene of planned seduction Sunday afternoon.

"Wake up, big shot! Park the car. Meet us in the restaurant." The brittle commands brought Herbie back to reality. Better forget Claire. Today belonged to Whitey. . Tumor row was another day.

As it turned out, the day also belonged to Alex Goodman. When Herbie got to the restaurant, it was a sea of babbling horseplayers. Goodman was in deep conversation with Whitey, Frank Bannerman and Mitch Weller. Whitey barely glanced at Herbie as he slid into an empty chair. Alex nodded briefly to the youth. The conference ended in a few minutes and Whitey introduced his son.

"This is big shot, my son, Herbie Roberts."

"We've met. How are you, Herbie?" Herbie thought he spied a sympathetic gleam in the tout's brown eyes, then banished the idea as wishful thinking. There was hardly an adult male of his acquaintance to whom he had not looked for support. More evidence of a lack of manly fiber, he concluded.

"Good to see you again," said Herbie stiffly.

Certainly he was rattled by the attention paid to Goodman, just a week after scoring with six winners. Anyhow, turf advisor Herbie Roberts got Whitey off to a poor start. In the first race, he could not make contact with Baal. The odds board lights stayed a depressingly dull orange as Herbie fought the fantasy of Claire sitting on his piano with her bosom spilling out of her blouse. There was undoubtedly a connection between the anger he felt at the shift of focus to Goodman and his erotic vision. He recalled that whenever he had felt a jealous twinge, as his father's attention was diverted elsewhere, compensatory erotic visions of females in stages of dishabille flashed through his mind. Now, it happened once more. And at Whitey's expense, as the suddenly powerless odds board prophet guessed, rather than prophesied.

Herbie's guesses failed in the first and second races. Whitey's thin lips got thinner. Herbie pleaded harder with Baal for a signal. In the third race, still no connection with Baal. Luckily, Herbie's frantic guess on a courageous filly named Saddle Tramp resulted in a second-place finish, as the filly was beaten a neck. Whiteys grim pre-race warning, "this is your last chance, big shot", was forgotten for one more race.

Despite the temporary reprieve, Herbie was overtaken by gloom. There was little question now that recurring visions of Claire were shutting off connection with Baal. But what could he do? Talk to his father?

"Say Dad, I'm sorry to tell you this, but I keep thinking about screwing this girl, and it interferes with my out-of-this-world method of picking winners." No, that would not cut it. Better bite the bullet and call off the date with Claire. He'd say:

"Hello Claire, Herbie Roberts. Sorry but my college tutor is having a big orientation at Dunster House for incoming freshmen.

We'll have to make it another time." Claire would be upset, but better she than Whitey.

The decision made, he felt relaxed enough to look about at the fans hanging over the rail to see the horses entering for the post parade. Whitey, seated majestically in a canvas chair, was holding court with his Satcor cronies. Myrtle stood at his side wearing her perpetual smile, waiting for Whitey's betting instructions.

Herbie now knows the parental pattern at the racetrack. Whitey sits for the full eight races, huddled with his buddies. . King of his fiefdom, he decides on whoever's wisdom is in vogue at the moment, then translates it into orders for Myrtle, two minutes before the horses reached the starting gate. By delaying the Satcor bet until almost the final moment, Whitey is able to assess the late odds board action that shows up the "good things", and give hearings to the various informants who hang around stables, trainers and jockeys. Alex Goodman has a place of honor in this hierarchy. Herbie admits to himself that he aspires to a similar niche and asks himself why it is that he is the only person in Whitey's world who gets the full load of Whitey's scorn.

"Make no mistakes," Whitey growled at Herbie before the first race. Herbie accepted this instruction as a vote of confidence, even while he realized that other sons, with other kinds of fathers, might have regarded it as a threat of violence.

Whitey did not worry about Myrtle getting to the ticket window on time. Scalplock Larson, on Whitey's payroll for at least ten years that Herbie was aware of, sold fifty-dollar tickets in the clubhouse. He supplemented his paycheck with the sale of favors, depending on the season. During the winter, he was a ticket taker for hockey, boxing, wrestling and other functions at the Boston Garden. He also took bribes from Whitey and other lovers of sports who appreciated the special largesse that Larson could dispense, one of which was to let friends and their families, into the sports palace by accepting blank cardboards at his admission gate, instead of legitimate tickets. Once inside, an usher, Gino Carmine, cousin to Freddy Carmine, a Whitey Roberts meat-cutter, found seats for Whitey's guests. Then in spring, summer and fall, Larson, as the "token" black among New England track cashiers, held a privileged spot. In this seat of power, he chose to be the fifty—dollar ticket seller in the clubhouse, where he made certain that genuine friends like Whitey Roberts never got shut out of a race. He did this by motioning them to the head of the line and by whispering the numbers of horses backed by heavy bettors presumably "in the know." This hospitality earned Larson a favored place at the Saturday morning payoff sessions at M. Roberts.

Now, as the post parade advanced in the backstretch, Herbie was rewarded by Baal for cleansing his mind of lustful thoughts with a brilliant orange 6-5 signal opposite number Three, Mac Truck. Whitey grimaced when his prophet told him that he even money favorite was his selection.

"I never touch a big favorite," he snapped. "Why do I need you to tell me to bet a 6-5 shot?" Jogged by a warning from the public address horns that "the horses are nearing the gate", and given the nod of approval from the men of Satcor, he handed Myrtle a sheaf of twenties and instructions to bet Number Nine at 5-1 odds. Mac Truck chugged home by three lengths and Herbie retreated miserably to the furthest corner of the clubhouse.

In the fifth, Alex Goodman's pick was Number Two, the third choice at 7-2 odds, which attracted a heavy pooled bet from Satcor. This was Satcor's target bet for the day, so Herbie knew his advice wasn't wanted. Nonetheless, he returned to this trackside spot on the rail opposite the odds board to test his will power against the tendency of erotic thoughts to come center stage at the wrong times.

Herbie did not have long to wait. The sensuous image of Claire Strong blocked his view of the entire odds board. In vain he repeated the tactics that worked so well before the fourth race—an imaginary phone call canceling his Sunday date with Claire.

Not only was the singer entirely nude, she made such violent love to Herbie that he felt himself approaching a climax. Catastrophe was prevented by a light tug on his shoulder from Frank Bannerman.

"We're on Number Two fairly heavy. What's your opinion?" Frank, like the others in Satcor, was aware that Herbie had picked Mac Truck in the fourth. And, like the others, he had benefited from Herbie's prophecies the past three Saturdays and was looking to Herbie for a hedge choice.

Herbie looked at the odds board. Might as well chance it. If his choice beat Goodman's, Whitey would know. If his choice lost, he was no worse off.

"Give me a minute," he muttered.

Bannerman's interruption had wiped Claire from his thoughts. Baal responded with a clear message that Number Eight, at 10-1, would win.

"Number Eight," said Herbie.

"The price is right," Bannerman said, and then departed.

Number Eight won by a length, with Goodman's pick second. Because of Bannerman, Satcor had a hundred on Number Eight. Satcor had bet a thousand on Number Two, so cleared just seventy dollars for the race.

In Herbie's opinion, his father should have been grateful, but instead, he was furious.

"Why couldn't you say something twenty minutes ago and give us a chance to make a real bet?"

Herbie's face reddened. But Whitey, disappointed at missing a killing, laid it on.

"Everything you do is last minute. You don't shine your shoes until you're half way out the door when I remind you. You stay up all night to study for an exam you're unprepared for. You never practice until the day before you take a lesson. Jesus Christ, Herbie, when the hell are you going to change?"

For Whitey to let the whole world know his deficiencies was too much. Herbie's ears reddened. His throat constricted. He could not reply. He was sure everyone in the clubhouse was looking.

"Leave the kid alone." Bannerman to the rescue.

"I told you we shouldn't have let him come," said Myrtle mildly.

Herbie sauntered painfully to his trackside retreat, covertly checking to see whose eyes had witnessed the tongue-lashing. But horseplayers, especially before a race, are in a world apart. No one, with the possible exception of Alex Goodman, the tout, now limping toward the Satcor group, had seen Herbie's humiliation.

Herbie decided it was better to lay low for the remaining races rather than risk more public punishment.

"I don't know anything," he responded when Bannerman asked his opinion before the next three races. This wasn't true, of course. Satcor missed out on three winners and Herbie showed up at Hibernian Manor for his job with Ken Riley's Royal Minstrels in a mood to chew nails.

* * *

With Lew Saccardo on drums, Harvey Hurtt on trumpet, Basil Swenson on sax and Herbie on piano, the Royal Minstrels were fraudulently named. But what came out of his band of all nationalities was, to Ken Riley's ears, "right from the ould sod." The pay was modest-Herbie would bring home six dollars for his night's work-but the hearty appreciation received by the Minstrels for their renditions of tunes like "Sweet and Lovely" and "Sophisticated Lady" made up for the meager pay. And, when the rest of the group dropped out while Herbie accompanied Ken's rich tenor in "When Irish Eyes Are Smiling", the gathering of several hundred Saturday nighters stopped dancing and crowded close to the heavenly sounds, anxious not to miss a golden note.

After six months of pounding on the old Chickering every Saturday night, and some Friday evenings as well, Herbie was accustomed to pretty girls pushing close to his bench, flashing inquisitive eyes and plump bosoms in a frank play of interest in the good-looking piano player. Tonight was no different. Near the close of the evening, as Herbie glanced at his watch, wearied from the day's disappointments, a black-haired, dark-eyed Irish lass with ivory skin pushed close beside him on the piano bench.

"Are you doin' anythin' tonight? I'm needin' someone to walk me home through the dark streets." Her soft breast brushed his arm. Once, then again. For a long minute, Herbie thought favorably of the idea. Until he came to the vision of himself stripped to his underwear, fumbling for a contraceptive that he did not have. Drugstores would be closed, and besides, how could you march arm and arm with a girl up to the prescription counter and say, "I'd like some rubbers, please?"

That delicious pressure on his arm, once more. Glancing around, Herbie saw Basil looking in his direction while fishing in his pocket. He held his wallet in Herbie's view, winked and put it back. Basil would give him rubbers. So would Lew, Harvey and Ken. They were older, wiser, and unafraid. And they were a brotherhood Herbie felt shut out from.

"Count the ways you are alone, Herbie." He had said it to himself a thousand times, especially in the six years since his mother's father had died. Lewine Nattelson had loved Herbie, appreciated him, and encouraged him. . The twice-a-month visits to the Nattelson home beside a park in Roxbury had been a pleasant focus for both Herbie and Larry. Larry, the extrovert, reveled in the challenge of the huge, smooth-humped glacial age boulders just outside the Nattelson front door. Once, inspired by the Tarzan stories, he had tried to swing from one limb of a tree to another. He had fallen and injured himself badly enough to required chiropractor attention for a full year.

Undeterred by his fall, Larry plunged into a rugged outdoor life. He was on both football and wrestling teams at Brookline High. Herbie envied Larry's physical feats. And his brother's sexual adventures as well, about which Larry was wont to brag. Herbie tried to imitate his brother by following him into the Boy Scouts. He failed to follow him into the Sea Scouts and envied his brother's weekend excursions on an old Coast Guard cutter along Boston's South Shore to Cape Cod.

Herbie reminded himself that he had even felt shut out from boys he had grown up with who, along with Herbie, were about to go on to college. Often, walking to a movie with Danny Lanin and Seymour Barnofsky, he had suddenly found himself alone while Danny and Seymour were in close, animated talk. Both would live at college. They often talked about the great times awaiting them. Herbie had no such illusions.

The satiny cheek brushed his own, bringing him back to the girl's invitation. Lilac perfume caressed him.

Herbie looked at Basil bleeping a few warm-up bars on his sax. Basil nodded encouragingly.

"Nothing I'd like better," Herbie said, managing a grin.

It was just a mile from Hibernian Manor to Kathy Collins' wood frame home on Mission Hill. Kathy chatted about the difficulties of maintaining professional dignity at Wheeling Hospital where she was a nurse's aid.

"The doctors are always trying to steer me into the linen closet. I'm trying to do my job and you know how hard it is to keep up with medical problems today."

Herbie hardly picked up a word she said, interjecting a sympathetic grunt here and there while attempting to slow his pounding pulse.

"Tachycardia, an accelerated heart beat." That was what the examining doctor said when he was screened for play on the Brookline High football team. This slight disturbance kept him off the squad.

A doctor's examination was one of the ways that Herbie's protective shell could be pierced. Herbie told himself that the slip of paper that kept him out of football and excused him from gym classes meant that he was afraid the doctor's stethoscope would reveal his deepest secret, his masturbation habit, his sensual thoughts about girls, and most of all, his subterranean intention to physically do away with his father for treating him as a stranger all his life.

The speeded up pulse brought on by his approaching rendezvous was, he suddenly realized, akin to his reaction to a doctor's examination. Both required that he take off his clothes. The thought made him smile. Kathy thought he smiled for her presence and tugged him along faster.

Still pursuing the objective of slowing his racing pulse, Herbie reasoned that shedding his virginity might be the catalyst that banished his erotic fantasies. Fantasies that too often came between Baal and him. What he was contemplating with Kathy, then, might erase the real obstacle to getting Whitey's love and respect. No erotic fantasies, more signals from Baal. More signals from Baal, more winners. And Whitey wanted winners perhaps more than he wanted anything else in his life.

Feeling clearer bout his objectives, Herbie patted the wallet in his back pocket as he and Kathy tiptoed hand in hand up the wooden stairs to her front door.

CHAPTER 7

Inside her room, Kathy switched on a soft lamp, revealing a sofa in one corner, its shadow frescoing a crucifix on the wall above it. A dresser and bed bordered the opposite wall. Herbie wondered: Will we "start" on the sofa, and then gradually work our way to the bed? Of course. That was it.

"Come see." That soft, but determined hand on his arm pulled him to the sofa.

"See what?" The half-light showed little else in the room but a chair and the door to a closet. And oh yes, a book-like object on a table before the sofa.

The object was an album of family photos, which Kathy flipped through from cover to cover, chirping with delight as she identified four generations of the family Collins for the puzzled young Jewish lad.

"Fine people, fine people." He muttered the unfelt platitude several times. Have to go along, he said to himself. It wouldn't be right to act like an animal no matter how animal-like he had been in his fantasies. Just the same, he wondered about the direction of the young girl snuggling close to him as she turned the pages of the album. Was this girl's ploy to throw him off guard? A subtle way to cool him down? Or best of all, was she trying to heighten his desire by playing hard to get?

"I like you, Herbie." He face was turned towards his. The most sensual mouth he had ever seen was partly open.

This was better. His arm circled her shoulders. She took his other hand and placed it lightly on her breast. Trembling, he leaned to kiss her but she drew back.

"Do you like me, Herbie?"

"Very much."

"How much?" She pressed his hand tightly to her breast.

"You're wonderful!" He mustered as much feeling as he could in this statement, thinking this is what she wanted to hear. And besides, the firm mound beneath his palm did feel quite wonderful. He tried gently to free his hand from hers, so that he could explore beneath her bodice, but the small hand stayed in control.

"Kiss me." She had reversed the traditional roles: now the woman was aggressive, the man yielding. Kathy was in charge.

They kissed, French style, tongues darting in and out of each other's mouth. Herbie's thoughts raced along with his pulse.

At what point do I put on the condom? The feelings in his groin would shortly be unmanageable. Despite his growing agitation, he sensed that Kathy held her composure.

Provoked by her perfume, her active tongue, the fullness of her breast, his breathing became heavy and rapid. He tried desperately to subjugate the Niagara in his groin and slow down to her pace. What should have been a blissful revel was now pure torment.

"Herbie, darling," she said, with a slight gasp that encouraged him to believe her excitement matched his. She continued: "I'd like you to . . . " her voice dropped off shyly.

At last, he exulted silently. A request for something sensational. Take off my dress, my bra, and my panties. Blood tingled his scalp.

" . . . meet my family." Her voice was low and sweet, but determined.

Ebb tide. His passion retreated, dwindled to a ripple, then evaporated.

"I'm only eighteen." He couldn't believe he said that. Here he was allowing himself to follow her lead into a conversation about formal courtship after an acquaintance of less than two hours.

"So I'm three years older. It won't make any difference. My father is younger than my mother." She gave his hand, still resting on her breast, an encouraging pat.

"That's not what I meant," he said, not knowing what to do with his anger any more than he did with his now defunct desire.

"You still think I'm wonderful?" This was spoken more for self-assurance than as a question. The undertone of doubt meant that she had noticed how the crest of passion beside her had lowered.

"Uh huh."

"And you do want to meet my parents, don't you?"

His hand, under hers, lay limp on her breast. He suddenly withdrew it, responding to her question with the fervor of a prisoner pleading for his life at the bar of justice.

"I'm only eighteen! Do you hear? I'm only eighteen!"

With this explosion, he fled out the door, leaving Kathy weeping face down on the family album.

The bells were tolling two o'clock from the church opposite Kathy's lodging when Herbie launched himself from the scene of failure in the general direction of Brookline Village. There he caught the bus that dropped him within a mile of the Roberts mansion.

Undressing in the bathroom so as not to disturb Larry, he sorrowfully withdrew the condom from his wallet. It didn't look very clean, so he flushed it down the toilet. Only the six crisp new dollars from the night' work meant anything. What if all girls were like Kathy? My God, he thought, I could have said the wrong thing and become engaged.

He slid quietly under the covers and pulled the top sheet over his head to blot out the evening's mistakes. The first place he went wrong was to let Kathy run the show. The second was in being there in the first place.

"Hey kid," the whisper from Larry was loaded with curiosity. "Howja make out?"

Then, as Herbie held his silence, he continued:

"Didja get laid? Break your maiden? Come on, tell big brother."

He was sorry he answered at all. When Larry was in a teasing mood, it went on forever. But answering was the only way he could get the sleep he needed to handle Sunday's heavy schedule.

"What do you think? Three times. That's right, three times. And excuse me, good night."

"No kidding? Three times. Gosh. Good work." This was followed by a summary of his own evening's pleasure with a girl he had picked up at Nantasket Beach.

But Herbie did not hear a word. He was asleep.

CHAPTER 8

Herbie threw in the clutch as he came to the end of the row, wiping sweat from his eyes so he could read his watch: quarter to eleven. Better hurry. The old man was a stickler for Sunday dinner at twelve, hitting the road immediately thereafter for Connecticut.

As Herbie wheeled the mower into the garage, his father's voice booming through opened windows held Larry captive. Larry's application for re-admission to Southern Cal having been turned down, he was being baptized into the beef business.

"Godammit, look at me when I'm talking to you. Remember that unless you're in the customer's place of business the same minute, the same hour, the same day of the week every week, you'll never make a living on the road. That's right, you've got to give the sonofabitch a pain in the stomach if you don't show up on time. You've got to marry the bastard. Why? He can get the same beef cheaper from the packer, so you've got to give him what he can't get from the packer—that's service!" Herbie could not make out any answer from Larry. This was normal. Herbie was certain that Larry was sitting absolutely silent and motionless, his eyes locked on his father. Whitey boiled over if anyone in the family looked away when addressed by him.

The voice of the Butcher Boy, as his cronies often greeted him, had stopped, so Herbie knew the lecture had ended. Then it would take Whitey ten minutes to shave with his old-fashioned straight razor. He didn't trust the newfangled safety razors that were sweeping the country.

Grasping a corn broom, Herbie whisked the mower clean, squirted oil into the ports stamped "oil here", tucked the mower into a corner of the garage, then bounded up the back stairs and through the screen door into the kitchen with such velocity that the thump of the door brought thunder from the bathroom.

"Godammit to hell, you cut me," roared Whitey, stemming a rivulet below his nostrils where the razor had nicked him.

Herbie's insides became a bag of ice. "I'm sorry," he said, his voice a toneless squeak.

"Don't stand there. Get yourself cleaned u p in the kitchen. I'm leaving in thirty minutes." The cold blue eyes squinted narrowly over a blanket of soap, spearing the youth momentarily, then releasing him so the business of shaving could be completed.

Time was, long before his own beard made a straggly debut, when the small boy huddled against the opened door to capture the thin gruel of closeness afforded by the sight of his father shaving. He would devour every inch of the ritual as the gleaming blade swept the baby-pink skin clean. But that cherished time was gone. Any chance he had to acquire love and respect from his father would have to come from Herbie's uncertain ability to communicate with Baal at the racetrack. And that chance might be lost unless he found a way to keep the image of Claire Strong from taunting him with her undressed charms.

Although he had mentally rehearsed postponing his date with Claire the day before, Herbie had no real intention of delaying his sexual destiny. If this marked a dishonest streak, he did not know. He would overcome it in time. But the two powerful currents on which he was being carried along could not be denied. One was the vision of Claire pleading for his caresses. The other was a relentless need for his father's affection. Both were omnipresent, insistent, waxing stronger every day.

* * *

When Claire had given him her address, Herbie recalled a drugstore across the street from the bus stop near her home. There he planned to purchase a packet of condoms. He had been exemplary in his bodily preparations, commencing thirty seconds after Whitey's Chrysler disappeared in the direction of Hartford. He took an hour to shower, shave and shape his straight, light-brown hair. This lengthy appropriation of the only bathroom with a full-length mirror drew impatient yowls from Reggie and Larry. Every Sunday following Whitey's departure, his children unchained themselves and fled in every direction, groomed to the teeth. Delia, their housekeeper, bolted the Roberts home after dinner cleanup like a cork popped from a bottle, uncaring whether she landed in a movie or on the lap of a sailor in Scollay Square.

Yes, Whitey had a way of making the hearts around him beat fonder for their freedom.

Until the shock wave of the gambling craze swept her along as it did many others during the Great Depression, Myrtle Roberts would also seek her own world Sunday afternoons. She did the bridge, whist and mahjong circuits so regularly, with such perseverance and skill, that she accumulated a closet full of gold- trimmed ashtrays, one- of-a-kind teacups and flower vases. This harvest was periodically reduced when Whitey went on a door-slamming tear.

Recently, however, Sunday afternoon was time for Myrtle to settle down over the form charts for Monday's horseracing. When her children asked why she was doing this, she replied with a sad, faraway look, "I do it to forget." The Roberts children did not have to ask what she was trying to forget. They had all witnessed angry exchanges over Whitey's supposed infidelities. These usually took place late at night, requiring the children to choose between intervention or hiding under the blankets. Only Herbie showed his face, attempting to cool the heat of the combatants or comforting his mother should Whitey elect to leave home for a day or two. This move hastened Myrtle's return to a state of forgiving penitence.

Now, her face buried in racing charts, Myrtle barely heard Herbie's "see you later, Mom."

"Bye dear," she answered, not looking up.

Alighting from the bus, Herbie glanced at Claire's house, which he assumed from her description was the neat two-family house with blue shutters that stood third from the intersection. He quickly crossed to the drugstore. A thin-faced man in a green eyeshade and gray sack coat was serving two sedate-looking ladies. Herbie busied himself at the magazines until they departed several minutes later.

Herbie walked to the counter as coolly as a sudden surge of excitement allowed.

"A packet of Trojans, please." Larry had flashed the popular condoms often enough for Herbie to know what was in style.

"Regular or Super?" The druggist asked quietly, not wishing to alert two young girls dawdling at the cosmetics counter.

"Regular, please," wondering immediately if he should have said "Super." He paid for his purchase and hurried from the store. What if "Super" meant insurance against failure of the condom? His anxiety still possessed him when Claire's face appeared in the foyer window in response to his ring.

"Herbie, darling, you're right on time." She took his hand, tugging him gaily inside. She gave no sign that his nervousness was noticed.

"I like it. Looks just like you," said Herbie gallantly.

The living room was all purples and pinks, a true horror. An upright piano sat along one wall, a vase of flowers over the soundboard.

A photo of four persons hung near the piano. The girl in the photo was Claire. The boy was her brother Horace, with whom she shared the apartment. Horace, a fireman, was on duty and would not be home until midnight. Pretending to study the picture of Claire's parents, who lived in New Jersey, Herbie spoke up:

"I can see why you're so pretty."

"You'd like Horace. He's a dear," said Claire, basking in Herbie's compliment.

Herbie thumbed through the music scores on the piano rack, noting that they were all by Richard Rodgers or Cole Porter.

"You've got excellent taste. I approve," said Herbie, feeling increased confidence.

"We're going to make beautiful music," he continued, seating himself at the piano.

"We certainly are," she said. Claire had seen Herbie go into the drugstore and divined his purpose. She knew that whether they performed in accord with her program or with Herbie's program, she would do her part well.

* * *

Claire chose a Rodgers tune, "It's Easy To Remember," to begin with, probably, thought Herbie, because all the notes were within one octave, and Claire's vocal range was a good deal more restricted than her bodily movements.

Uncomfortable in the original key, E flat, Claire said:

"Herbie, I'd really be happier singing in the key of G. Any problem?"

After a small struggle, Herbie transposed successfully. He felt, however, that Claire's style was unsuited to the gentle lyric, and spoke up:

"'I see you've got the music from Rodgers' new show. I'd like to hear you sing 'It's got to be love'. More your kind of song."

What he meant was that Claire's bouncy rhythm would blend better with the swinging beat of the Rodgers tune.

Musically, this proved a good choice. Claire projected her husky voice, aided considerably by her suggestive swaying breasts loosely bound in a floppy gray sweater.

Herbie found his attention wandering to Claire's physical rather than musical output. This caused an occasional misalliance between his beat and the singer's phrasing. Claire ignored these mistakes, so pleased was she with the opportunity to rehearse.

After a dynamic, driving rendition of "Lover", which Herbie recognized as an imitation of an extraordinary version recorded by Peggy Lee, Claire drew a long breath.

"I don't know about you, but I'd like a break. What will you have?"

"Make mine coke, if you've got it." Herbie was glad for the interruption. His concentration on the musical requirements had deteriorated rapidly in the previous number.

"How about a spot of rum?" The bottle was already poised over Herbie's glass?

"Of course," he said, unwilling to seem naive. He rarely declined a challenge. It was as though he always needed to prove himself. As a man, a person of character, a great companion. And now, his intuition said that he was about to be tested as a lover.

They sat on the piano bench, sipping their drinks slowly. The day was growing hot and their conversation lagged. Both singer and piano player were content to sip, rattle the ice and smile at each other. . .

Herbie was feeling warm. He hung his jacket over a chair and returned to the bench beside Claire.

Claire pointed to the score of Cole Porter's "What Is This Thing Called Love."

"Don't you agree that Porter was very unfair to open the chorus on such a difficult interval?"

Herbie squinted closely at the score. Humidity had clouded his glasses. He removed them, wiped them dry, put them on again.

"Yup, you're right." He shook his head. "Pretty unusual to open on the diminished seventh."

He realized that Claire's musical education very likely did not include study in depth of chord structure, but he was eager to prove that she mad made a good choice of accompanists. Besides, he thought, a display of sophisticated musical ability might go a long way to erase their age difference.

"You're very good looking without your glasses," she said, leaning forward to remove them, unconsciously pressing against his shoulder with her breast.

The resulting tremble was an early warning to Herbie. He recalled the first mate's shouted instruction to the hands in "Three Years Before The Mast"—"steady as she goes," he cautioned himself.

Aloud: "I haven't always worn them."

"It was reading in poor light because I did not want to wake up my brother Larry: that made my eyes go bad." However, she paid little notice to his explanation, merely smiled gravely, as she loosened and removed his tie, and then opened the top buttons on his shirt.

"Doesn't that feel better?"

"Uh huh." A sudden prickly sensation behind his collar might have been due to the heat of the day. Then too, it might be a response to the touch of her fingers on his bared skin.

Claire laughed. "Bet you've got lots of girls, Herbie." She wasn't poking fun, just telling him she was glad to be sitting alongside. The musicians with whom she had barnstormed around New England would, to a man, have tried to take advantage under the same circumstances. Herbie's reserve provoked and challenged.

"Kiss me, Herbie." Claire's pale, unpainted mouth, lips parted, did not wait for Herbie to act, but continued on, touching Herbie's mouth lightly, then withdrew.

This was new. Herbie usually took the initiative in necking bouts with girls he had paired off with at parties. Now he hesitated, uncertain—the object of his fantasies was making the first move.

Once again, the lips that tasted slightly of Cuba's leading beverage were against his own, this time making demands to which he was not ready to respond.

"You're very sweet," Claire murmured, inclining her head in the crook of his arm. She removed his glasses and looked into his green-blue eyes with her smiling brown eyes.

"You're sweet," he managed, chokingly, wondering what he should do to recapture the initiative. Who ever heard of a real man accepting the advances of a woman?

"Come." She stood up and pulled Herbie to his feet. Without relinquishing his hand, she led him to the sofa, slip-covered with the biggest roses Herbie had ever seen. Herbie sat down, still dazed by Claire's first kiss.

Claire did not sit down but stood over him, the full contours of her breasts outlined in the fluffy wool sweater. Then, looking deeply into Herbie's eyes, she lifted the sweater over her head, allowing her bare breasts to tumble into view.

Herbie remained frozen, disbelieving both the abundance of Claire's breasts and the reality of the challenge so playfully posed to him.

"Take it," she said softly, maneuvering one nipple, hard with passion, close to Herbie's mouth. Virtually surrounded by her awesome bosom, Herbie had no recourse but to take her nipple in his mouth. At first reacting in a very tentative way, barely tasting the nipple's light dusting of bath powder, Herbie quickly became so greedy that Claire was persuaded to undress completely.

Even though she stood naked and Herbie was fully dressed, there was no question in his mind but that Claire held the upper hand. The idea that he had to be seduced in order to cast off his virginity caused him to momentarily break the spell that Claire was weaving.

"This . . . doesn't seem right," he said weakly.

"No?" A mischievous smile. "Let's talk about it," she continued, seating herself close to the youth. He folded his hands in his lap to avoid her rounded hip and the delicious slope beyond.

She leaned back, affecting an attitude of thoughtful attention that was belied by excited breathing.

With difficulty, Herbie forced his gaze upward from the fascinating darkness of her crotch, past the dimpled navel, and the beckoning half moons of her breasts to finally light on the carefree brown eyes.

"Yes?" from Claire with a note of whimsy that masked the flame now licking over her body in tandem with Herbie's gaze.

"I uh," he hesitated. He wondered what would happen if he allowed his hands to roam at will over the expanse of heaving flesh. As if she got his message, Claire twisted her generous thighs from side to side in slow, undulating movement. She arched her back, the stately mounds rising every higher, nipples stiffened into small spikes of desire.

Ever so slowly, Herbie caressed a thigh, a hip, finally reaching the hollow between her breasts where his hand meet Claire's. Now her hand led his over every hill, into every valley, the pace at first sedate and measured, then faster and wilder as Claire's excitement was transmitted to Herbie's fingers.

Herbie shook free of Claire's grasp to capture a generous expanse of her firm breast on his own. Then, as Claire's hand curved around his neck, bringing his face close to hers, Herbie found her mouth in a long kiss. From her mouth, Herbie's lips traveled lightly over every part of Claire, evoking sighs of delight and whispers of encouragement.

His exploration of Claire was having an effect on Herbie's own body. The rising heat in his groin suddenly reminded him that his long journey would end in disaster unless he could reach the pocket of his jacket where he had hidden the condoms.

"Gosh," he said in panic, raising his head from her belly to look for the chair with his jacket.

"This what you want?" A hand dangled the packet of condoms in front of his nose. In the semi-darkness, his blush went unseen. She knew everything and was aiding his purpose.

"You're quite a girl," he said admiringly, standing to remove his clothing, a process she watched avidly.

While not as heavily muscled as his brother Larry, who worked out with weights, Herbie was ruggedly built, with smooth skin, unlike his brother's hairy mat. As he stepped out of his briefs, Claire said, with kindling excitement, "Herbie, you really are something."

They went into Claire's bedroom. She stretched out, Herbie embracing her, luxuriating in her warm contours. Then, the primeval manly force in command, he was over her and between her thighs. He moved with her, feeling her passions rise to a surmountable peak.

"More, more!" She cried out, urging him to still greater excesses of wildness, until her moans of pleasure mingled with his own.

CHAPTER 9

The next day was a blur for Herbie and a puzzle for his teachers. They could find little resemblance between the intelligent, alert student they had prepared for Harvard and the sleepy-eyed youth who slumped in his chair one class after another. The truth was, simply, that Herbie was played out from his afternoon with Claire Strong. Moreover, he was troubled by anxiety over the worth of his adventure.

While not consciously probing for some cosmic meaning to his first intimacy with a woman, the parade of events starting with Kathy Collins on Saturday night went by in unbidden mental review a hundred times. Herbie was not sure that the uninhibited sex with Claire represented a high point in his life or a low point. Certainly there was little congruence between the largely intellectual pursuits that had dominated his adolescent years and the animal-like quality of his encounter with Claire. Their parting had included a promise from Claire to call him with the result of her audition at the Golden Bull on Wednesday.

Myrtle was on the phone with Warner Sarnow when Herbie dropped wearily into a kitchen chair at three o'clock. He had killed an hour after school talking with Marvin Reach about the value of sampling courses during his first year of college versus concentrating in one area that might become his "major" as an upperclassman. Marvin had decided to go into his father's dressmaking business after college. Herbie said he had no intention of going into his father's business. This elicited disbelief. "Geez, Herbie, my dad says your dad is the biggest beef man in the city."

Herbie mumbled something about the need to think the problem through before making up your mind. This was the advice he had received from George Atlas, who was in investments and lived next door. Herbie liked the quiet, deliberate way Mr. Atlas spoke and felt that this must be one of the reasons why his son Lenny showed such casual grace on the tennis court, beating Herbie consistently.

The wife of the biggest beef man in the city was in tearful disarray when she got off the phone with Warner Sarnow.

"What's wrong, Mom?" Herbie knew what was wrong. She had just received the result of the second race at Atlantic Downs and was reaching for the smelling salts.

"I've lost a hundred dollars on two races, Herbie. I told your father I didn't like that Midnight Cracker."

"Why don't you stop for the rest of the day?" Whatever Herbie told Myrtle would have no effect. It rarely ever did.

"I've got to do what he says. I've got to carry on."

The brilliant smile Myrtle usually wore was rarely seen the rest of the week as she continued her losing ways, all at Whitey's behest. Of this, Herbie was certain. Herbie thought her losses must have totaled over a thousand dollars through Friday night. And every dollar loss showed in the strain lines at the corners of Whitey's eyes.

Claire phoned Wednesday night to say that she had won the singing job at the Golden Bull, and Herbie had brought her good luck that would have to be repaid, and soon. By Wednesday, Herbie had regained his sense of physical well being Claire's remark about repaying him for her good luck stirred fantasies of a repeat performance. He was a little surprised at himself for conjuring up visions of the remarkably endowed Claire dedicating her body to his whims. He had thought that once initiated into the Great Mystery of adulthood, he would be over that nonsense.

* * *

Myrtle woke up Saturday morning with a sore throat. Whitey told her to stay home and take care of herself. Herbie hunched into the

Chrysler beside Whitey thinking how awful to take all of Whitey's firepower by himself. But it didn't turn out that way—Whitey's volcano took a catnap all the way to the track. This gave Herbie the thought that his mother's frequent dumb remarks, like "don't take me to that terrible place for lobster any more" had something to do with his father's explosions.

Of course Herbie had to assume Myrtle's duties as runner for Satcor. This meant staying close to Whitey's perch, along with Bannerman, Michaels, Weller and Dana until they made their collective mind up on how they wanted to bet. Then he'd make a fast trip to the 50-dollar window where Scalplock Larson would motion him to the front of the line and punch out the tickets. This added assignment required him to budget his time. Instead of being able to hang back until five minutes before post time, when the odds didn't change as frequently, he had to make his connection with Baal earlier, when rapid odds changes tended to upset his concentration. As a result, he never did make the Baal connection before the first race. But Satcor was in luck, because Alex Goodman gave them the winner, Rosy Posy, who went off at 9-2.

When he appeared at Scalplock's window to place the four hundred dollar bet on Rosy Posy, a wizened little man in a checkered golf cap was shoveling handfuls of big bills at Scalplock. The ticket-seller punched out a hundred and twenty win tickets on Rosy Posy, six thousand dollars worth. It took so long for Scalplock to punch the tickets that Herbie was the last bettor served before the buzzer locked the machines. Scalplock recognized Herbie, of course. Herbie had been a regular for free admittance at the Boston Garden hockey games the previous winter.

As the closing buzzer shut out several big bettors behind Herbie, who went away with angry and disappointed comments, Scalplock pushed close, giving Herbie a good view of the well-oiled topknot that was his trademark. He said in his most confidential tone, "Very big customer. Get me? Very big", referring to the runt in the golf cap.

When Herbie cashed the tickets on Rosy Posy and returned to Satcor, he saw Whitey disappear upstairs to the Paddock Club. With him was Louie Septimo.

"Your father's gone upstairs on business," said Bannerman, who acted as Satcor treasurer. While Bannerman paid off Alex Goodman, Herbie took off for his favorite trackside post to try for an early message from Baal on the second race.

This was his first try to reach Baal so early in the betting and it was unfruitful. He stared hard at the odds board and twelve dull orange signals stared back.

This was a worry. If Baal wasn't ready to communicate with him until late in the betting, when Herbie was supposed to be buying tickets for Satcor; the whole afternoon could be a washout. He sent a stream of word thoughts, using his best biblical style, at the somnolent witch of the infield.

"I am grateful, Baal, for all you have done. But this is a day when I need your help very badly because I am unable to contact you at our usual meeting times." He paused, then, seeing no effect, went on, somewhat critically. "Can it be that the great Baal is mired down in such trivia that he cannot free himself for the important work that goes on between him and Herbie Roberts? You must know, Baal, that my whole future depends on the resumption of our cordial relations."

Nothing. Now Herbie tried the tactful insult: "Even the beasts in the fields will flick their tails at the flies that sting them. I am a mere fly, Baal. You are a mighty spirit. Cannot a mighty spirit speak to a fly? Are you not a god with obligations to lesser beings?"

Bingo. Baal flashed a bright orange 5-1 on Number 2, Trimatree, and a two-year old maiden.

As he worked his way through clusters of bettors to the Satcor bunch, Herbie asked himself why it was that he could not be as eloquent in his relationships with others, especially men, as he had just demonstrated with Baal. Without being able to spell out the specifics, he realized that it had to do with his father relationship. He wondered if Whitey's attitude towards him would improve if he won a great deal of money from Herbie's prophecies. The past four Saturdays must have put several thousand dollars into Whitey's hands, but it had gone through his fingers like water, probably into Louie Septimo's coffers by way of Warner Sarnow. Desperate to augment his Saturday successes, and thus achieve a net gain for his father despite Whitey's profligate betting during the week, Herbie had opened a new page in his extra- sensory life. He tried scanning the names and numbers of the horses entered in weekday cards at Atlantic Downs. Perhaps Baal would signal Herbie by darkening the ink on particular names, numbers, or opening odds, as printed on the Globe sports page.

In the privacy of his bedroom, Herbie had stared at the sports section with what he hoped was the same dispassionate receptiveness he relied on at the track. But this produced no differences, either in the color of ink, or size of type. He tried squinting, with no success. He tried various means of blocking out the distraction of unrelated information, blanking out the names of the horses and post positions and perusing only the opening odds, and vice versa. Nothing. The "heavy ink" theory having collapsed, he borrowed the "divining rod" principle from "dowsers", people who made their living by locating bodies of underground water with a forked stick. He tried with a branch from one of the apple trees in the backyard, then a forked twig from the privet hedge, finally, his own forefinger. Nothing.

Conclusion: the only place he would find Baal was at the racetrack. Whether this was due to the actual presence of the horses at the track, or to some unknown esoteric scientific principle, he did not know. What he did know was that there was no way Whitey could get Herbie to give up going to college in order to appear at the racetrack on weekdays.

Mitch Weller interrupted Herbie's reverie.

"What's the good word, Herbie?"

"The word is number two, Mitch," he replied, thinking that it would be great to work for a newspaper and make a lot of money, like Mitch.

"Do you like him just a little, or a lot?" The second questioner was Sam Dana, a direct receiver of western cattle. He sold Whitey much of the prime beef that Whitey resold to leading hotels and clubs. Sam could tell just by looking the approximate weight of a quarter section of beef, fore or hind. He would recommend a Satcor bet in an amount proportionate to Herbie's confidence. Herbie realized that bettors who read past performance charts fluctuated in their degree of confidence in the outcome because of fluctuations in the performance of horses being considered. He had no such obstacles to his thinking.

"He'll win," he said, in a matter of fact tone. He had no reason to think otherwise. It was a fact that Trimatree would win because Baal had said so.

"You're not very enthusiastic," probed Sam.

"What difference would that make? He'll win because he's got it in him to win, not because I might express enthusiasm." This was a long speech for Herbie, and it went over quite well, especially with Jake Michaels.

"I say we put the Rosy Posy bundle on Trimatree." There was a small dissent from Sam Dana, but Jake's recommendation prevailed.

The twenty-two hundred dollars in his pocket made Herbie sweat some as he made his way to Scalplock's window.

There were still eight minutes to post time, but the man in the golf cap was at Scalplock's window before Herbie. When he finally got to bet, Scalplock whispered, "Number five" in answer to the question he thought he read in Herbie's eyes. Herbie laid his bundle down before Scalplock and said, "Number two, please, to win. Forty-eight times." Scalplock punched out the tickets with a disgusted expression.

Trimatree won and paid $9, which meant a $10,800 payoff for Satcor. Jubilance was widespread. Even Sam Dana smiled. Frank Bannerman said he would collect and let Herbie refresh himself at the snack stand. There was still no sign of Whitey. His business with Septimo must have been important for Whitey to miss the race.

When he finished his hotdog, Herbie visited the men's room.

"Hi Herbie, meet my friend." It was Alex Goodman. Alex introduced a stubby little man, Dennis Larkin. Herbie had seen Dennis on a number of occasions, always in the men's room. Dennis, who had the wide shoulders and wasp waist of a jockey, was the men's room attendant.

"Pleased to meetcha, Herbie." His handshake was firm; smile lines etched deeply around blue eyes.

"You've got a good grip," said Herbie smothering inclination to ask if Dennis had been a jockey. The question might have embarrassed Alex, even if it didn't bother Dennis to be thus reminded that he had come down in the world since his riding days. And even though his contacts with Alex had been cursory Herbie had an instinctive respect for the quiet, dignified mien of the tout as he plied his trade.

Herbie thought his father would be back with Satcor when he passed by the group on his way to communicate with Baal. But Whitey was still absent, probably with Septimo. Talking about what?

Since Septimo had been described as a racket boss by Frank Bannerman, all the associations of "Mafia", "underworld" and "gangsters" gleaned from newspapers, movies and radio were fused by Herbie into one image: the thickset, flab-faced Septimo.

The piercing trumpet signaling the post parade turned Herbie's attention to the need to consolidate whatever gains he had made in Whitey's esteem as a prophet with honor. But when he canvassed the odds board for Baal's bright orange message, he came up empty. Again he searched the odds board, and again he came up empty, coming away instead with a vision of a heavy-faced man with dark, coarse, flabby cheeks who showed the gold in his teeth as he grinned evilly at Herbie.

Herbie instinctively felt that Septimo was a threat to him personally, regardless of his business with Whitey. But where was Whitey and what was the lengthy meeting with Septimo all about?

Seeing the Satcor group looking expectantly his way, Herbie scanned the odds digits again. But they continued to blink noncommittally in a dull orange monotone. In vain, Herbie first pleaded with, then railed at the Baal of the tote board. All that happened was that Septimo's image got larger and more malevolent. With five minutes to go to post time, Herbie gave it up and told the Satcor folks the race was "just too tough". They were disappointed but decided to put two thousand on Alex Goodman's choice, Icy Talk.

When Herbie got to Scalplock's window, the long shot plunger in the golf cap was nowhere in sight. Herbie figured he must have been discouraged by his huge loss on Number 5 in the second race. Scalplock punched up the two thousand without comment, but as Herbie turned to leave, the man in the golf cap rushed up to take his place.

By this time in his initiation into gambling, Herbie was accustomed to the look of happy anticipation on the faces of many who hurried to place last-minute bets. These were people who obviously had received information that was dependable. Surprisingly, the man in the golf cap wore a bored expression. Herbie hung around until the man left. He hoped Scalplock would unravel the puzzle of a bettor who, with total unconcern, laid down ten thousand dollars and walked away with scraps of cardboard.

"Who is he, Scalplock?" Herbie kept his voice low, so as not to be heard by bettors in line behind him.

"Layoff!" hissed the ticket seller.

Herbie was taken aback by Larson's refusal to give his customary cooperation and left the window.

When he brought the tickets to Frank Bannerman, Frank cleared up Scalplock's apparent refusal to explain the mystery of the man in the golf cap. Larson was simply telling Herbie that the heavy bettor was a representative of a bookie syndicate hedging its commitments so as to come out a winner regardless which horse won. The money so invested was layoff money, and the bettor's role was that of a layoff flunky.

Whitey had returned to his cronies. "Herbie, get me a cold drink like a good boy." This request puzzled, rather than annoyed

Herbie. Whitey had been with Septimo in the restaurant for an hour, evidently so preoccupied that he could not take time to satisfy his thirst. Whatever was on Septimo's mind was important enough for Whitey to subjugate his personal needs to practical considerations. In Herbie's eighteen years, he could not recall a single instance when Whitey's appetites did not demand and get immediate satisfaction.

The third race was run before Herbie could return with his father's coke, so he did not see Icy Talk run third. He did, however, see Icy Talk's number posted for third place. He walked by Alex Goodman who was looking into space. Icy Talk had gone off at 20-1. Had he won, there would have been a big payoff for the tout.

"Too bad," sympathized Herbie. Alex nodded briefly and returned to contemplation of empty space.

Obsessed with the question of what Septimo wanted with his father, Herbie was blanked by Baal for the rest of the afternoon. After he told Bannerman for the fourth consecutive race that the race was too tough for him to make a selection, he was tempted to take a stab in the eighth. Number three, a handsome bay filly named Kitty B, caught his eye in the post parade. Without a supporting signal from Baal, however, he dared not risk losing face with Whitey's pals. They had lost four out of five. Herbie did not want to be responsible for a losing day. So, even though he would lose ground in his campaign to be the preferred source of information, Herbie said once more, "too tough", when asked for his choice.

Kitty B won and paid $15.60. Hiding his disappointment, Herbie said blithely, "Better luck next time, men." The Satcor cronies called it a day, having gone down on Goodman's fourth straight loser.

Win or lose, Jake Michaels usually kept the minds of his buddies on positive goals.

"Is this any way to end less than a perfect day? Of course not! I say we go to Wonderland and make them pay."

"Fine with me," said Whitey. Turning to Herbie: "You'll take the car home. Frank will drive me. Tell your mother we're working on a business deal." The joke was well received by the others, but Herbie found cause to be concerned. Whitey would be out to salvage something from a week of losses. The others were in it for the fellowship. At the end of the road, Herbie was certain his father would confront the sinister figure of Louie Septimo.

When she saw Herbie arrive without Whitey, Myrtle went a bit paler than her cold had already made her. Herbie could tell from the sad droop of her mouth that the story of the "business deal" was accepted with more than a drop of suspicion.

The day had been dismal enough that Herbie would have welcomed a little necking with one of the unattached girls who crowded around the piano player at Hibernian Manor. But the fates weren't smiling tonight. No firm bosom pressed against him. Nor did he see the ivory skin and raven black hair of Kathy Collins, whose broken heart would likely need more than a week to heal from the sting of Herbie's rejection.

Since it was the last night when the Royal Minstrels would play at Hibernian Hall for several months, Ken Riley suggested that Herbie join the others for a nightcap at Riley's house in Jamaica Plain. But Herbie, uneasy over the mysterious meeting between Septimo and his father, said, "Thanks a million. Please call me if you have an audition. I've got to hurry home to take care of my sick mother."

CHAPTER 10

It was after one-thirty when Herbie dropped from the bus and set out on the ten-minute walk along darkened Bessenden Street to the Roberts house. It had rained during the evening. The sidewalk was pockmarked with puddles. Herbie rolled up the cuffs of his white trousers, mindful that if he got them dirty, he would be expected to pay for the dry-cleaning.

Occasionally during the walk home, the headlights of an oncoming car winked through the darkness, throwing a stray beam at Herbie puddle-hopping through the misty darkness While it took all his attention to avoid the water hazards, a formless fear began to tug him homeward ever faster.

When he was in sight of his house, the only car on the street was parked in front; facing Herbie. The roof light identified it as a taxi.

Something told Herbie to remove himself from the taxi driver's line of vision. After no more than a minute, the front door of the Roberts house opened, then closed noisily as Whitey clopped down the stairs. He crossed the street and got into the taxi. Herbie's impulse was to cry out. But the day's events had been so disquieting that he felt it wiser to stand back and try to make sense of them. He needed one solid clue to the connection between Whitey's departure at this moment and the meetings between Whitey and Septimo. As the taxi slowly accelerated, the flattened nose and high cheekbones of the driver were illuminated in light reflected from street water. A cord dangled from a knob-like ear. It was Joe Rocco, ex-prizefighter, boxing instructor, taxi driver and, from inferences dropped by Whitey, also an enforcer for an unnamed loan shark. This shark, said Herbie to himself, could only be Louie Septimo.

* * *

Claire Strong's career as a nightclub singer began serenely enough. Dominick LaRenza, manager of the Golden Bull, greeted her with a friendly handshake, wished her good luck and assigned her a dressing room with "C. Strong" on the door. Sy Kasselman, the bandleader, showed a touch of humanity. When Claire suffered an attack of stage fright in her debut, he steered her to a table well out of range of the spotlight that had triggered her nervousness.

"I'm so ashamed." Tears muddied her eye shadow. "This has never happened to me."

"That's because this is a 'first' for you. Isn't that right?"

"Right, Mr. Kasselman." A few dabs of a handkerchief restored her calm. "I'll be fine. Thank you."

"Of course you'll be fine. Just put it across the same as you did in your tryout."

She went back to the mike, and then belted out a rollicking, bosom-bouncing version of "Little White Lies." The ripple of applause from the audience brought a smile from Claire.

After her first shaky experience in the spotlight, Claire settled into a comfortable groove. Sy and the bandsmen, it seemed to her, were pleased because her meat-shaking-on-the bone style drew vociferous applause for the entire ensemble. She felt that Dominick treated her with Old World courtesy. And she was aware that the bartender, Biff Larson's strategic view of her on the bandstand gave him an ample return, at least for the present, on his investment in her drinks.

On two occasions during those first weeks, Claire went to the phone to call Herbie Roberts. The memory of their sensuous time together was still vivid and exciting. Just as important, Claire told herself, Herbie represented all that Claire felt was wholesome and good, even a possible escape some day from the flesh-for-advancement barter system by which she made her way. But each time she fingered the dial to call Herbie, she lost heart. She said to herself, "It's wrong to push myself on Herbie. If anything good is to come of our being together, Herbie should make the next move."

The next man to figure importantly in Claire's life was Dimmy Garino, a narrow-featured pretty boy whose respected status in the underworld was earned by dedicated service to Louie Septimo. Backed by the might of his boss, Dimmy found few door closed to him, few favors withheld .If he wanted a new wardrobe, the most exclusive tailors in the city leaped to serve him. If he wanted to see Joe Louis fight, the promoters rushed ringside seats to him by taxi. If he wanted a woman, he had the pick of the girls in Septimo's Back Bay brothels.

When Septimo decided to shift his headquarters from the West End to the South End of Boston to be closer to his downtown betting parlors, the Golden Bull was the logical choice. Septimo had acquired it when the first owner defaulted on a loan from Septimo's "bank." The default was accelerated by a vicious gun thrashing from Garino that left the former owner a beaten pulp outside the City Hospital's emergency ward. Technically the club was in the name of Dominick LaRenza. In fact, Septimo owned every inch.

One Saturday evening in early September, Claire's career took a new turn. Dominick LaRenza greeted her on her arrival at the Golden Bull.

"You're moving up in the world, Claire. Come with me, someone important wants to meet you." The perpetual smile behind his thick glasses seemed to Claire wider than usual.

Claire followed LaRenza to the table occupied by Louie Septimo and a, lean, dark-skinned man, eyes glued to the singer.

Claire knew her place. "Evening, Mr. Septimo." The story of the rise of the blocky, smooth-tongued Sicilian immigrant from numbers game clerk to head man of the New England Mafia family had been gleaned by Claire in bits and pieces from the Golden Bull staff over the past weeks.

"Claire Strong, Dimmy Garino." This was pure business for Septimo. No waste of words. Just another payoff.

"How nice to meetcha, Mr. Garino." These few words plus her sweetest, most innocent smile and Claire was excused. . Garino simply nodded, but his glistening black eyes followed her every step to the bandstand.

At the ten o'clock break, Claire was stopped on her way back from the ladies' room by light-as-silk pressure on her arm. It was Dimmy Garino.

"Tell Sy you'll be back in an hour." In tough-guy fashion, the words came out of the corner of his mouth. Objectionable in polite circles, it added a note of authority in dealings with others, as it did now.

"I-I'm sorry," Claire stammered. "I don't understand,"

The silken pressure on her arm became steely.

"It's all right. Sy understands. Tell him you'll be with me."

Bewildered, Claire did as she was told. She returned with a mystified expression. A small note of uneasiness crept into her voice. "Please explain," she said.

"Come with me. I'll explain." The pressure on her arm was silken again, but insistent. Claire followed Dimmy down the softly lit, thickly carpeted corridor to the club's hospitality suite, reserved for important visitors. Claire hadn't been inside the suite since her tryout, when Sy and Dominick had talked salary following her audition.

Dimmy unlocked the door and motioned her to follow, then pushed the door shut. The sound of the door self-locking raised an incipient alarm in Claire's stomach. What she saw inside the suite raised an opposing signal of delight.

The room was furnished with embroidered wall tapestries, huge leather sofas, half a dozen lamps with enormous burnished metal shades, a large oval marble-topped table with chairs and a record player.

Opulence has its natural children: Claire was one. She lifted her arms as though to embrace the luxury around her and cooed with pleasure.

"Nice, Dimmy, real nice," she said. She spoke his name tentatively, with unsure ness that is a hallmark of the innocent.

"I'm glad you like it, sweets. Watcha gonna drink?" He was already at the bar, mixing his own.

"Rum with coke, please."

Settling deep into leather cushions filled with goose down, sipping her drink greedily, Claire relaxed and surveyed her companion with a foolish smile.

Coerced by the elegance of these unexpected fringe benefits, Claire now thought Dimmy extraordinarily handsome. A full mouth, the lower lip wide and sensual, softened the narrowness of his face, accentuated by high cheekbones. His straight black hair, brushed close to a long narrow skull and parted exactly in the middle, gave him a look of uncompromising rectitude some persons associate with a department store mannequin. Agate-bright black eyes looked out at the world and called it their own.

Just now, Dimmy's eyes gleamed with barely controlled desire.

"All right, sweets," he said," it's time."

"Time for what?"

Claire, wrapped in self-satisfaction topped with alcohol, could not see that she had been steered down a road from which she could not hope to return.

"Strip, sweets. Off with the rags." These words, spoken with authority, penetrated the alcoholic haze.

"I-I don't think so." Alarm had taken root, making her reply more negative than the words implied.

Claire now discovered that incipient rebellion is easily mastered by prompt, decisive, counter-action. Dimmy, practiced at the art, slapped Claire hard on each cheek.

"Now. Strip now." The black eyes hardened dangerously. There could be only one answer to Claire's predicament. She rose unsteadily and slipped her gown from her shoulders until it puddled at her high-heeled pumps. Her bosom rose and fell violently, impelled by fear dissembling as passion.

"The bras and panties, sweets. Off with them, now!"

She unhooked her bras, stepped from her panties and stood naked for his examination.

He stood very close, holding her soft brown eyes in his hard dark eyes. Then he brushed his fingers on the soft skin of her throat, a deceptively tender gesture veiled with menace. Claire's breasts heaved intemperately. His fingers lingered on the contours of those firm white mountains, paused a few seconds at her stiffening nipples, swept across the velvet skin of her belly, lazed around the firm columns of her thighs and explored the womanly folds of her dark crotch. Suddenly, he stepped away and rapped the marble-topped table.

"Here. Stand here."

"My God, what now?" The; words were silent, but deeply felt. Claire's best friend was her God. Where was he now? Moving like a zombie, she pulled herself clumsily onto the tabletop, then to her feet. She looked down stupidly at Garino, now as naked as she, a lean dark foil to her golden Titianesque figure.

The hot, pulsing rhythm of a rumba filled the room. He had switched on the record player.

"Dance," he hissed.

Slowly, she began to sway to and fro. She twisted her thighs in sinuous ecstasy. Then, as the throbbing drums spurred her most primitive inclinations, her gyrations became faster and wilder. She shook her bobbing, quivering breasts at him, and then pirouetted to toss her buttocks in his face. Then round about again, until finally he grasped her flailing arms and slowly pulled her down to the tabletop until she lay supine, thighs parted, panting for him to enter her. She felt him mount her quickly, and then thrust hard and deep quickly, until his harsh cries of pleasure mingled with the "hiya's" of the rumba bandsmen.

Thus hammered and tempered on the anvil, Claire found her true master.

CHAPTER 11

When Whitey blasted out of the house, muttering that hell would freeze over before he'd return to such a crazy woman, Myrtle gave way to a flood of tears at the scene of their quarrel, which happened to be the kitchen in the rear. So she did not see what Herbie had seen—Whitey boarding the waiting taxi.

"Oh Herbie! He's gone to that woman. Please stop him."

While he gathered his mother in his arms, Herbie told himself to keep quiet on the subject of Whitey's all too timely taxi.

"Let him go. It's time you handled him differently." Even as he said this, Herbie was aware that Whitey had dealt with this event differently than with preceding quarrels. This time the argument had not flared up as the result of anonymous perfume on a suit coat, or some such nonsense. This argument had been instigated by Whitey. . Herbie didn't have to know the whole story. The sight of Joe Rocco and the meetings between his father and Septimo were evidence of collusion. But where was the cab taking Whitey? To a meeting with gangsters? To Whitey's customary cooling off place, the home of Nick Civitello? What was behind the whole affair?

The scenario had too many possibilities for Herbie to follow. He urged Myrtle to go to bed. He assured her that Whitey would be back and all would be well. "But he said such terrible things." Finally, Herbie was able to coax her upstairs to bed. There wasn't a sound from Larry or Reggie to indicate they were aware their father had gone off in a huff, real or invented.

Delia, up on the third floor, probably had heard nothing. Even if she had, she was too ring wise after three years in the Roberts household to do any more than root silently for Myrtle from her attic perch.

Sleep came hard to Herbie. He was certain that something unsavory would come from the week's doings. First, there was the string of losses with the bookie. Then Whitey's disappearance with Septimo at the track. And finally Joe Rocco picking up Whitey by prearrangement following a staged quarrel with Myrtle.

Although the boxing lessons had stopped years earlier, Rocco had popped up in the fortunes of the Roberts family in the intervening years. Once to organize strikebreakers who kept the meat cutters' union out of M. Roberts. Another time to introduce Warner Sarnow as a reliable bookie who would pay off Whitey's "action." And occasionally to drive Whitey home from East Boston after an appropriate cooling-off period between a blowup with Myrtle and Whitey's desire to assume the family reins once more. But there was an ominous new element in tonight's incident. The faked quarrel had a certain use for Whitey and, feared Herbie, for the racketeer Septimo. Herbie tried desperately to substitute a vision of Claire for Septimo, and fell asleep as the two battled to possess his thoughts.

The next morning, it came as no surprise when his father, red-eyed from lack of sleep, reappeared at about eleven o'clock to assume command. Then the script went as Herbie expected.

Myrtle was at first effusive in her greeting, then suspicious. "Daddy, you know I love you", quickly followed by the question, "tell me where you slept?"

"Nick's place. Where else?" His smile was too broad, too disarming.

Myrtle clucked her disapproval, and then hastened to check the roast beef. It had to be just the right degree of rareness for her Daddy. Whitey retreated to the bathroom to shower and to scrape the blond stubble from the baby pink skin.

The storm that erupted less than twelve hours previously was replaced at the dinner table by a benign calm. How phony, thought Herbie.

Whitey seemed to be making an effort to be less stern than usual, even managing a few playful digs.

"Larry, with all your nightly activity, I expect you'll be bringing home a girl soon to meet us." Over the years, Larry had discovered that his ear-to-ear grin was a satisfactory alternative to a stumbling reply sure to draw Whitey's fire. So he grinned. It was obviously the right answer, as Whitey turned to Reggie.

"It won't be long before you can go for your driver's license, Reggie. Who would you rather have for your teacher—Larry or Herbie? Your mother? Or maybe there's somebody else?"

Reggie, who would be sixteen in October, flushed deeply, more in anger than embarrassment at her father's probing about a mystery beau. She had stored up memories of too many whippings and denunciations for supposed sexual misconduct to accept his jibe as legitimate fatherly concern.

"I'm not in a hurry. There's plenty of time," she said coolly.

Herbie figured Whitey would have to drop this banter quickly- it was out of character-at least, with his family. The next item from Whitey's mouth was the clue for which Herbie was waiting.

"Mother needs a break. So Tuesday night we'll be having dinner at the Supreme when I get back from my trip."

Myrtle beamed. Reggie, who had been feeling especially persecuted, nodded approval. Whitey's temper was usually under control when they were out in public.

Larry grinned. He enjoyed the competition with Herbie for the fresh-baked rolls served at the Supreme. And the Supreme waitresses were known for their ample bosoms.

"Here we go again, Herbie," said Larry. "Don't stuff yourself before Tuesday." Such needling was Larry's way of saying he resented Whitey's favoritism for Herbie. . Larry's interests in weightlifting, wrestling and chasing girls didn't seem to rate as highly as Herbie's straight A's and piano playing, now beginning to bring a monetary return.

As was his custom, Herbie ignored Larry's thrust. It was important to study the significance of his father's announcement. It was delivered a shade too casually for his peace of mind. This must be it: whatever had transpired between Whitey and Septimo would be explained by events after dinner at the Supreme Tuesday night.

* * *

Tuesday night at the Supreme saw Whitey at his best as father and husband. He complimented Myrtle on her blue silk dress, patted Reggie's neatly waved curls, and smiled like a great cat as Larry and Herbie exchanged appreciative whispers about the ripe figure of their waitress when she refilled their plates with sugared rolls.

Herbie was sure this display of family togetherness meant Whitey was up to no good. Possibly he would announce that the family was broke and he was giving up his business to take a job. This would not surprise, since cracks in his empire had been showing for the past year. Their house needed repainting, the dents in Myrtle's car were six months old, and, when the question of living at college had come up, Whitey had snapped, "It's more important for you to join the union and get weekend jobs. "

But the apple pie heaped high with ice cream arrived and quickly disappeared without an answer to the question troubling Herbie. Whitey paused to talk business for a moment with the manager while the others piled into the big Chrysler parked before the entrance, but this encounter was too routine to provide a clue to the puzzle of Whitey's sudden switch to tonight's humane actions. The ride home was uneventful, except for Whitey Roberts as the offended motorist. He exploded with curses at the driver of a car that had dared to disappear from Whitey's path without signaling his turn. A presentment of disaster that had begun in the pit of Herbie's stomach grew to a near-choking sensation as the car turned into Bessenden from Commonwealth. He could smell danger when traffic crawled to a stop, the way blocked by a police car angled across the road. Bells clanged. Sirens wailed. Red lights blinked brilliantly in the darkness. Then Herbie smelled smoke.

"It's us, Daddy. Oh my God, it's our beautiful home." Sobbing, Myrtle bolted from the car, pushed through a knot of onlookers huddled in the glow of flames dimly seen in the front window of the Roberts house.

Herbie was two steps behind his mother as a huge policeman interrupted her stumbling flight over fire hoses in the general direction of her most prized possession-the Steinway grand piano. Its shape was now clearly seen—flames licked the graceful black slant of the upraised soundboard.

"You can't go in, lady, no how." The huge policeman was gruff and unmoving.

A flurry of fists on his chest identified her as the injured homeowner and softened his tone.

"We've got to give the fire department cooperation-they'll have it under control shortly." Reassurance sounded empty to Myrtle, observing the arrival of still another engine company, bringing to five the number of crimson dreadnaughts spewing hose, ladders and firefighters over and into the beleaguered mansion.

Half a dozen policemen formed an impenetrable line on the sidewalk. Another half dozen on the opposite curb kept a curious throng from getting closer to what Herbie believed was the choicest take-in of the season for neighborhood gawkers.

White it was getting quite dark, it was still only eight forty-five, a weeknight, making for the largest possible audience to the Roberts misfortune. Students from the Railey College of The Spoken Word, across the street, were the most vocal.

"To be or not to be, that is the question." The voice floated across the police lines, balanced sonorously above the hallooing and barking of the darting firemen and brought a snort of disgust from Whitey who, to this point, thought Herbie, was strangely quiet for one accustomed to taking charge.

"Teach a donkey to bray and this is what you get." The voice was friendly. It belonged to Mr. Atlas next door who, with Lenny, stood alongside the Roberts family, hiding their anxiety lest the fire leap across the gap between houses.

"I smelled the smoke and called the engines. I always wanted to break the glass and pull the alarm." Lenny's still-shrill fifteen-year old voice was stuffed with pride.

"Good boy," muttered Whitey dispiritedly. Herbie wondered: was his father downcast because the fire represented a blow to family security or because he was disappointed in the progress of the fire, which seemed to be coming under control?

It had been scarcely twenty minutes since the Roberts family had come on the scene, and already their house, a genteel giant on a street of like homes, had passed from vigorous mid-age to senility and decay. But the flames were also in decline, surrendering ground rapidly to the firefighters, who now appeared in broken-out attic windows, evoking cheers from the crowd with their triumphantly brandished pikes and axes.

The sound of Myrtle's weeping, which had been covered up by shouts and cheers, the shattering of glass and thudding of axe heads on wood, now penetrated the night, turning most of the onlookers homeward, dissipating appetite for awesome destruction in others.

Offers of assistance, of places to sleep, came forward. The family was quickly parceled out: Regina to the Lynches, Larry to the Jacksons, Myrtle and Whitey to the Levines. Herbie said "sure, great" to the offer of lodging with the Atlas family. He was not the least bit convinced by the statement of the fire chief that the fire had probably been caused by faulty wiring. "You know—these old houses should all be inspected," he affirmed.

As Herbie peered through the smoky darkness at the vanishing watchers across the street, his eye caught a lone figure trapped in the circling beam of light from a departing fire engine. There was no mistaking the battered features and telltale cord suspended from a cauliflower ear. It was Joe Rocco.

CHAPTER 12

On Friday evening, 72 hours after the Roberts family had dispersed to various neighbors' homes, Whitey had his family together in their new house, a modest white Georgian style house with red shutters, within a half-mile of the fire-scarred Roberts mansion.

And still more remarkably, the new house was furnished fresh and new, from the Mason and Hamlin baby grand in the living room to the pink shower curtains in the master bath adjoining Myrtle's second-floor bedroom. Frank Bannerman, who handled Whitey's insurance, had established a new record in settling the claim so speedily, whispered by Myrtle to Herbie as "very generous, I think about ninety thousand." Bannerman had found the new Roberts home among his own holdings, fortunately redecorated and empty, aching for an occupant.

Herbie admitted to himself that while the fire was certainly no accident, the availability of Bannerman's property might simply have been a crazy coincidence, in keeping with Whitey's history of being able to rise from the ashes in a jiffy.

Herbie recalled from his family's history that when the margarine company for which Whitey was a star salesman failed years earlier, his father had traded the six cases of margarine representing his severance pay for a single loin of beef. He had carried the 80-pound loin on his shoulder into the kitchen of a downtown steak house and made the sale that founded M. Roberts & Company. When the Great Crash wiped out Whitey's reserves, he borrowed $3,000 from Myrtle's father, which enabled him to meet his payroll for a month and re-float his firm. He rebounded with such fervor that M. Roberts quickly grew to be the leader among Boston's wholesale beef purveyors.

Against these legends of superhuman achievement, Herbie's achievement in gaining a coveted place in the Class of 1940 at Harvard College was entirely dwarfed.

Whitey quickly organized the immediate future for each member of the household. Herbie was assigned a large tract of grass and weeds to attend to, starting in the morning. Larry got time off from chores at M. Roberts in order to put the basement storage space in order. Reggie spent Saturday hanging curtains and drapes with Delia. Myrtle was charged with restocking the larder—special attention to snacks for the pinochle crowd. Yes, it would be auction pinochle Saturday night just as though a Tudor mansion had not burned out from under the Roberts family less than four days earlier.

As low as she had been during the fire, Myrtle's mood was elevated to new heights in her new home. She flitted about, eyes sparkling, giving orders to Delia, whose lost belongings had been replaced.

Herbie's mood gave him cause to worry. He should feel bitter towards his father. But even though many items of personal importance were gone—the Steinway piano, his books, clothing and childhood trinkets—Herbie felt grudging admiration for the coup pulled off by his father Herbie believed his father's duplicity in this instance amounted to the riskiest gamble of a lifetime. What if the arson had been suspected and proven? Not only would the Roberts family have lost everything, but also Whitey may have gone to prison. Then, without Whitey at the helm, M. Roberts would have foundered. Reggie and Herbie would have lost any chance to go on to college.

Still, when Whitey and Myrtle climbed into the Chrysler shortly after twelve o'clock, bound for the racetrack, Herbie was not surprised. Any man who would risk his family's future on the ability of an arsonist to perform without being discovered, could be expected to disregard being thought callous for leaving his children working while he went off to play.

Being only a minor miracle maker at the racetrack thus far, Herbie was dispensable for this one Saturday afternoon.

As July waned, Herbie found himself refereeing frequent squabbles between his parents about mistresses Whitey was said to make love to during selling visits in Connecticut. Larry made himself absent on these occasions. Regina hid in her room. And Herbie, while protecting Myrtle from potentially violent Whitey Roberts, remained neutral, unwilling to disbelieve his father, stopping short of asking his mother to switch her imagination to healthier matters.

Occasionally, Myrtle registered her accusations with such vehemence that Whitey left the house for several days. He went to his office as usual during these episodes, sleeping at the East Boston home of his foreman, Nick Civitello. By Saturday morning, he was back home, ready for the expedition to the racetrack, and Myrtle was always prepared to greet him with open arms, modifying the warmth of her greeting with a bittersweet smile and a brave statement, like "Here is my wandering boy again."

The illogic of Myrtle's behavior, swinging like a pendulum from accusing wife to loving sweetheart, troubled Herbie. It raised a question about her stability. When Herbie was much younger, Myrtle even then found solace from Whitey's wrath and her sorrows by taking her son in her arms and weeping as though her heart would break.

She told Herbie, not ten years old, that she stayed with his father "only because of you children. Who would support us if I left him?" She no longer said this to Herbie, relying on his growing understanding of the sometimes-rocky road traveled in marriage.

Largely due to her dependence on Herbie during these crises, Myrtle had assumed the niche of a younger sister to Herbie. Thinking back to those times long ago, Herbie remembered that the period marked the beginning of a recurrent dream that he now traced to the arguments between his parents. In his dream, a dark, swirling cloud mass hovered over his head, ready to attack and destroy him. Just when Herbie would be about to shriek out loud in terror, the angry, rough-looking cloud would be transformed into a fleecy, smooth-textured cloud with a serene disposition which allowed Herbie to drop into a quiet sleep.

In Herbie's view, the devil cloud, as he termed it, was the fear he felt when his parents screamed at each other, fear that it would result in Herbie being abandoned without father, mother or means of support. The friendly, non-combative cloud was the relief he felt when the argument was over.

That there might be an even darker explanation of his dream sometimes gnawed at him. He harbored a subterranean resentment against Whitey for the harsh whippings and biting criticism that were the warp and woof of his childhood. After one especially bitter parental battle, his mother told Herbie a story about his infancy that burned in his consciousness for years.

"When you were a baby, we lived in Beachtown. One night, I believe it was in August; there was a terrible storm. You were disturbed by the thunder and lightning and began to cry. I tried to quiet you, because your father hates to hear children crying, but the storm was too much for me. Your father took you from me, and then gave you a terrible beating with a belt. It was awful—I wanted to leave him then, but what could I do? Larry and you needed support. I stayed with him."

"How old was I, Mom?"

"Just five months old, my darling."

The whippings had ceased as Herbie neared the size and strength of a grown man. And the criticism dulled to an occasional "Godammit, I told you not to do it," as Herbie's scholastic honors, athletic and musical talents pointed to the emergence of a person to be reckoned with.

Mondays and Tuesdays during the summer were Herbie's best days. Weather permitting; he would advance his tennis skills with Lenny Atlas. When it rained, he read Dos Passos or Turgenev or played around on the Mason and Hamlin that had replaced the Steinway lost in the fire.

Wednesdays, Thursdays and Fridays he was kept busy by Whitey with gardening work. Saturdays were reserved for trips to Atlantic Downs. In mid-August the racing would shift to Narragansett Park. Herbie wondered if he was expected to give up Harvard football games for duties as Whitey's handicapper in the fall.

The last Sunday in July lay under the spell of the rain gods. Herbie was grateful. The drumming of rain against his bedroom windows meant no gardening. The day before had been "a hard day at the office" at Atlantic Downs. Herbie had muffed three of the first four races. He did not receive a clear signal from Baal. But because he was unwilling to back down from the lofty position of the All-Knowing that he felt he had carved for himself with the Satcor guys, Herbie made the mistake of picking horses on the "hunch" method. Herbie deeply regretted this strategy as Whitey continued to tear up tickets and glare at him. Before the fifth race, Whitey saw Goodman for advice. Much as he was aware that Alex was a solid handicapper, Herbie became anxious when Whitey sought him out.

Herbie took immediate action to right his sinking ship. He fixed his eyes on the huge odds board, and found himself in silent conversation with the ancient deity who had befriended him on so many occasions.

"Why is it, Baal, that I find myself without your assistance on this important Saturday, less than two months before I embark on my new life at Harvard College?"

An approaching rain cloud emitted a roll of thunder, no doubt causing uneasiness in the horses on parade to the post, but more importantly, lending weight to Baal's response.

"You are too preoccupied with earthly matters to hear my message." There was a definite flutter of the 8-1 odds digits for Number 4, a horse called Dandikins. Some might have ascribed it to the interference of the approaching electrical storm. But Herbie knew it was simply Baal's way of communicating with an underscore.

Be gone, then, thoughts of Claire Strong and her firm breasts. Be gone thoughts of tension-filled moments standing between Whitey and Myrtle. Be gone concern about what would happen to his chances to win Whitey over if he lost his prophetic powers. Be gone anticipation of loneliness in high-ceilinged Harvard lecture halls.

Thus self-purged, Herbie glanced again at the tote board. The odds on Number 4, now 6-1, had become bright orange, filling Herbie's heart with elation and sending him on wings to see his father. Whitey, holding tickets for Alex's choice, Number One, was all for disregarding Herbie's advice. But the fervor of the zealot won out, resulting in a hurried trip by Myrtle to the ticket window. The victory of Dandikins put Whitey back in Herbie's camp for the balance of the afternoon. A happy, if exhausted Herbie had then run off consecutive victories in the final three races.

Lulled by the pounding sheets of rain on his bedroom window, Herbie lapsed into a pleasant fantasy. He was a super hero for the Harvard football team, throwing passes for six touchdowns against Yale. He fell asleep and slept until almost noon. Myrtle's throaty voice woke him.

"You have got to get up, Herbie. You know your father has to leave by one." Whitey was always concerned with making his departures and arrivals matters of precise timing. You might say he lived for the moments.

At twelve, Herbie was seated at the dining room table in the strained silence that usually embraced the Roberts family at Sunday dinner. The tension was greater than usual—Whitey and Myrtle had been squabbling nightly since his return from Connecticut Tuesday evening.

Following the destruction of food, the others braced themselves for the parting orders that would hold things together until Whitey returned Tuesday.

He snapped at Reggie:

"I expect you to walk to school with someone other than Valerie Blue. I don't want you associating with a girl who writes filthy letters to her friends."

Valerie had penned a mischievous scrawl to a neighbor's daughter, Mindy Wax, describing in detail how Mindy would lose her virginity. The letter had been passed among the parents in the neighborhood, producing appropriate clucks of horror.

"Larry, you will start on the cutting board tomorrow morning. And be certain you are there at seven sharp. Nick is expecting you."

"Herbert, the yard is a disgrace. Do I have to say any more?"

"Myrtle, I am tired of looking at bare windows in the breakfast nook. Call Jordan's and get curtains up for Chris sakes."

Minutes later, Whitey was on his way, the black Chrysler quickly nosing through the downpour to route 9, headed southwest to Connecticut.

With the boss gone, slaves quickly scattered: Reggie to a matinee at the Richwood Theatre, Larry to Levine's drugstore to refill his tobacco pouch, Myrtle to her bedroom with a guidebook on Central America; she hoped to take a cruise. Herbie retreated to the kitchen with The History of Harvard College by McKinlay Storrow. Herbie was deep into the administration of Charles William Eliot who became president of Harvard in 1869, when the phone interrupted his reading.

"I'll take it, it's for me." Herbie spoke loudly Myrtle monitored every scrap of mail, every phone call possible; to corroborate her suspicions about Whitey's philandering.

"Roberts residence. Herbie Roberts here."

A woman's voice replied, with a slight brogue.

"H'lo there. I know about you, Herbie, from your father. Is he in??

Herbie had a premonition of disaster. Who could she be, this woman who knew about him from his father's lips? He steeled himself, forcing politeness.

"He's out of town. Would you like to leave a message?"

She laughed. "He's already got the message . . . and a heck of a lot more."

The insinuation of intimacy hit Herbie with stunning force, making him mute. The woman broke the silence. Her tone was cajoling.

"I know about you, Herbie. I'm Myra. I'd like to see you."

Her words echoed and re-echoed. "I'd like to see you." Over and over, stripping Herbie naked, scattering his thoughts. One thought remained: Whitey had lied to him. There was another woman he went to. Likely more than one other. The bitterness swelling in his chest constricted his lungs and cracked his voice.

"Why did you call?" He asked hoarsely.

"To talk with your father. I love him and he loves me." Her words were like whips. "I'm surprised you don't know about me. I live in Brighton."

Out of my life—whore, devil, and succubus. You, nothing but a vessel for any man's lust, have lain touching my father. I, a perfect son, am rewarded for pursuing my father like a shadow with nothing but this hateful revelation. I hate you, Myra. My hate will destroy you and my father together.

The revulsion he felt became a knife that almost severed his vocal cords, leaving a barely whispered command,

"Don't call any more," he said. Then hung up.

"Who was that, Herbie?" Myrtle had come out of her bathroom, toweling her hair. Herbie was thankful she couldn't see his face, contorted with pain. He forced a casual tone.

"It was just Lenny." Then he fled outside into the warm rain, now settled into a soaking drizzle.

Unseeing, he stumbled around in the garage until he found a small spade. With this he would dig the pain out of his chest.

The spade dug savagely at the wet turf spotted with summer weeds, uprooting dozens of thickly matted clumps in a few minutes. Panting with his effort, muddy slime covering his arms to his elbows, knees drenched, he did not hear his brother's approach, just returned from a lengthy review of the girlie magazines at Levine's drugstore.

"Say, Herbie. You really are going at it, old boy. What's the idea—you trying to score double brownie points wit4h the old man?"

A tease from Larry at any other time would have been parried with a joke at the other's expense. But this riposte bit too deeply. Herbie let out a wild roar that Larry instantly translated into big trouble. He scrambled up the back stairs into the kitchen, slamming and locking the door, which was half plate glass. From this fortress, his grinning features taunted Herbie, who tugged in vain at the doorknob.

"Open the door, damn you!" Herbie's fists beat a tattoo on the wooden half of the door, then, blindly obedient to a lower law of nature, shattered the plate glass itself, showering fragments inside.

Unhurt, Herbie lurched into the kitchen just as his brother's form vanished rapidly on the stairs to the second floor.

"It wasn't you, Larry," he gasped, staggering with his load of hate, fatigue and regret.

The storm was over. Outside the rain ebbed and stopped. He saw that the blue Dresden kitchen clock, a gift to Myrtle from the Enterprise Club, said 4:29.

* * *

A long, black Chrysler bearing a Massachusetts license plate sped through the rainy, murky Connecticut afternoon. The pavement of the Jenkins Parkway was pockmarked with pools of water where the alternation of winter and summer temperatures had depressed the surface. Inside sat the driver, powerful shoulders bent over the wheel, steel blue eyes squinting through the swishing wiper for a glimpse now and then of the white center line dividing the road. Despite the unsavory road conditions, he gunned the black car along straight-aways and around curves at better than sixty miles an hour. Whitey Roberts was a man in a hurry.

Behind him was another steamy argument with Myrtle. In all his years of traveling, he had never provided her with any direct evidence of playing around. But there had been plenty of indirect evidence. Traces of lipstick on a handkerchief or a shirt collar which he had laughed off as razor nicks. This evidence was left by Ellie Sessions, the wispy brunette with the great body who cashiered for Mack's Grill in New London. Occasionally Myra Brown's perfume had lingered on his clothes. Myra was becoming too possessive. Have to dump her, which would be too bad. A good lay and handy to the office when he needed relief from the strain of keeping the plant humming with orders. His biggest problem was his own dwindling energy. He had rarely been in the mood lately to make love to Myrtle. This, he realized, gave Myrtle her most solid proof of infidelity. And it was getting to be a battle to keep Herbie in his corner.

Herbie was too bright to swallow his stories about Myrtle's crazy family much longer.

The car lurched suddenly, as a pool of water grabbed at the heavy tires, interrupting his thoughts, demanding all his strength and feel for the road to straighten his course. Onrushing traffic blinked dangerously close to the centerline, reminding him to switch on his own headlights. And still he kept the speedometer above sixty.

He told himself he had to make Farmington by four to see Johnson Stayes, owner of the plush Robinson Hotel. Stayes had been immune to his pitch for a long time. But Stayes had finally consented to give him a trial order today. It probably wouldn't be a large order, but Whitey could depend on his foreman to ship prime stuff, quality that would make Stayes' eyes pop. Once he had Stayes' order in his pocket, he could relax for the balance of the day with Julia Dannon, head bookkeeper at the Dunes Club. Julia was really something, with an appetite that matched his own. Like Whitey, Julia was also smitten with horseracing and occasionally met Whitey on a Monday when Narragansett was open. After the races, they would stay overnight at a roadside inn outside

Warwick. Julia's brother Carlo owned the Dunes Club and had a small string of horses that he sometimes raced at Narragansett.

The car swerved again in the wet clutch of the highway, forcing him to abandon his reverie. Too dangerous to split his thoughts between driving and the broads. He switched off Julia and switched on the radio.

" . . . heavy showers are blanketing New England and will continue through most of the night. Hail and electric storms have damaged tobacco and truck crops in the Connecticut Valley. . . . In Plymouth, Massachusetts, A. Lawrence Lowell, president emeritus of Harvard, was injured when his car skidded on a slippery road. He is reported in satisfactory condition. In sports, Harold Vanderbilt's Ranger and T.O.M. Sopwith's Endeavor will compete at Newport tomorrow in the second race for the America's Cup. We close with a warning from the State Police that heavy rain has brought flooding and dangerous road conditions to many parts of Connecticut. This has been the news and the weather. It is now four twenty-nine." The announcer continued with a sports roundup, but Whitey never heard it. The big car left the road and telescoped against a huge elm tree.

In less than a minute, police arrived and set up a wall of flashing lights around the wrecked car. . The body of Whitey Roberts lay motionless, impaled on the hub of the shattered steering wheel.

* * *

"No, I'm not going. I called Frank Bannerman. He's driving you and Mother. Whatever has to be done when you get to the hospital, Frank will do. I have to stay with Reggie."

This statement, spoken with an air of finality by Herbie, could sit unkindly with his brother.

Larry looked incredulously at him. The phone call from Farmington Hospital said their father was dying. And yet Herbie, Whitey's chosen one, their mother's old dependable, was shrinking from the final act.

He looked questioningly at Herbie. "What's the real reason?"

Herbie's jaw tightened. Maybe Larry sensed the part he had played in the violent end of Whitey Roberts. Maybe not. The important thing was that he couldn't face his father on his deathbed. He needed time to sort out the mad-glad-sad feelings that ate him up inside.

He said firmly, "I told you—I'm needed here with Reggie." His sister, smothering a deep sob, buried her face on his shoulder.

Larry shrugged. "Suit yourself." His eyes, deep-set and blue-green, like Herbie's eyes, still puzzled over his brother's backing off from Whitey's final hours.

There was a tearful time with Myrtle when Frank Bannerman arrived ten minutes later. Her pretty features were distorted with grief and she clung to Herbie as though he were her last hope for living. Nonetheless, she had dressed neatly and packed an overnight bag. Herbie spoke encouragingly, though disbelieving his own words.

"Now mom, I want you to know that dad is going to be all right." He's too strong to let anything happen"

Herbie wondered at his ability to rise to the occasion. He was normally uncomfortable referring to Whitey as "dad", an endearment that the core of him could not stomach. He and Larry shared the feeling. They said "our father" or "the old man".

"Keep a stiff upper lip, Herbie," said Bannerman. Herbie felt his brother's probing glance once more, as, one arm around Reggie, he kissed Myrtle goodbye.

It wasn't going to be easy to keep the truth from Larry, particularly when Herbie himself knew that he had willed his father to die when he put his fist through the glass in the kitchen door.

CHAPTER 13

The unexpected recovery of Melton Roberts from injuries that prove fatal to ordinary men further bolstered Herbie's impression of his father as an indestructible, if sinister force.

The miracle patient's doctors were frankly puzzled by his refutation of their early estimates that he could not survive the shattering and subsequent removal of most of the sternum, extensive lung damage and loss of blood. What they failed to take into account, because they did not really know the man, was the plain fact that Whitey Roberts was simply not ready to surrender his place at the head of the line where are issued the foods, money and women that make life worth living. Yes, his appetites kept him alive. Plus the steel constitution inherited from his forebears, hardy peasants who farmed the lowlands of the Austrian Alps.

While Herbie did not believe his mother's accusations of wholesale unfaithfulness, he had been in his father's company often enough to assess his interest in pretty women and their willingness, no matter how politely veiled, to respond. Too, his father's reputation as a fabulous trencherman, at Masonic and Temple dinners, was frequently attested by quips from his pals when dining or playing cards in the Roberts home. And Herbie, pressured to provide winning horses every Saturday right up until the day before the accident, could testify to the fact that what really kept Whitey alive was an insatiable hunger for money.

Whitey Roberts had made a lot of money, mostly from an ability to paint vivid word pictures of the fabulous beef handing in his coolers, partly from a way he had of converting honest chefs and stewards into petty thieves. If young Herbie had ever noticed a halo around his father's head, it quickly disappeared, as Herbie became old enough to hear and interpret scraps of conversations between his father and his foreman, Nick Civitello. These tidbits had been available on Herbie's infrequent visits to .M. Roberts & Company, and were now available to anyone who, like Herbie, walked by Whitey's bedroom when he was on the phone.

"On the order to the Bonton Club, keep in mind that George, the chef, is on our list. This meant, figured Herbie, first that George was pocketing bribe money from M. Roberts, and second, that he would overlook such trivialities as short weight and under grade beef.

"Nick, when I was in the New Yorker Hotel before my accident, I took a look at our strips in their cooler. They aren't riney enough for us to make money." "Not riney enough" meant that they were too well trimmed. By leaving more fat on the steaks, profits would escalate.

Not that Melton Roberts believed he was doing anything wrong.

"No sir, it's not what you know, it's who you know that's important." This advice, from Boynton Harrison, one of Whitey's first employers, .was obviously close to Whitey's heart. He had built Boston's biggest list of "grafters" to go along with Boston's biggest wholesale beef operation.

Some men, like next door neighbor Baird Atlas – Herbie was certain Baird was of this stripe – plan wisely to achieve their goals. Others, like Whitey Roberts, maneuver and scramble Indeed, he bribed, he stole, he covered his tracks, he cajoled, he orated, he roared, he purred his way to the top. All this Herbie knew about his father. And still he courted his father's approval and fretted when his father had business reversals.

One early September afternoon, when Whitey was in his sixth week of "recuperative leave", as he called it, he hailed Herbie, arrived home from a day of discussions about curriculum with his freshman advisor-to-be.

"Come in, Herbie, I've got something important to discuss."

"Yes, sir," Herbie acknowledged hesitantly, not knowing whether his summons was for good or ill.

Whitey, resplendent in a blue silk jacket, looking fat and pink, beckoned him to a chair next to his at a card table where he occasionally played gin with Myrtle. His tone was confidential. Herbie expected the worst.

"You know, Herbie, I was happy to make the decision to send you to college," he began. His seriousness intensified: "Even though the way business is I had no right to do so."

"I didn't realize," Herbie stammered.

"You never do," was the blunt rejoinder. This was the old Whitey. Go ahead, said Herbie to himself, turn the screw.

The cobalt eyes studied him.

"You wouldn't like it if you couldn't go to school, would you?" No reply was expected to this jolt, as his father continued.

"We might not have to do that. We'll see." Thin lips pursed. The cobalt rays shifted from Herbie to a cobweb on the ceiling. His tone became reflective.

"About six months ago, the packers put the squeeze on. Dropped their prices to our best customers. That's right, the dirty bastards I've been feeding for fifteen years put on a drive to sell my customers, cutting us out. Not that they can give the service we give. Not by a long shot. But Hartford House listened to them. So did the Vance Hotel, the Journeys End Club. All told, about eight thousand dollars a week down the drain. So what could we do? We stepped up our business in Vermont and New Hampshire, where the packers don't get much play. We pushed the grafters for more volume. We cut a few corners." Here, he paused, unwilling to pursue this line of thought.

"You know, I've got one hell of an overhead, and every man is important to the operation. On top of all this, I've got to pay out nine thousand in medical bills." He shook his head, and then went on.

"The packers want their money every week or else we've got nothing to sell. On the other hand, our customers pay us once a month. We're between the devil and the deep blue."

"So what do we do?" He looked furiously at Herbie as though he had helped to create the problem. Indeed, it seemed to be no longer a problem, but a crisis.

Herbie felt his own two feet being pushed closer to the edge of the precipice.

A manicured forefinger measured Herbie.

"There's one thing I won't do. I won't close the doors of M. Roberts, packers or no packers, depression or no depression."

"I've put in too goddamned many years building a business to let a few lousy bastards piss it away on me. Yes, I've got a problem. Big expenses. Not much cash I can lay my hands on. Everything tied up in coolers, in freezers, in cold storage. Half a million. And the goddamned banks won't cough up what I need. So what can I do? I'll

Tell you what, Herbie," his anger cooled. He looked at Herbie through half-closed eyes.

"When things got rough last spring, I went in hock with the bookies, trying to make it that way. I wasn't lucky . . . " His voice trailed off into a question. Had Herbie been aware that the mob had ordered him to have an insurance fire so that he could pay his gambling debts? He had respect for Herbie's intuitive gifts, but certainly there was no way he could know.

Feeling that he was expected to break his silence, Herbie offered meekly:

"What can I do?"

"I want to be fair with you, Herbie." The voice was solemn. "How many subjects will you be carrying – four?"

"I know some guys who are carrying five."" What was his father up to? Herbie's thoughts flashed ahead, trying to get on track with Whitey's direction. Maybe he wanted Herbie to carry another language, like Spanish, so he could help him develop business in Cuba and the Caribbean. Herbie expected to go on with French and his father knew it. He had dropped his interest in German because of the hell that Hitler was raising with the Jews Maybe Whitey wanted him to take another music course, so he could step up his qualifications to play with the big bands. He was unprepared for what came next.

Reaching to the bottom of a stack of papers on the table, Whitey pulled out a newspaper and handed it to his son.

"Here's your textbook," he said.

Herbie looked. It was the Morning Telegraph, the "Telly", as its readers termed it – the nation's most popular compilation of past performances on racehorses. Herbie saw that the dateline was current – September 8, 1936.

There was nothing unusual about seeing the Telegraph in the Roberts home. Myrtle was up at dawn each day to get her husband's breakfast. She drove him to his office then stopped at the newsstand in Back Bay Station to pick up the Telegraph. Racing had been her focus for the past three years. They went to the races every Saturday from April to the end of October. When racing was nearby, she drove to the racetrack several days a week. Otherwise she played with the bookies, with whom she was given a daily sixty-dollar limit by her husband. When Herbie had remonstrated with her about her unhealthy absorption in horseracing, she replied:

"This is how I forget what your father is doing to me." .

Herbie now blanked out this ancient history. What was happening this moment had to be faced. This was the proposition: use your wits to make me money or there's no Harvard College for you, son. Herbie wondered briefly if any of his classmates would also be taking Gambling I. Then, feeling weak against his father's will as always, he tendered his acceptance in as "up": a voice as he could muster:

"When do I start?"

"Tonight. Alex Goodman is coming to dinner."

* * *

Alex Goodman was a slim, quiet man with bushy brows and a neat brown mustache that twitched when he was enjoying a good meal or savoring a good winner.

Just now, under the influence of Myrtle's cooking, his mustache twitched left and right like a baton conducting a string orchestra. Myrtle was not present to take her bows because Whitey had asked her to host dinner in the kitchen for Larry and Reggie while he chaired the meeting between Alex and Herbie at the dining room table . . .

Over a forkful of roast potato, Whitey summed up Herbie's months-long successes on behalf of Satcor in twenty-two words, delivered in his most pontifical tone.

"You've done some lucky guessing, Herbie, but guessing is too risky for my plan. I need scientific handicapping, not a rabbit's foot."

Herbie felt as though he had been slapped. So all he had been to his father's Saturday gambling success for three months, right up until his accident, was some kind of lucky charm. Of course, Herbie had never told anyone how he had selected sixty-one winners out of eighty races. The secret of Baal's support was locked in his breast forever. But it certainly was not "lucky guessing." How many "scientific" handicappers could equal what he had done?

Suppressing anger, Herbie said nothing and averted his eyes from Whitey. He looked at Goodman for any sign that the tout also considered Herbie nothing more than a lucky charm. But Alex hardly glanced at Herbie and continued to eat with gusto while Whitey held forth.

"I want you to know, Herbert, that Alex is the top handicapper in the country. Consider yourself fortunate that he will be your instructor."

The compliment reddened Alex's stubbly cheeks. He stopped chewing long enough, his mouth still full, to mumble his thanks, then went on eating.

Reminding himself that when he had seen Goodman at the races the tout had looked half-starved, even desperate, Herbie mentally took him down a few pegs from Whitey's ranking and placed him somewhere in the middle of the pack. Alex was certainly not Numero Uno, not with frayed shirt cuffs peering out from neat but worn coat sleeves.

But if Whitey Roberts was going to gamble a lot of money on whatever he, Herbie, could learn from the tout, then Goodman had to be on the up and up. Whitey Roberts demanded and got his due from the people who worked for him.

Herbie ventured: "I've heard great things about you, Mister Goodman."

"Call me Alex."

"All right, Alex it is." Herbie smiled. "Alex and Herbie," he said, "we could do the circuit."

Alex's deep-set brown eyes twinkled. The twinkle owed more to Myrtle's hearty cooking than to the feeble joke, thought Herbie.

"We'll do all right, Herbie," said the tout.

"You've got to do better than all right," said Whitey, with a grim smile. He had twenty bucks an hour invested in Herbie's instructor. He had better set them straight.

"Alex has agreed to give you two hours of his time each night for the next six nights, excluding any night you're playing piano. Then he's leaving for Hot Springs. I expect you to be a first-class handicapper after this instruction, provided you do your homework." Whitey allowed himself a chuckle.

The joke is on me, thought Herbie. Add several hours of what could be daily duties as Whitey's handicapper to his study load when school begins, and what do I have left? Only time for practicing, sleeping, working weekend nights with the bands. What about Harvard football games? Dates with girls? He slumped in silent disgust.

The cold blue eyes fastened on Herbie's discomfort and read the signs of revolt.

"You've got no gripe, Herbie. Look at Alex. Had a full-time job nights ushering in a movie house while he went to college. Right Alex?"

"Uh huh. N.Y.U."

Surprise. There was nothing about Alex Goodman's appearance to suggest the educated man. Herbie shot one of his rare inquisitorial glances at Goodman, who appeared to flinch slightly. His eyes, when Herbie's eyes met them, were full of intelligence. His speech, devoted strictly to horserace business, was pure Brooklynese. He said, "foist" instead of "first", "Booston" instead of "Boston." His dress, as Herbie had noted at the track, was neat but shabby No giveaways there. Here was a can with no easily opened ends, reasoned Herbie. Whatever he would discover about Alex's past would have to be voluntarily proffered. It was not surprising that Whitey had some knowledge of the tout's background. They had been together at the Florida tracks the past four winters when Myrtle and Whitey took their winter vacations.

Whitey rubbed out any further resistance from Herbie with an abrupt hail to the kitchen.

"Delia, please clear the table. We've got to get down to business," One final glare in Herbie's direction.

"Okay, fine," Herbie, muttered. And that was that.

It would be a long evening for Herbie. First the session with Alex, then he had at least two hours of work to finish an arrangement of "My Blue Heaven" for Ken Reilly.

Reilly's Royal Minstrels had an audition for the Blue Rock House in Scituate Tuesday afternoon. Let's get with it, Alex; his impatience was barely concealed.

"You don't have to begin with the first racing thoroughbreds," he said. "I know about Matchem, Herod and Eclipse."

Whitey didn't hear Herbie's sarcasm, having headed for bed.

A flicker of annoyance shot from the quiet brown eyes. "I suggest you take notes. This is not a snap course."

"Before we begin," said Herbie warily, "what's your opinion of extra-sensory perception?" Might as well see if Alex is acquainted with Baal.

"You've done well with it. That's all the evidence you need that it has validity."

Alex paused, then added, "I imagine most of us occasionally have had the feeling we're reading another person's mind."

There was no rancor in Alex's tone. But Herbie sensed from a sudden tightening of the other's mouth that he had opened up an old sore. Herbie's successes for Satcor had cost Alex profit opportunities the past three months.

"How do you know that I depend on extra sensory perception?" Something made Herbie pursue the topic, which would, he resolved, never be raised again after tonight.

"I've seen you stare at the odds board, finding answers in what you saw there."

Bingo. That was close. And here he thought he had been able to hide his secret in the anonymity of a racetrack crowd. Goodman is sharp; can't underestimate this guy, Herbie.

"There will be six parts to what I have to say," said Alex, looking directly at the pen and pad in front of Herbie. He paused until the other poised, ready to make notes.

"We'll start with a discussion of different horses and their racing styles." Herbie noted there was some distaste in the way Alex had uttered "horses", as though he wanted to put some distance between himself and the seamy side of the sport of kings.

Alex continued: "When you understand running styles, you'll be prepared to learn how to chart the real speed of races on a particular day, regardless of track conditions. You'll learn what it means to be on the pace, close to the pace, off the pace. You'll find out what happens when different running styles compete against each other.

You'll learn to convert class into speed figures and you'll learn about weight on a horse's back and its effect on speed."

"Since fifty percent of the races in New England are run at six furlongs, we'll confine our study to factors influencing six furlong results."

Herbie suddenly found a similarity between the man in the shabby gray suit seated before him and Dr. Hector Phillips, a distinguished Shakespearean scholar who had guest-lectured to Herbie's graduation class. Both knew how to teach.

"Perhaps you've heard," said Alex, "that all horses are either quitters or closers?"

He waited for Herbie's assenting nod, then went on:

"This is strictly a human viewpoint, based on the willingness of most people to think in only two values, black or white, bad or good. The objective viewpoint, which is all that you and I can be concerned with, is that the natural speed of a horse is constant, or decays or matures at different points over the six-furlong course," Alex went on to categorize ten different running styles that resolve the outcome of all races, although it was unlikely that all ten would be entered in any one race.

"These are useful code numbers for the various running styles: 'one' races fairly level quarters, 'two': decays more or less evenly from the start of the race, 'three' races the first quarter faster than the second or third quarters, the latter two are raced at level figures. 'Four' races the first two quarters at level speed, decays in the final quarter. 'Five", 'six" and 'seven' show their best speed in one of three quarters, varieties of decay or maturation in other quarters. 'Eight', 'nine' and 'ten' exhibit maturing speed in one or more quarters, otherwise hold their speed level."

Throughout this discourse, Herbie remained silent, his busy pencil making the most of what he gradually discerned to be the "real stuff". He asked himself: why should Alex tell his trade secrets for what Herbie knew had to be a pittance? The question evidently showed in Herbie's face.

"If you've been asking yourself why it is that I spill my brains for forty bucks a night, let me tell you that even when you have everything I can teach you, which may be more than you can get from anyone else in the business, you'll still have nothing."

"Why is this so?"

Alex's upraised hand put the brakes on a rush of questioning. His features hardened. "Because with all the crookedness in business and government, we can't expect any improvement in racing ethics. It's the most dishonest business in the country."

Fishing through a small red notebook, heavily indexed, dug from his pocket, Alex quickly found what he wanted.

"Take last Friday at Bimoniam. Of nine races, two were won by favorites—both horses made favorites in the final odds change just before the start. Of nine legitimate favorites, only two finished in the money, both thirds. Maybe one or two had bad racing luck, but nine? Now let's look at the times for the races. For the seven races at six furlongs, the average time was one minute, twelve and three-fifths seconds. The day before, for comparable class horses, there were six six-furlong races. Average time: one minute, eleven and four-fifths. And six favorites won that day. You're going to say the track was faster that day? Wind conditions were the same both days. And no rain. The answer? At least seven, maybe nine fixed races on Friday. A whole card."

Paying no attention to Herbie's sagging jaw, he continued:

"So Friday was an example of the boat-race, the hold-back fix. Now what about the stimulation-fix?" He thumbed to another page. "Saturday, August, 12, at Atlantic Downs."

Herbie became extremely attentive. He had been present for that day's racing.

"Fourth race. Nine entered. Wide open betting. Three horses are three to one, the other six up to forty to one. An animal named Brush Me. His sixth start of the meeting. Best finish: eighth. His best time: one minute fourteen and three-fifths. So what happens? Brush Me wins by three lengths. Time: one minute, twelve and four-fifths. Payoff: eighty-four dollars."

Herbie recalled the race. It was one of only three races that day when Herbie had failed to deliver the winner to Satcor, courtesy of Baal.

Herbie felt empty, totally defeated. He wondered: why am I sitting here? His dejection provoked a friendly smile from Alex.

"You know, Herbie, I didn't really mean that you'd have absolutely nothing when you learn to handicap. If you learn good, you'll be better off than most bettors who get their kicks from the races. What I want you to know is that I can't give you any clues when the jockeys, the trainers or the owners are going to fix a race. I can give you clues on when an animal is deliberately held back to increase the odds next time he runs."

Seeing Herbie's mood brighten, he said, "You'll find this out another night. Tomorrow night the main subject will be race dynamics. What happens when horses with different racing styles compete against each other?"

Herbie grinned. "Professor, you know how to put it across."

"I should. Otherwise I wasted five years teaching at Richmond Banks High!"

CHAPTER 14

Now that he had broken the ice with Alex, Herbie began to feel comfortable with this association, more comfortable than with any other man he had known with the exception of his mother's father. Perhaps he was influenced by similarities with his grandfather that he saw in Alex: the quiet manner and certain physical characteristics. Goodman, like Lewine Nattelson, was slight of build, and mustached.

As Herbie's tutelage in scientific handicapping advanced, he discovered that Goodman was interested in whatever he let drop about his college plans. His intent to concentrate in English literature, with minor emphasis on music theory, drew questions from Goodman.

"What are you going to do with English? Teach" You may be able to criticize Shakespeare, but you're not the dramatic type. My experience teaching math and physics convinced me that unless you had a flair for acting, you don't belong in teaching."

Piqued by this allusion to his natural reticence, Herbie drew his reply from a recollection of his high school teacher's praise of a piece he had written. Grace Aborn, a wispy, white-haired lady with a warm spot for the solemn-faced Roberts boy, had scrawled the one word "Delightful!" next to his grade mark on Herbie's paper, "On Going For The Newspaper." Herbie had written this piece in what he hoped was a close imitation of a popular 19th century essayist.

"My teachers felt I'd make a writer. But I don't know."

"Turf writer? Book writer?" The tout smiled his questions.

Herbie returned a helpless smile.

"I don't know what I'm headed for." Herbie stared into the friendly brown eyes with a feeling of hope. Maybe this stranger could read signs in him to which Herbie had been blind.

"You're headed for trouble with me if you don't get down to business."

Herbie shook visibly. Whitey's voice was deceptively quiet in its intrusion through the partly opened door.

Seeing the youth's fear, Alex hastened to stop the bleeding.

"You've got your style, Whitey. I've got mine. Leave us alone."

The massive presence in the hallway seemed to falter at the unexpected show of strength from the tout, then retreated to the accompaniment of a rumbling cough, testimony to Whitey's chain-smoking habit.

Muscles in Herbie's shoulders that had tensed up, relaxed. Relief spread across his face. Seeing this, Goodman took his cue to return to the study of racing dynamics. This was the tout's term for what happens when horses with different running styles interact with each other.

Even though he had reservations about the tout's handicapping methods rivaling his own intuitive method, Herbie was a natural student. If understanding what happens when front-running horses are challenged by late-runners would help bridge the chasm between Herbie and his father, then let's get to it.

"See what happens when a front runner is challenged in the first quarter." Alex traced the developments on a sketchpad. On the pad he had drawn the shape of a one-mile racecourse.

"At the start of the race, a horse is a full tank of gasoline. You know that the faster you drive a car, the faster you empty the tank. The jockey's job is to hold his front position at the slowest pace possible, so that his mount will have something left for the stretch run."

Herbie's quick nod told the tout he need not dwell on this point. Alex paused to indicate his next point was especially important.

"But no matter how slow the first quarter, it's still the fastest quarter in the race." His digression to show why this was so, due to the conformation of the racetrack, interested his student.

"You're saying that most of the second quarter is around the turn, which slows down the pace."

"That's usual," admitted Alex.

Presented with time charts proving the next point, that despite being run mostly on the stretch straightaway, the final quarter was the slowest, Herbie asked a question that drew a smile from beneath the mustache.

"If there are other horses who force the early pace, doesn't this make it easy for a closer to win?"

"Easier, not easy," assented Alex. He then sketched various situations on his pad to indicate how different "mixes" of running styles produced different fractions at the quarters and different final placing results.

"Now let's look at the distances behind the lead horse at each quarter."

"I guess we have to check these distances on the result chart—like this chart, for example?" Herbie pointed to a Morning Telegraph result chart for Atlantic Downs on the table before teacher and pupil.

"Exactly," said Alex. Because his pupil was absorbing information rapidly, Alex decided to introduce the salient topic of assigning a numbered value to the lead horse at each quarter of a six-furlong race, a subject he had intended for the next lesson.

"If you make it through this next subject, you're an apprentice handicapper."

This promise perked up Herbie, who showed signs of late night fatigue.

"We're going into simple arithmetic—the assignment is to describe an animal's running style by his relative speed at the first, second and final quarters. In order to do this equably, we've got to compensate for the factors which influence those fractions, causing them to vary race to race for the same class of horses." This was a head-breaker. So Alex waited for it to sink in.

Herbie nodded. "Wind, rain, different mixes of styles, differences in post position, differences in the size of the field. Right?"

Alex smiled approval, continuing:

"We do this by averaging the fractions for six furlong races for each day's racing and assigning a value based on the average class of horse running that day."

When the lesson was over, Herbie looked at his watch, which said two-thirty. It was already "Tercentenary fireworks day" and he could be a participant, for the first time, in a historic occasion at Harvard College.

"Weather permitting, how about having tonight's lesson outdoors at Harvard Square?" His grin grabbed at Alex.

The brown eyes twinkled. "I'm in the mood. I always wanted to teach in the Ivy League."

* * *

For two weeks, distinguished scholars had congregated in Cambridge to make statements of significance to mankind, while honoring the graybeard of American higher education on its 300th birthday.

For Herbie, the events leading up to today's Alumni Day festivities, two days before the program was to culminate with the appearance of President Roosevelt, had gone by in a glaze of impressions to which he felt himself an outsider. Etienne Gilson, France's leading philosopher, warned the world against the Nazis. The brilliant English astronomer Arthur Eddington had spoken words of wisdom. Professor Edward Krasner of Columbia, who had astounded the mathematical world by originating a method of measuring the horn angle, had appeared at the Tercentenary lectern. He was the only famous Jewish scholar to appear. Albert Einstein was supposed to come, but sent apologies, giving no reason for his absence. Werner Heisenberg, Germany's second-ranking physicist behind Einstein, winner of the Nobel in 1932, had been invited but was unable to appear. The same fate befell Otto Warburg, son of the founder of Zionism. Warburg had won the Nobel in medicine in 1931 for his cancer discoveries.

The only names that Herbie paid any real heed to were names like Carry The Day, Ebony Rock and Discovery, champion racehorses. These were the "real stuff" of Alex Goodman's evening lessons. If Alex had not said "yes" to Herbie's suggestion, Herbie was certain that this historic occasion would have passed him by entirely. Just one more instance of events of vast significance having only a pianissimo effect on the youth, walled out from much of the real world by his internal wars.

It was seven-thirty when Goodman limped from the subway entrance in the center of the Square and hailed Herbie waiting across the street.

"Ho, there, Herbie!"

"Great. I'm happy you made it. How did your day go at 'Gansett?"

"It was a pisser. Imagine trying to find half a dozen regular customers in a crowd of 30,000 people!"

"Oh right—today was the running of the Gansett Special. What happened?"

Herbie had discovered that the faces of most racetrack goers reflected their fortunes at the mutuel windows. But Alex Goodman's crisis-toughened features never showed whether fate had smiled for him or not. Tonight was no exception, as he commented:

"Rosemont won the Special at 8-1." His eyes shone triumphantly. . "It wouldn't have happened except that Rosemont was an Alex Goodman special!"

"Nice work, Alex. It's good to be in the classroom with a winner."

They shared a good laugh, secure in their friendship.

Herbie took a good look at his teacher's dress for the evening and grinned.

"You noticed my crimson tie? What do you think—I don't know protocol on a huge occasion like this?" Goodman had always been tie less, even as a supper guest at the Roberts home.

"When I'm invited to Harvard, I go all the way," he said lightly. "Let's get a sandwich. I'm buying."

"Okay, teacher." Herbie grasped the other's elbow and steered him down Dunster Street through the maze of cars and merrymakers in the direction of a greasy spoon favored by undergraduates. Herbie felt a glow. The tout's red tie, fashioned in a huge knot below his chin, was as much a sign of the other's regard for Herbie as a courtesy to Harvard.

The restaurant was filled with students, teachers, alumni, and their guests. The take-out counter, however, was uncrowded, so the pair grabbed sandwiches and drinks and shouldered their way onto the street.

"Let's find a spot on the Charles where we can enjoy our meal and watch the fireworks." Herbie credited his familiarity with the topography around the Square to half a dozen scouting trips in the weeks leading up to today.

Picking out a knoll diagonally across the Charles River from Weld Boat House, Herbie could not refrain from a backward glance to see if this cozy time harbored any promise of interruption from the specter of Whitey Roberts.

"Tell me what we're going to see," said Alex, hoping to change the subject he reasoned was on Herbie's mind. Alex gestured toward a huge barge moored at the boathouse. Japanese lanterns strung crazily over the bow and stern illuminated a horde of red-jacketed young men clutching French horns, clarinets, saxophones, trumpets, trombones, tubas, fifes and drums as they scrambled into chairs set up on the barge. A huge green plaster replica of the figure of John Harvard sat in the bow. Warm-up tweets and toots drew huzzas from throngs of students, their dates and alumni couples hanging over the parapet of Larz Anderson Bridge.

Peering through the eight o'clock dusk, Herbie took in the barge scene, and then glanced to his left and right and across the river. From the Weeks Bridge, near Herbie and Alex, to the Larz Anderson upstream, both riverbanks were jammed to the water's edge with thousands of spectators. They crowded close to roped-off semi-circles where student crews manned rocket-launchers protected by police escorts.

A second huge barge sat in front of Alex and Herbie, studded with fireworks platforms. On a flat, grassy area between the Weeks Bridge and where Herbie and Alex waited was a massive, 30-foot high "Veritas" sign, the motto of Harvard College.

The figures of the fireworks teams on the barge suddenly began moving rapidly, their movements mirrored in pockets of reflected moonlight rippling across the Charles.

"They're in the starting gate," Alex said lightly.

No sooner had he spoken than a succession of detonations shook the lagoon, ricocheting from one side of the river to the other. These signaled a shower of flares from a procession of motor launches now moving downstream under Weeks Bridge.

The bombs jarred Herbie. He shivered violently. His nervous system, conditioned since infancy to expect the worst from his father, ill-prepared him for this noisy assault. He looked at Alex to see if the other were similarly affected.

But the tout was smiling, as Herbie had never seen him. His mustache quivered with excitement. "This is what I came for," he said.

If Alex said anything else in the next few minutes, Herbie could not have heard him. As though orchestrating the chaotic scene, the bandsmen on the lead barge struck up a familiar Harvard football song, "In Crimson Triumph Flashing." This touched off loud singing from merrymakers pressing close to Herbie and Alex, echoed by crowds on the opposite bank. Simultaneously, hundreds of torches suddenly glowed over Larz Anderson Bridge.

The fireworks barge erupted in dazzling rockets and Roman candles, then flung an ever-increasing crescendo of delayed-action bombs high over the river. These exploded, cascading streamers of multi-colored lights over the watchers.

A succession of golden starfish burst over the river, bringing vast sighs of delight from upturned faces. . The ivied, red brick buildings on both banks glowed satanically in the illumination of dozens of floodlights.

To Herbie it was both Heaven and Hell. Heavenly release from perpetual anxiety, and an endless disgorgement of luxuriously savage visions. Spectacle followed spectacle in mounting fury. Each rocket burst seemed to liberate a long-smothered ball of anger from his unplumbed depths.

Riveted to the sky show, Herbie was not aware that his companion had been distracted from his own pleasure in the happenings by harsh cries springing unconsciously from Herbie's throat in concert with rocket bursts.

"Aaagh! God in Heaven! Aaagh! God in Heaven!"

"Hey Herbie! Don't miss what's coming up right below us." Alex's shout, a desperate attempt to liberate the youth from his obviously personal struggle, failed to penetrate. Then Alex, inches shorter, grasped Herbie's shoulders and shook him.

"Here, here! Herbie, here!"

Jarred from his wild reverie, Herbie blinked rapidly, blinded by the yellowish light of a giant pinwheel descending on a parachute within twenty feet of the pair. Now a cluster of revolving pinwheels drifted over the scene, spreading out before Alex and Herbie like a grotesque Gustav Dore canvas. Flotillas of launches, manned by police and reunion classes, cut in and out of the line of barges which had completed their parade downstream. The eerily lit, massive green figure of John Harvard led the procession.

The bandsmen played "Ode To Harvard", music composed to accompany a poem written for the Tercentenary by Robert Frost.

The pulsating yellow fingers of Roman candles arching the stream seemed to clutch at the thousands of spectators, who alternately cheered and gasped at each fresh burst.

Though golden ribbons of light continued to arch from the riverbanks, the tempo of the celebration appeared to reach its peak and begin its decline, pausing before the final act.

"Something's wrong. The Veritas lighting is supposed to be the finale," said Herbie. He pointed to a half dozen figures swarming around the huge replica of John Harvard at the water's edge, fifty yards below Alex and Herbie.

Alex went into action, limping briskly down the sloping bank toward the Veritas. Herbie followed. He suddenly had a crazy feeling—something important would happen and Alex would play the lead role!

They were now close enough to see that whatever had delayed the finale in the fireworks program was a complete mystery to the fireworks team. A man seated in a canvas chair who wore a baseball cap issued staccato instructions. His men scrambled hither and yon seeking the answer to the puzzle:

"Why won't this damn thing work?" The man in the baseball cap was speaking for the assembled thousands. Repeatedly, he pressed a switch box in his lap but nothing happened.

Several motor launches darted in an out near the shore, the occupants shouting encouragement and well-meaning, if futile instructions. Hastily improvising, riverbank rocket crews sent up fresh salvos of Roman candles to mollify the disappointed throngs.

Herbie's attention was drawn to the Harvard bandsmen. Having debarked and assembled at the foot of Boylston Street, they struck up "Fair Harvard." alma mater of generations of Harvard men. The army of torches massed along the bridge from Harvard Stadium to Boylston Street shivered in anticipation. The hairs on the back of Herbie's neck stiffened. He looked to see if Alex was similarly moved, but Alex had disappeared.

A sense of panic that filled his breast at being deserted gave way to relief as he glimpsed a limping figure vaulting onto the platform supporting the giant set piece. Herbie watched closely as Alex conversed with the man in the baseball cap. The cap nodded. Then Alex's ordinarily deliberate movements became quick and authoritative. He inspected the rigging, then the fuse points, the latticework of pyrotechnic cable woven in the shape of "1936" and "1636". His head dipped out of sight for a few seconds, and then reappeared. He gestured towards the man in the cap, who closed the switch in his lap with one hand and waved to Alex with the other.

The river basin erupted in cheers as the mammoth Veritas burst into a brilliant orange. This glorious finale was saluted by a flurry of aerial bombs and a final splash of blue, green and crimson ribbons that bridged the river from the roofs of the Business School structures behind Herbie to the spires of Eliot House across the river.

Almost before Herbie could catch his breath at the drama of Alex's role in what had been developing as an embarrassing situation for Harvard College, Alex reappeared.

He was quietly exultant.

"What was that all about?" asked Herbie.

Alex grinned.

"Not much. I've been hooked on fireworks since I was in the 181st engineers in France. We blew up a few bridges."

CHAPTER 15

Herbie and Alex walked up Boylston Street from the Charles, treading carefully to avoid burned-out torches discarded by the merrymakers that preceded them. Nearing the Square, the din was still great, though diminishing. Behind them, the darkness over the river was now complete. The last man-made stars had fallen. The giant "Veritas" was extinguished and thousands of onlookers had vanished. Only a handful of police launches remained in the lagoon, nosing shoreward to see if any tipsy celebrants needed a helping hand, scooping up still-smoldering debris near the silent rocket stands and disposing of it in the river. It was well they did. Strong winds were now coming from the south, whipping the ordinarily placid Charles into choppy black wavelets and threatening to whisk stray sparks from spent rockets onto the Harvard dormitories along the river. A hurricane was predicted to hit Nantucket. Heavy rains were scheduled for Boston.

Herbie and Alex spoke not a word on their way to Harvard Square. The smacking of Herbie's leather heels on concrete was the loudest sound from the pair all the way from Memorial Bridge to Mount Auburn Street. For Herbie, a world of words bubbled just below the threshold of speech. He glanced at Alex. The gleam of triumph still burned in Alex's eyes, as he stared straight ahead, the corners of his mouth working slightly in pleasant contemplation of the night's work just past.

The Square was alive with alumni, some whose crew cuts stamped them as recent grads, and others whose white hair and stiff-jointed paces marked them from well before the turn of the century. The joy of the occasion was general and complete, flowing in and out of the entrances to half a dozen pubs fronting on the streets funneling into this most cherished and cosmopolitan landmark of Harvardians. Alex looked about with interest. He had intended to cross the street to the subway kiosk and take the train back to Boston and his hotel. But, like Herbie, he had a sense of need to add another chapter to the evening. Harvard was entering its fourth century. Herbie and Alex were entering a new era as well. Neither knew it or could put it into words, but the feeling of closeness they had shared would be something they would return to again and again.

Having decided that the evening was still young, Alex allowed Herbie to steer him to a booth in the Wursthaus, where the level of happiness seemed to approximate their own.

Young eyes, looking for truth, have a certain irresistible quality. Though Herbie said nothing, His eyes asked everything. Alex felt impelled to respond.

"You have a right to know some things about me, Herbie." The brown eyes narrowed seriously." But only in those areas where we bump up against each other."

This meant Herbie was to accept what was proffered and not ask for more. He nodded that he understood the terms of Alex's confidences.

Over foaming steins of beer, Herbie learned why his unprepossessing companion with the bottomless store of surprises had become a tout.

"I was drafted into the U.S. Corps of Engineers in January, 1918. Soon after basic training, I shipped overseas with the 181st Regiment I did construction work at the port of LeHavre, and saw action in several battles, especially in one engagement you may have read about:—the fighting near Chateau-Thierry and the crossing of the Marne."

Herbie's nod and smile of anticipation pushed Alex on.

"I was wounded and they shipped me home. After I was mustered out of the service, I went back to N.Y.U. And got my master's degree. This qualified me to teach math and physics at Richmond Banks High in the Bronx. I had five good years of teaching there, with enough time off accumulated through leaves of absence, and supplemented by night school, to earn a doctorate." Herbie's eyes widened. Alex smiled: "My thesis was on the rates of combustion of various gun powders for rocket applications."

Herbie grinned. What had happened at the lagoon an hour earlier had been child's play for Doctor Goodman? "I was riding high, so I thought. I was next in line to become head of the science department when Linus McNair, the head at the time, retired in one more year. Boy, was I wrong!" He shook his head. "I was passed over for the job—they gave it to a person with two years teaching experience and just a master's degree." Herbie's expression of complete incredulity was answered quickly.

"How did it happen? Cherchez la femme." He said this with a wry smile that failed to hide the bitterness underneath. "I had fallen in love with Angela LaTurca, an unusual person with brains as well as beauty. Angela was a senior in my math class. I was aware of the prohibition against dating students, but the chemistry between us was too strong. We married. Then came disaster. First, because my family did not welcome Angela. Second, because she was snubbed and we were not invited to the windup dinner given in June for faculty who earned PhD's the preceding year."

Herbie sensed his friend's swelling anger with his next recollection.

"Not one rejection, two rejections. Naturally I resigned from Richmond Banks High. I took a job as a civil engineer with a company doing highway work for the State of New York. This didn't last very long. I was out of there the first of the year—why? At the Christmas party, Angela was cut cold by the wives of my bosses."

"You know what was behind all this, don't you?"

The question from Alex caught Herbie unprepared. He covered his mouth with his hand and his expression saddened. Herbie had known the answer for the past twenty minutes.

"Yes," said Alex, "Angela is black. And what I had done for her was to take her great pride and cover it with dirt."

Alex became very solemn. Flinty sparks shot from his grave brown eyes. "That's when I began to think about an entirely new career—as turf advisor." Alex smiled and managed a smile at this self-platitude. Herbie tried to restore the happy mood with which they had entered the restaurant. He ordered another round of beers as Alex continued:

"When I was at N.Y.U., I played hooky from classes with an old army friend. We visited the races at Aqueduct. We never bet. The idea was to try and match the conformation and apparent condition of the horses to their likely performance in the races." He chuckled. "No, this theory never proved out. Probably because I majored in physics instead of chemistry, and it was the invisible chemical additives in the diet of the horses that threw us off track." He smiled broadly at his joke, and was pleased to see Herbie respond with his own big smile.

"But nonetheless, it was a happy experience. My friend got bitten by the urge to become a jockey .I just got bitten."

The eyes of Herbie's friend clouded as he returned to the circumstances of his tailspin following the brief career of civil engineer.

"In just six months, I went from one odd job to the next—tree surgeon, dock worker, fuse maker in a fireworks factory. Finally, I made the bottom of the ladder, washing dishes at the Waldorf-Astoria.

"Our marriage? Very bad Even though we had two young children, Max and Dinah, Angela took a job as an inventory clerk at Stern Brothers. While her mother took care of the children, Angela insisted on separation. It was the only answer for our troubles. Angela would not suffer repeated degradation. I would not be handicapped trying to build a career in a society that would not accept me with a black wife. I fought Angela on this one; she insisted."

"Imagine," Alex said softly, coming close to topics of intimacy he had obviously tried to avoid

"Two people who loved each so much and we had to separate." Herbie sympathized. "It's a rotten world. It wasn't your fault." He was unhappy with himself because his first reaction to the disclosure that Alex had been married to a black woman was one of mild revulsion. Then he realized he was simply echoing the prejudice dictated by the white bourgeois middle-class society that said whom you should share your life with, whom you should cut out of your life. He felt ashamed and would have done or said anything to prove to Alex that he was on his side.

Alex had been talking with his gaze absently fixed on his beer glass. Now he looked at Herbie, who met the other's eyes without hesitancy, something he was unable to do when addressed by his father.

"If someone held a lighted match so that the flame touched your fingers, what would you do?" He did not wait for Herbie's reply. "You'd take your hand away—right?"

"Of course."

"That's what I did. I took myself away from what was hurting. I accepted the separation. But where did I go? What did I do?" He smiled grimly.

"I spent the first afternoon of my so-called 'freedom' in Loew's theater on Lexington Avenue at 51st Street. Ronald Colman and Vilma Banky were in a movie called "Night of Love" and there was an "Our Gang" comedy." He paused, resolved to lighten the mood.

"In those days, if you went to see a western, the sound of galloping horses was in the left hand of the piano player who sat below the screen pounding the rhythm of the chase. If you went to see a love story, it was in the right hand, playing the high notes in trills and waterfall effects. There were a lot of waterfalls in "Night of Love." He was gratified to see Herbie's smile.

"I had supper in a beanery across the street. Then I walked down to Times Square. What did I do? I went into the Rialto and saw a movie called "Children of Divorce.' Clara Bow was in it. I came out of there a wreck. I could see what might happen to my kids. That's how I decided not to apply for a job as a motion picture projectionist."

"The next day I looked through the help wanted ads to find something in which I could forget my troubles and make money to send to Angela and the kids. Hoover was asking for engineers to come to New Orleans and build flood levees. But these jobs would have brought me too close to the same people I had worked with or studied with. Then it was that I realized I wanted to get away from my own kind."

Herbie was unused to beer and took off for the men's room. On his way back he met Claire Strong. She was just leaving with her escort, a smooth-featured, black-haired man dressed in a tight-shouldered zoot suit of some shiny material that Herbie thought was pretty sleazy.

Claire broke out a wistful smile, making the introductions:

"Herbie Roberts—Dimmy Garino. Dimmy is in the office at the Golden Bull, and we're at Harvard Square because Dimmy has a thing for fireworks."

Garino grunted assent: "You can say that again."

Alex rose when he saw Herbie with the couple and extended his hand to Garino.

"How've you been, Dimmy?" Alex was coolly cordial.

"Aces. How're you hittin' 'em?" Dimmy's words slid out from the corner of his mouth like a snake uncoiling from behind a rock.

Herbie introduced Alex to Claire. The four stood and exchanged superlatives about the fireworks display. Then Garino, whose eyes betrayed a chronic impatience, put his hand on Claire's arm in a familiar way and said, "We better scram, sweets. You gotta get your beauty sleep."

Claire smiled her sweetest at Herbie: "Congratulations and the best of luck at Harvard. Nice to meetcha, Mister Goodman." Herbie and Alex bid Garino goodnight and settled back to their beers. Alex spoke first: "You're surprised I know Dimmy Garino? We had the same boss, Louie Septimo, at Jamaica." Alex chuckled. "Yes, when I got through the help wanted pages, I turned to the sports pages. Jamaica was open, and I was open to suggestion. So that's where I went, and it was just what I needed—there are no sharp edges at a racetrack."

Jamaica was on Long Island, near Manhattan. So Garino was a New Yorker. His looks had repelled Herbie. He wondered how Claire had fallen for him.

Alex described his introduction into racetrack life. Cool, sweet mornings in the half-light when he joined others with a stop-watch to clock the runners; the hot, sweaty afternoons hunched over the rail, binoculars following the pack's mad dash down straight-aways, around turns, down the stretch to the finish line; nights and days poring over racing charts to arrive at a working method of handicapping.

"I was an apprentice for three weeks. Then one day I selected for a fifty percent winning percentage. I was ready to be a tout.

One of his first clients was Septimo, who, it turned out, was testing Alex and other touts before he selected Alex as his professional "opinion" a function that Alex was unaware of and backed away from when he found out Septimo's motive.

"I thought he was a find—a rich man who loved to bet. He turned out to be a track bookie .I got his number when he began to ask me how I liked certain horses, instead of asking me for my selection. Then I realized he wanted my opinion so he'd layoff money bet with him on those that had a good chance to win, and hold the money bet on horses who I believed did not have a chance."

Herbie was surprised. "I don't understand how an illegal bookie can operate in competition with the racetrack?"

Alex shrugged. "Where there's big money, you'll find the mobs looking for a way in. Septimo was a bookie in New York. The people he works for set him up as a "senator" in New England."

"What's a 'senator'?" Herbie thought it curious. "The 'senator' runs the syndicate's network at a racetrack. Who's in the network? Spotters who locate the big bettors who won't bet through the regular ticket sellers because they don't want to lower the odds, the runners who take the bets, the layoff men who bet the insurance money on likely winners with the ticket sellers, the muscle who protect the operation."

The image of the black-haired, pasty-faced Garino who talked out of the corner of his mouth flashed in Herbie's mind.

"So Garino is muscle for Septimo?"

Alex nodded. He paused. "One more duty for the 'senator'—he makes the arrangements with track personnel at the security level so that the mob can operate."

Herbie shook his head. Such devious, cold-blooded corruption was beyond belief. And his own father was close to Septimo. He shuddered.

"Herbie, would you like to know what a tout really is?"

"Sure." An interesting tidbit coming up—the twitching mustache said as much.

"I don't mean the phony touts—the con men looking for a scam who pose as jockeys or trainers so they can make a fast killing. Then, when the authorities find them out, they repeat their act at another track. And I don't mean the shotgun artists, who tout every horse in a race, one to a client, so there's always at least one client who's happy. These people use up their welcome very quickly."

"The professional tout is a sign reader, like the guide who hires out to city people who want to kill a bear but don't know how to read the signs on the back roads and in the woods. If a tout has grown up among thoroughbreds, he has an edge, because he can read the signs of fitness and infirmities." He laughed. "My best recommendation in this respect is that I lived for two years in the vicinity of army mules. "Continuing his dissertation on touts, Alex said, "Different horseplayers look at touts in different ways. To some he is a high priest, with a ritual all his own, dispensing hope. When he wins, the tout is Mr. Omnipotence—sublime, a genius. When he loses, he's a bag of hot air, a faker, a clown who's made the mistake of simulating a king."

Herbie thought he should offer his own interpretation. "Isn't the tout a descendant of the prophets in the Bible? Ezekiel, Isaiah, Jeremiah, Amos?"

"You're forgetting, Herbie, that the prophets were intermediaries between God and the people of Israel. I'd say that the tout is a weigher and a measurer, a scientist on a very junior level" He paused, eyeing Herbie shrewdly, "I'd say your prophesying, as much as I understand it, is allied fairly closely to the ways of the old prophets."

"Because it appears as though I'm receiving a message from somebody?" Herbie told himself that this was as far as he should go. He wasn't admitting anything, just making conversation.

"That's the way it appears." Alex hesitated, unwilling to make Herbie uncomfortable but constrained to demonstrate his own lifelong training to believe only the evidence of his senses. "I see what I see, and I see just you, doing some rather remarkable prophesying."

Herbie didn't know if this was intended to be complimentary or a way of saying to him:" take another look at yourself, you're missing something important."

After a long silence, Herbie broke it. "I'll vote for the high priest idea. You listen like a priest to your clients when they tell you their stories about how they almost hit the big winners, or how they would have done so if only someone hadn't come along and touted them off the winner." He stopped, thinking he had insulted the tout, but Alex laughed.

"Almost and 'if'—that sums it up pretty well. The near misses that keep me in business." He glanced at his watch. "Let's leave it at this: a tout supplies a little more hope than the player brings with him to the track. And how much is this hope worth, even if it lasts for only a few minutes?" Herbie had no answer for this at the time. Alex had a way of leaving him dangling; forcing him to think, and that wasn't bad.

CHAPTER 16

During his recuperation, Whitey's day began with a leisurely breakfast fetched to his bedroom by Delia. He rarely appeared around the house in other than a blue silk robe that Myrtle had purchased for her Daddy when he returned from the hospital. On this rainy Friday morning, however, he sat across the breakfast table from Herbie in one of his new custom-made suits. This would be his first day at the office since his accident, a relatively easy day, dominated by a sales meeting. But the first business on his mind had nothing to do with beef, everything to do with horseflesh.

"Isn't tonight your last lesson with Alex?" The blue eyes bored right through his son.

"Uh huh. And tomorrow we go to Narragansett to see what I've learned." Might as well spill it out—that's where the next question would lead to anyway.

Herbie thought his father was pleased that he might start to reap the fruits of Herbie's cram course in handicapping, but the stern mouth didn't show it.

"And when do you register?"

This question was leading to how much money was needed for tuition. His father knew the facts, but he would insist on Herbie laying it out again, as a way of emphasizing the strain of being Herbie's father. So Herbie blurted out the whole picture.

"I register next Friday morning, the 26th. Tuition for the year is four hundred, plus forty for fees—mostly phys ed. and health stuff. The forty is due now, the tuition in four installments."

"And how much have you got towards the first payment?"

Herbie gritted his teeth and tried not to show frustration.

"Seventy-five. I need forty for clothes, so a hundred -five will do it."

"I guess we can manage that." The grim lines at the corners of the thin mouth relaxed. "Who knows, tomorrow you might earn it yourself."

Although the rain had begun to fall heavily, prompting Myrtle to make an attempt to keep her Daddy home, Whitey brushed her off and left for Boston.

Herbie tried to pull himself together. As often as he had been cross-examined by his father, he had never been able to shake off the trembling and anger that followed. He tried to recall the stirring events of the night before. How proud he was to bring Alex to his college. How good it had been to share confidences with Alex. He looked out the window. The rain was slanting in sheets, driven by high winds. The weather would force today's Tercentenary exercises inside. Herbie felt sorry that President Roosevelt would be addressing just those guests who could fit inside the New Lecture Hall.

He looked forward to the evening, when Alex would come. Tomorrow would be the last day of their "official" teacher-and-student time together, since Alex was leaving for Arkansas the next day. Saturday night would see Herbie back at the same old piano bench in Hibernian Manor, pounding it out for Ken Reilly's Royal Minstrels.

Herbie doubted he would ever match Alex Goodman as an honest-to-goodness handicapper. Goodman had the advantage of twenty years of education and training in physical sciences—what Alex called 'weighing and measuring'. And, as the tout unfolded the mysteries of weight allowances for such apparently trivial differences as age, sex, class and recent winning performances among the entries in a particular race, and how those differences figured to separate the horses at the finish line by anything from a whisker to a city block, Herbie was all the more certain he'd be a fool to abandon the simplicity of his arrangement with Baal. Too, the whole question of the importance of weight seemed nebulous. What difference could it make to a powerful 1200-pound animal whether it carried 114 or 117 pounds? His skepticism showed.

Beginning the lesson, Alex felt the seriousness of Herbie's challenge. "I realize it's hard to swallow. How could an animal as big and muscular as a racehorse be sensitive to miniscule variations in the package it carries on its back?" Alex paused to correct himself. "I should say, rather, variations in the package of weight that it lifts."

"What do you mean—lifts?"

Alex speculated for a moment on the best way to make the point.

"Let's try something. Bring back two sticks of butter from the kitchen."

This was crazy. How was Herbie expected to grasp such an elusive idea by staring at two quarter-pound sticks of butter? But Alex had made good sense throughout his cram course. And his rescue of Harvard's fireworks shows the night before told Herbie never to underestimate the tout. Seated across from Alex with the butter on a plate between them, Herbie's look of anticipation drew a smile from Alex.

"I hope you're not expecting the table to rise or anything like that?"

Herbie relaxed. "Just a few raps from the departed will be quite satisfactory."

"Put one hand on the table, palm down."

Herbie did as instructed. Alex placed a single stick of butter on the back of Herbie's hand.

"What do you feel?"

Truthfully, Herbie barely noticed the weight of the butter and said so. "Not much. It feels like a feather"

"Now lift it in the palm of your hand."

"It feels like something," Herbie admitted. "There is a difference."

"Now let's do the same with two sticks."

The same comparison done with two sticks of butter demonstrated clearly that weight lifted in Herbie's palm felt more than twice as heavy as the same weight on the back of his hand.

Alex summed up: "Exactly. That's the difference between weight at rest and weight that's carried—or in motion, lifted weight."

Score another big one for Alex. The guy can really teach, thought Herbie.

There were all kinds of variations to look out for in weighting a horse. Like when the jockey weighs in heavier than his assigned weight. There were the horses that seemingly "read" the weight assignments and absolutely, positively wouldn't raise more than a gallop if the assigned weight were higher than their "ceiling" weight of 110 or 115 pounds. And how about the horses that ran the same steady 1:12 for six furlongs whether carrying 110 or 125 pounds? For every principle that seemed to apply in most instances, there were exceptions. Alex was always able to supply the keys to deciphering even these puzzles.

"Boy," sighed Herbie as the tout seemingly was bent on filling him with vital facts until he burst. "Sure is a lot to think about."

Seeing Herbie's fatigue and interpreting it correctly as mostly boredom, Alex shifted into he "dessert" for this lesson.

"To this point everything you've learned tells you to assume that every entry in the race has a chance. Is that right?"

Something was up. Better zero in, Herbie. He nodded yes.

"Let's talk about the important special case when only one entry gets your attention, and he gets it because you've been carrying his name next to your heart for some time." The tout smiled. His mustache twitched. He was enjoying being teacher again.

"The name you carry on your specials list has to earn it." He paused, waiting for Herbie to contribute.

"By showing exceptional real speed in two or more recent races?"

"That you already know," said the tout in a scolding tone. "This is a lesson on weighting."

"How about excellent performances carrying top weight in two or more recent races?" As he asked the question, he knew that he was wrong, then said the words he knew were on the tout's lips.

"I know—beware the obvious."

Alex made a circle with thumb and forefinger to acknowledge that Herbie had read his mind. Alex then continued:

"I'll make two statements I won't qualify. The first is that the best entry in a race runs well even with the most handicaps, which may or may not include carrying top weight." This was a puzzle and Herbie's bewilderment showed.

Ale had used the plural "handicaps." Could he mean that a front-runner performing well in a race made to order for come-from-behind horses was one of those handicaps? Or that the converse could be a handicap for a late runner who performs well in a race made to order for a front-runner?

Herbie was thinking. Good. Alex smiled. "You're probably getting the idea.

It's any tough condition equal to swimming against the tide. The torture test. Doing well when the pace is unsuited. But the most important clue is doing well in a race carrying high weight when the odds board shows that the majority of entries carrying light weight are all favored over the high weight."

The odds board? Herbie was suddenly flustered. He had thought he was receiving the only valuable message sent by the odds board. Yet obviously he was missing out.

"Listen to me, Herbie." Alex was aware he had touched a nerve. Herbie had intimated that his prophecies had something to do with signals read from the odds board.

"Here's my flat, unqualified statement number two: the best handicapper at any racetrack is the odds board as you see it when the race actually starts." Alex waited for this to take effect.

Herbie grunted. The lights were beginning to go on. "What you're saying is that by the time the race starts, the truth comes out on every solid horse, on every sleeper, on every class horse who's really fit, on every horse who's improving himself out of his class." His satisfied expression told Alex that the youth had not simply read the tout's mind. He had thought out the problem.

Alex grinned: "Absolutely, positively right."

Herbie grinned back and put up his hand to hold the floor for another moment.

"To put it succinctly, as my English teacher used to say, 'money talks'." Alex roared and slapped the table so hard that Whitey, in the living room below, bellowed up the staircase:

"Easy! What in hell's going on?"

There was quite a lot going on, Herbie said to himself. And more to come please God.

CHAPTER 17

If anyone were to ask Whitey and his Satcor cronies what they thought of Herbie's test run at Narragansett Park as a "graduate" handicapper, they'd call it a bust. But if that same person were to ask Herbie or Alex if he were satisfied with the day's results, the answer would be "yes."

With Alex mostly looking on and not helping out, Herbie came up with exactly one winner, one second, three thirds and two clunkers on a track surface that was a sea of mud. When the eighth race came around, the Satcor guys stayed away as though Herbie had measles. Alex said to Herbie with his told-you-so smile: "Now you know how a tout feels after one long, rotten, lousy day at the races."

Herbie agreed. "It was a long, rotten, lousy day for we touts." Then added, "But not for Herbie and Alex."

Between the first and eighth, there had been plenty of profit for both.

When Herbie muffed the first two races, he threw down his Telegraph, well marked up with the" tracks" of the handicapper, and stared moodily at the odds board. Herbie's disgust was interpreted by Alex as rebellion rather than guilt at having cost Satcor a wad. Alex picked up the newspaper and returned it to Herbie who continued to stare at the odds board.

"Now you know how the colonials felt when they had their Boston tea party," Alex said.

"What is that supposed to mean?" Herbie showed annoyance, as he struggled to decipher Alex's words.

"OK, let's spell it out," said Alex patiently, secretly delighted that Herbie's guarded reserve was showing a few cracks.

"One, the colonials felt that taxation without representation was worth at least a small rebellion against the king. Two, the rebellion took the form of dumping the tea on which they were supposed to pay a tax. Three, you've been feeling all along that being ordered by the king to perform like a monkey on the stick was worth a rebellion. Four, you threw the tea into the harbor when you threw the paper on the ground. And lastly. . . ."

He could not go on, as Herbie, bent over with laughter, gasped, "No more. Oh, no more, please, Alex!"

Herbie managed to figure out a second place finisher for Satcor in the third, which did something for his morale, but nothing for Satcor, because they played to win only.

Alex gave Herbie a nudge and nodded in the direction of the Satcor guys, now buzzing around Whitey with gestures of impatience. Herbie figured that they were asking Whitey to abandon the quest for the golden goose with Herbie as their leader.

"The troops are getting restless," said the tout. "Tell you what—I'll make a selection and not tell you. You do your prophecy stuff for this race only. If we match, you give them the selection. If we don't match, I will. All right?"

Herbie grinned. He could see a flaw.

"Just one thing—if you pick first and then our picks coincide, you'll never know whether I got my pick the usual way or whether I read your mind." Herbie shook his head: "And I won't know how I got the pick either."

A thoughtful scowl from Alex. "Then I'll pick after you, instead of before you." His logic told him that now was the time for Herbie to share his secret. But his instinct told him to wait for Herbie's decision on this important matter.

Herbie framed the three rows of odds digits in his vision. Number 5 shone brightly. He turned to Alex, who had been watching intently.

"Number five," he said. Number five was Calico Sue, at 10-1.

After five minutes of study, Alex looked up and smiled. "Calico Sue." he said. Calico Sue won and paid $18.40, which brought

Satcor back alive. However, they had little cause to smile the rest of the day.

During the three races that followed, Alex learned the source of Herbie's prophetic powers.

Alex was especially interested in Baal's role as the custodian of the golden secrets.

"How is it that Baal, or whatever his name, seems to punish you sometimes by not coming through with the signals?"

Herbie sighed. "Punish" was a clever choice of words. Herbie believed that Goodman had seen enough of the relationship between Herbie and his father to know that Herbie was the product of an old-fashioned reward and punishment method. Do as I tell you, and I reward you. Disobey and you get punished. Alex had seen Whitey act out this pattern a number of times. Alex was linking Baal with the personage of Whitey Roberts. But if this were actually true, the existence of a being or spirit in the odds board would be simply a creation of Herbie's imagination. No way, Herbie insisted to himself. Whether its name was Baal, or Mr. Big, it was sending Herbie a signal the same way anyone perceives objects or signals, with the eyes. Now that he had disclosed the source of his prophecies, Herbie wondered if Alex thought he were a nut, or perhaps even crazy.

"You think I'm crazy," Herbie said, but without conviction.

Alex seemed to ignore Herbie's statement. He said, "I don't believe very much is known about psychic phenomena. I haven't studied it, so I really know nothing. There'd be no reason for me to doubt you." Whitey's style was to put his sons on the witness stand. Alex would not make this mistake. He went on:

"On a few occasions, I've had the experience of getting a message from some people before they opened their mouths. I think this happens with many people. Some have it happen quite a lot. Like you do." This was an invitation for Herbie to talk about such experiences.

Since the day of his first clandestine look at the odds board, Herbie had sought out articles on psychic phenomena. J.B. Rhine, a professor at Duke University, seemed to be the leader of a group doing research. Herbie's reading had produced words for his experiences. Like "extra sensory perception" and "telekinesis." They seemed to describe events in his life leading up to the discovery of Baal in the tote board.

For Alex's benefit, he recalled some of the happenings that he had paid little notice to at the time. Now they appeared to add up to a facet of his personality that would be with him forever.

In the summer of 1931, at Boy Scout camp, an eleven-year old tenderfoot named Calvin Roach was missing from morning roll call. While search parties combed the woods, Herbie received a flash of a fully clothed scout floating face down under the boat pier. When Herbie steered his scoutmaster to the spot, they found Calvin Roach drowned as Herbie had visualized

On a spring afternoon in 1932, Herbie was playing catch in the backyard with Eddie Gilman when Larry hollered from the back porch that grandpa Nattelson had gone to the hospital for a prostate operation. Herbie had a sudden vision of his beloved grandfather's face, cold and white, lying with eyes closed in a plain pine coffin. The experience choked him up and he left his game without explanation. The next morning before breakfast, the Roberts family got a phone call from the hospital. Lewine Nattelson had died on the operating table

Herbie had often startled Alice Fitzgerald, his eighth grade English teacher, by voicing her thought just before she was about to speak. After this happened about a dozen times, upsetting Miss Fitzgerald to the point where she would clap her hand over her mouth and not say anything for a couple of minutes, Herbie put a lock on his own mouth and assumed the role of a dummy.

Up to this point, Herbie had been able to skirt references to his father. But if this new feeling of trust in Alex were to flourish, there could be no holding back.

"It's too long a story," he began hesitantly. "But I haven't got along very well with my father." Alex nodded understandingly.

Herbie went on: "To the point where, at half-past four, on Sunday, July 30, I put my fist through glass and wished my father dead."

There was a long moment before Alex spoke. What he had just heard was not just another psychic incident. He had been permitted a glimpse of the raw, bleeding conscience of another human being. Handle with care, Alex. "That was not one of your better days, Herbie," he said, injecting a light note that he did not truly feel, but which he believed would keep their relationship alive and growing.

"Your wish didn't come true."

Herbie smiled, more because he was relieved that Alex grasped the significance of his confession without the necessity for a maudlin recital than out of appreciation for the other's wit.

"Which brings me up to today and Calico Sue," said Herbie. His revelations left him feeling empty but relaxed. Alex looked at him with a speculative smile.

"Do you know what I think of the place where your Baal lives?"

"Tell me."

"It's a Super-Straw. You think there's something there in those bright flashing figures. But when you reach for it, there's nothing there. Absolutely nothing."

Alex warmed to the task.

"Look at all those people staring at that thing." He waved his hand at the crowds. Herbie turned and looked. Alex had cued him to notice for the first time in the months he had been going to the races how the gaze of 20,000 people was focused, even riveted, on the wicked witch of the infield.

"Look at their expressions," Alex continued.

Herbie did as Alex said. For as far as he could see, across the apron of the clubhouse and into the grandstand, everyone wore the same expression. A look of blank, blind supplication, everyone seeking confirmation of his or her hopes in the gleaming numbers that seemed to promise everything.

"Scary," said Herbie.

"Yes, it is scary," said Alex. "Because they believe there's something special about the money they might win. They think gambling money is a different kind of money than the money they get from being doctors, ditch diggers, salesmen, secretaries, engineers."

"Do I sound as though I don't like my profession?" He said this aloud, but with a bemused, thoughtful expression. When Herbie did not reply, Alex smiled.

"You know, at one time I knew why I went into this business. But now, more and more, I believe I was covering up the real reason."

His direct gaze commanded Herbie's close attention.

"As I think about it, a lot of people are here, at the track, living out some kind of fantasy because the real world has been too tough."

Ales wasn't about to say, but Herbie knew that he meant confronting the problem of living with Angela was "the real world." And that because Herbie couldn't achieve a comfortable relationship with his father, he was going down Fantasy Road as well. Once more, Alex had prodded Herbie into asking himself why. The tout would be missed in the coming winter months.

CHAPTER 18

On Friday, September 26th, Herbie Roberts was among 1008 freshmen from forty-four states and six foreign countries that registered as the Harvard Class of 1940. A pleasant, middle-aged lady took Herbie's first semester payment at University Hall and gave him a slip of paper that would admit him to classes.

After spending a suitable few moments walking through the Yard, sizing up his classmates, Herbie signed for courses in basic harmony, 19th Century English literature, psychology and French. Herbie thought he might major in music or English when he became an upperclassman. Harmony and English lit would start him in either direction. And his current interest in music should lead somewhere. His advisor, Morris Danzig, encouraged him to keep past successes in high school English in view when making final choice of a major.

From Herbie's initial observations, the Harvard student body was made up of three main groups: the ruling preppies from Exeter, Groton, Governor Dummer and the like, middle-class Wasps from the Midwest and far west, and the ethnic hodgepodge from Boston area high schools and foreign countries.

Herbie had said to his advisor: "I hope my origins in this third group won't prevent me from making friends in the other groups. Isn't this the only way to have a full and rewarding life at Harvard."

"Ain't necessarily so," Danzig had replied. "Life at Harvard is like life itself. It's what you yourself make it."

Herbie's hopes that his new status as a college student would insulate him from his father's demands were denied less than a week after he made his first appearance in a Harvard classroom.

Whitey moved quickly to claim his due in Herbie's handicapping education.

"I'm not asking much. Just a couple winners during the week. But they've got to be choice, so make no mistakes!"

Herbie's logical side nagged him to protest this trampling of expectations for a monastic academic existence, untroubled by old demands. But his ongoing need for his father's approval surfaced as always, forcing the response,

' "No problem. It'll be taken care of."

It was, of course, a problem. First, it was necessary to maintain a pocket journal of the results daily at Narragansett. Analysis of the race result charts published in the daily newspapers gave Herbie the base for handicapping by Alex Goodman's method. Then there was the Morning Telegraph to buy Wednesday, Thursday and Friday, when Whitey was hanging on the phone at M. Roberts waiting for his noontime call. There was the Armstrong sheet with scratches and overweights to buy mid-morning. Then select one or two races from the card – take them apart, quarter-by-quarter, filtering the gold from the dross. All in all, seventy or eighty minutes of feverish, undercover doings that Herbie kept wholly unseen from his peers going about their simple student lives.

If Herbie found himself in a cluster of classmates on arriving at the Square in the morning, he had to detach himself and return ten minutes later to purchase the Telegraph at the newsstand next to the bus stop. It had to be done surreptitiously, you see.

The Narragansett past performances usually took up three pages. After folding these pages to fit in his pants pocket, he had to dispose of the rest of the newspaper without attracting attention. The toilets in the commuter center and Boylston Hall reading room became settings of daily panic as Herbie pressed for answers to Whitey's constant question, "Who is it today?"

Because the messages he phoned to his father contained the seed of happiness, Herbie found it essential to keep his hopes high the rest of the afternoon, nursing fantasies of favorable outcomes. His thoughts followed a pattern: relaxation of his father's usual grimness, a powerful arm around his shoulders after supper, a pledge that together Herbie and Whitey Roberts would lick the world. But puffing up his hopes when he was supposed to be absorbing an important educational experience had only one predictable result: embarrassment when an instructor's voice sliced through his fantasies: "Roberts! Get back on the same wave length with the rest of us."

Herbie's daily flights of anticipation would flourish or fade when he read the results of his morning's hard work on his father's face across the supper table. Mostly, he received messages of failure. As diligently as he stuck by Alex's teaching, Herbie was mismatched against the uncontrollable combination of bad racing luck and the corrupt base of what Alex had called "the most dishonest business in the country." A growing feeling of helplessness began to overwhelm him as the precisely constructed vessels of his handicapping skill foundered on the hard rocks of reality.

He felt he was a stray log drifting into a raging downstream current, tossed hither and thither by the irreconcilable forces of Whitey's needs, his own needs, and by the pulls and tugs of academic demands. On Saturdays, Herbie shrugged off the small pain of separation from a boy's dream of seeing Harvard football, and made the mandated visits to the racetrack with his parents. On these occasions he chucked science in favor of his old intuitive relationship with the Baal of the tote board. The resulting shower of money into Satcor wallets softened the grimness in his father's expression and quickened Herbie's faint hopes of eventual nirvana.

After these victories, Myrtle attempted to stuff money into his pocket. Herbie customarily said, "no thanks, mom. I've got to do it my own way." Herbie really didn't know why he rejected the money. He remembered accepting a payment early in his racetrack experience and feeling tainted. Was Harvard bringing out an inborn steak of snobbishness? Was it my inner core rejecting capitulation to others? Alex had mentioned during their last afternoon together that he begin to understand and respect that inner core.

Refusing his winner's share strained Herbie's ability to cover his expenses. Hibernian Manor was closed for repairs, so Herbie had to depend on a miscellany of band dates supplied by the musicians' union for money to buy books, articles of clothing and the means to join Karnofsky and Lanin on infrequent triple dates. There were also odd jobs as a night counterman in a cafeteria, and as a clerk in a meat market owned by Frank Cardinale, one of Whitey's racetrack buddies. And sometimes Herbie subbed for his cousin, Rob Romanoff, as a runner between doctors' offices in Kenmore Square and a laboratory in Roxbury.

The relative state of affluence supported by this mélange of careers lasted only a few weeks. A customer found cat hairs in her salad one day, and the board of health closed the cafeteria. A week later Herbie found his innate sense of gentility being tested as a purveyor of Cardinale's hamburger. It was Friday night and the many faces peering intently into the refrigerated glass case presided over by Herbie Roberts gradually lost their separate identities and became simply voices, divided by preferences for 19-cent, 29-cent or 39-cent hamburger. Of course only the insiders, including Herbie, knew it was all the same hamburger. But as the management shrewdly estimated would happen, the customers saw important differences between the three mounds of juicy beef. Their preferences were equally divided among the three different prices.

Such quirks of behavior were assiduously studied and exploited as a new retail science. Cardinale was a leading practitioner.

Occasional resentment at being made party to the flimflam boiled up inside Herbie and was quickly repressed. He performed like a machine, scooping hamburger onto squares of parchment, weighing, reading out the total price, wrapping, exchanging packages for assorted denominations of coins and bills. Though he had been up since six, his day as bus rider, student, turf advisor and meat clerk seemed to have taken little toll of his energy.

Now, at ten o'clock, one hour to go before quitting time, his eye for the specified pound or two pounds, or whatever, was so keen that he found himself receiving recognition from the blur of faces observing his proficiency.

"Look, a regular Houdini," said one.

"Say kid, I'd like to be your manager. How about it?" asked another?

"One pound on the nose. Remarkable!"

Herbie was beginning to think that maybe he was doing something exceptional when he himself fell victim to management science.

"A pound and a quarter of the thirty-nine." The man's voice was low and intense.

Thrown a bit off-stride by the unusual request, Herbie bent to the scooping, vaguely aware of small, dark eyes following his movements.

The purchase weighed and wrapped, Herbie announced the total of "forty-nine cents, please," and held out his hand for the expected dollar bill. Instead, a trickle of coins clinked onto the glass, a process deliberately slowed as the customer fished in his purse for more coins, his eyes never leaving Herbie.

People waiting their turn crowded up to the counter, voicing impatience as the stream of pennies gradually formed a puddle of coppery shadows over the mound of 39-cent hamburger.

"Hey, I've only got a three-day pass. How about it?"

"What the heck's going on? I haven't got all night!"

Herbie ignored the rising din of impatience. His fingers poised over the coins, feeling an urgency to restore the incredibly smooth, swift pattern of movement that was so pleasing moments earlier. His eye took in what appeared to be forty pennies. Nine to go. His gaze met that of the customer, whose eyes shone with subdued joy. The customer parceled out the final coppers.

Herbie scraped up the coins impatiently, finding it difficult as condensation had left a vapor film on the glass. He counted slowly as he picked up the coins.

"Only forty-eight cents. Another penny," he said, holding back anger.

The penny dropped onto the glass. Why not into his outstretched palm? The customer, unperturbed by Herbie's goodbye glare, disappeared into the crowded store with his purchase.

Herbie thought no more of the incident until, at quitting time; he opened his pay envelope to find a pink slip with a typewritten message:

THIS IS YOUR TERMINATION NOTICE. CUSTOMER SERVICE VIOLATION. SIGNED: FRANK CARDINALE.

The crossfire from Whitey over the loss of work at Cardinale's Market was as expected. And even though his telling of the circumstances drew nods of understanding from Myrtle, Larry and Reggie at Sunday dinner, Whitey succeeded in draping a layer of guilt over Herbie's shoulders.

"The fact that you lost the job is the only thing that counts," his father said.

Whitey's losses with the bookie during the week doubtless reinforced the vehemence of his reproach, thought Herbie.

"I don't know if I can get you another chance. With Frank Cardinale or anyone else. Unless you learn to stand on your own two feet, you'll end up another bum on the Boston Common."

For the briefest instant, as Whitey's car disappeared in the general direction of Southwest Connecticut, Herbie had a vision of himself, disheveled and unshaven, slumped on a bench among the other failures of the world who assembled daily on the Common.

The following Wednesday, wrapping up a pressurized day of class work and horse work, Herbie found himself in a struggle to salvage the job he shared with Rob as a runner for the ITC Laboratory.

In the beginning, it was only a struggle to keep his feet and protect his medical cargo tucked into a shopping bag, as the trolley lurched crazily on its underground run from Kenmore to Park Street.

Ordinarily, Herbie found riding the subway a blissful experience. Free from the probing eyes of people who knew him, surrounded by a delightful neutrality of faces and bodies, Herbie indulged his propensity to rearrange the innocuous as drama.

Most of the men were thin-faced laborers in rough wool jackets, caps pulled down over their ears against the nippy late October cold. They were bound for their homes in the poorer parts of the city after a day behind WPA shovels. The women were mostly secretaries and clerks in offices along Commonwealth Avenue. White shoes and stockings beneath plain cloth coats identified some as dental assistants or nurses from hospitals and doctors' offices around Kenmore. A furtive little man in a worn Chesterfield that hung below his knees seemed to be the pickpocket type, beady black eyes darting left and right as he burrowed into a cluster of straphangers a few feet from Herbie. A knot of hard-eyed men in seamen's jackets, carrying suspicious-looking leather suitcases, whispered among themselves. Herbie hazarded that they were headed downtown to blow a bank safe and make their getaway aboard a freighter. A sad-eyed woman with a child tugging on each hand was big with child. Herbie ascribed her woeful expression to the sudden death of her husband. He wished he were seated in front of her so he could rise gallantly and offer his seat.

Those lucky enough to find seats stared blankly at the ads for this or that shop, chewing gum and soft drinks that filled the spaces above the sterile black holes of windows.

Having catalogued the scene, Herbie shifted his gaze to the newspaper of a passenger occupying a window seat several feet distant. The car swayed from side to side, straining Herbie's ability to snatch glimpses of headlines forecasting Landon's victory in the following week's national elections. The headline quoted a poll by the Literary Digest. As he leaned closer to follow the headline down into smaller type, Herbie's bulky cargo intruded on a young woman reading a pulp novel just beneath him.

"Do you remind removing your groceries from my lap?" Her icy sarcasm was reinforced by a firm push against his shopping bag. Its guardian was thus harshly alerted to the dangers of exposing the nature of the mission for which he was being paid two dollars.

"Very sorry," mumbled Herbie, avoiding eye contact below. The woman took in his scuffed saddle shoes and leather patched on his sleeves.

"You fraternity boys don't learn the right things," she snapped, "just how to load up for a binge."

Thoroughly frosted, Herbie shrank into a corner with his parcel. He was relieved when the girl got off at Boylston Street. A fresh load of passengers, mostly shop girls and secretaries, got on to the accompaniment of protests from those already on board about being pushed around like cattle. The conductor, hoping to bring order out of chaos, yelled out orders:

"Find space to stand – move left and right—; let's make room for all the folks. Can't close the doors and get moving until we do this!"

Herbie positioned himself near an exit. It was now five-thirty and there was no time to waste. The lab closed at six-thirty. It was a good half hour ride from Park Street to the lab across the street from Franklin Park. If the lab were closed when he arrived, he's have to take the specimens home and deliver them early the next morning.

The Bluehill Avenue car pulled out as Herbie's trolley arrived at Park Street.

"Damn," he muttered. A sympathetic voice said, "Only fifteen minutes to wait for the next one."

Herbie squeezed into a space on the bench. He was grateful for the seat, even though the bench was jammed and the smell of whiskey from the man to his right was uncomfortably reminiscent of the drunks who sat alongside on his piano bench when he played at Tony's Harbor Club until four in the morning.

Herbie turned his head away and half-held his breath to reduce his intake of the offensive smells from the other.

A seamed, leathery face sat bulbous-nosed on a thick-chested body. Puffy, pale-green eyes licked hungrily over the parcel tucked close to Herbie's bosom.

"Watcha got there?" The hoarse question warned Herbie that he was about to confront a Waterloo.

"Groceries," answered Herbie. "For my mother," he added hopefully.

A grimy forefinger snaked out of the over-long sleeve of the man's coat and proceeded to explore the contours of the bottles containing the hopes and fears of the sick.

"Who ya kiddin'?" The man's face was now close enough to reveal the spiny network of red veins in the corners of his eyes. Alcoholic vapors accompanying his words deposited a gummy film on Herbie's face.

Herbie shuddered and tried to get up. He was restrained by a grip of iron.

"Whassa hurry? Less talk it over."

"Nothing to talk about. I've got to catch my car." Herbie's car was nowhere in sight, but the prisoner was determined to escape.

"Don't be a goddam cheapskate. Gimme just one bottle." Red-lined eyelids lowered, closing the drunk's eyes to narrow slits.

"Let go my arm," Herbie said in his most menacing tone.

The atmosphere of growing bellicosity spiked with the smell of rotgut whiskey quickly emptied the bench of other patrons. A thin circle of spectators stood around and took sides in a class war, the workingman against the college kid.

"You friggin jerk, gimme a bottle;"

"Hey jerk," echoed a bystander, "give the man a bottle."

Herbie scanned the area hopelessly for sight of a policeman who wasn't there, while wrapping his arms around his parcel to forestall the other's nonstop clawing to get inside.

"Mac, better leave the kid alone."

This tidbit of support from a faceless onlooker encouraged Herbie to get to his feet with the drunk clutching his arm.

A brief, violent struggle ensued, with Herbie balancing his

instincts to flee against the heavy moral charge to protect his medical cargo. Finally, the drunk succeeded in extracting a single flask from beneath Herbie's arms. He waved the bottle and its cloudy golden contents triumphantly aloft to the cheers of a coterie of followers recruited on the spot.

"Geez, home brew," said one, noting the absence of any label except a small, unreadable sticker.

"Betcha it's got a kick like a mule." Said another enviously.

"Please give it back. Don't open it. You'll get sick," pleaded Herbie. But the drunk had already nestled into a corner to savor his prize.

Herbie shrugged, gave himself silent congratulations for an honest effort. He hoisted the remainder of his cargo of urine onto the Roxbury-bound trolley, and then twisted around for a last look in the direction of the victor.

He saw the arm extended on high, bottle uncapped, the drunk's mouth agape to receive the precious liquid.

He looked quickly away. It had always been difficult for him to watch the misery of others.

CHAPTER 19

Not long after the robins departed from their nests in the trees surrounding the Roberts house, Whitey and Myrtle followed them south. They would be winter residents of Miami Beach until the first week in March.

Technically speaking, this four-month vacation was a business trip. Whitey Roberts did not find it difficult to ingratiate himself with the owners of large hotels catering to Northerners who expected the best cuisine. After all, M. Roberts was offering beef bred and fed in the nation's Midwest corn belt. The grass-fed cattle of southern Florida could not match this quality. Working just a few hours each week usually generated enough telephoned orders to more than pay for Whitey's stay in the most costly accommodations. These phone calls to his foreman, Nick Civitello, were also the occasion for the transmission of messages to the Roberts kids at home.

One evening early in December, Nick called to speak with Herbie.

"How goes it at school, Herbie?"

"Not bad, Nick. What's up?"

"Your old man has some specific instructions."

"I'm not surprised. Let 'er rip."

"Horses, winners, Herbie, that's all he wants. You're to phone him at the Fontainebleau every Tuesday, Thursday and Saturday at 12 noon. Just three winners a day for Tropical Park. Not much to ask, right, Herbie?"

"Hey, it could be worse. I'll talk to you again, Nick."

Herbie had expected this to happen. The two-week hiatus from his father's demands had been too good to last. Herbie would have to satisfy his father's horse track needs as well as his own need to survive as a Harvard freshman. Correspondence with Alex gave him his best moments of the long winter months.

12 IMPERIAL COURT
Hallandale, Fla., December 16, 1936

Dear Herbie:

How are you getting on in your classes? I am occasionally made aware by your father that you are keeping your hand in as my prize student. Last Saturday he had a nice winner you sent him—Crazy Alice, which paid $23.40. From your specials list, I assume, since it was also on Professor Goodman's list

It is clear that racing has become something other than the sport of kings. At Tropical, you can see professional gamblers, loan sharks, prostitutes, bankers, and priests—even Harvard men. The Harvard Club of Miami had a "day" last week. A few became clients. They are "regular" fellows for Harvard men!

Where Dennis and I live is 15 minutes from Tropical. It will be a longer trip when Hialeah opens next month. Dennis has applied for a trainer's license in Florida. He won't know for a few months. I hope he makes it. This is no life for him.

All the best,
Alex.

55 GREEN STREET
Brookline, Mass., December 28, 1936

Dear Alex:

My courses in psych and harmony are the most interesting .I asked Dr. Hartford a question about ESP. He told me I should have gone to Duke if that were my interest! All freshmen have a compulsory exercise period, one day a week. Mine is swimming. Last Thursday two of us swimming on our backs bumped heads. I said "sorry". He said, "Pardon me." He turned out to be Jack Kennedy, a son of Ambassador Kennedy. His older brother is an end on the football squad.

What you say about Harvard men at the track isn't surprising. Besides the ruling class of preppies, who give everybody the public image of Harvard, I have kids in my classes on scholarship from Dorchester, a few from China and Afghanistan, a load of Midwesterners, quite a few smart kids from Boston Latin. It's hard to know the ones you want to know unless you live at school.

I dug out Crazy Alice and a dozen others on my specials list while I was sitting in a French lecture. I may be the first professional handicapper to go through Harvard.

Best regards,
Herbie.

12 IMPERIAL COURT
Hallendale, Fla., January 9, 1937

Dear Herbie:

I'm glad to hear that you're in the swim with the filthy rich. I bump up against some of the rich ones, too. As you might guess, South Florida is popular with rich Cubans during the racing season. The depression doesn't seem to have affected the upper class. They know their racing. I've got to be on my toes to please them. Yesterday there was a demonstration downtown caused by some Cubans who don't like the way they're treated at home. One of these days Batista will wake up and discover that he doesn't have a country.

The best thing about celebrating New Year's in Miami Beach is the fireworks display at the racetrack. Not as elegant as what you and I saw at Harvard, but a fair show.

All the best,
Alex

*   *   *

On the occasions when Herbie and Alex had shared confidences, Herbie experienced a kind of happiness that was new to him. More or less unconsciously, he was trying to reestablish that close relationship in his letters to Alex. It seemed like a risk—opening the curtain on long-repressed thoughts—but sooner or later he had to get to this point. The impersonal tone of their correspondence wasn't getting him anywhere. The risk apparently paid off. When Herbie dropped his protective shell, so did Alex.

55 GREEN STREET
Brookline, Mass., January 23, 1937

Dear Alex:

Two of my classmates have quit school and joined the group called the Abraham Lincoln Brigade to fight in Spain against Franco. The brigade is part of the Spanish Peoples Army. I feel sympathetic towards the Spanish people, but I can't see myself fighting somebody else's war.

To tell the truth, I find it hard to get emotionally involved, even when I think it would do my future some good. The best example is that I find it difficult to be interested in what my professors are talking about. As a result, it doesn't take much for me to decide to cut a particular lecture. I look around and the faces are very interested, even excited. It's always been this way for me. I've never told this to anyone, but I really feel cut off from what others feel is important.

Excuse this nonsense. But I count on you as my good friend.

Best regards,
Herbie

12 IMPERIAL COURT
Hallendale, Fla., February 5, 1937

Dear Herbie:

Thanks for your letter of the 23rd. You remind me of the way I cut myself off from the real world ten years ago. We have something in common. We both took a bump, and we found it hard, if not impossible, to come back for more. A good deal of "scar tissue" has formed. Let's hope it's not so thick that we can't feel an honest feeling and respond to it any more.

Nobody makes all the right decisions. I've certainly made some wrong ones. My suggestion, for you and me, is that we try to hear that "inner voice." I divided my reading time last night between Henry Thoreau and the Telegraph. This quote from Thoreau seems to have some application for you and me.

"If one listens to the faintest but constant suggestions of his genius, which are certainly true, he sees not to what extremes, or even insanity, it may lead him; and yet that way as he grows more resolute and faithful, his road lies."

All the best, my friend.
Alex

55 GREEN STREET
Brookline, Mass., February 12, 1937

Dear Alex:

Thanks for the Thoreau quote and the good advice. You remind me that I should be doing my required reading for more reasons than degree credit. Speaking of degrees, providing I pass the midyear exams I finished up with last week, I've done one-eighth of my work towards my A.B.

This is a big "if" because I crammed all night before the exams. Nothing but chronic procrastination, due to chronic discomfort in the lecture hall. I have probably cut more than half the lectures. If I get through college, it'll be a miracle, unless I change.

Whether or not I continue as my father's handicapper, I'm grateful that the track was the reason we became friends. I'm looking forward to the opening of the racing season only because I'd like to have our talks again. Will you be coming back to these parts?

Your friend,
Herbie.

12 'IMPERIAL COURT
Hallendale, Fla., February 19, 1937

Dear Herbie:

Your letter came in the same mail with valentines from Max and Dinah. I have been thinking about my family lately, along with thoughts about making a career change, maybe back to civil engineering. But I've had this thought for five or six years, and nothing has come of it. So the chances are that Dennis and I will be coming back to New England in April.

I don't know if it's because I'm getting older or getting more upset with the "racial purity" nonsense that the Miami newspaper reports from Adolph Hitler. But the segregation thing bothers me more than ever. I'll never get used to it. I think of my kids not being able to ride up front on the Hallendale bus. Not being allowed to go with their father to the same beach.

Our friendship has meant a good deal, to me as well. It would please me if some day you met my family. They'd like you, and you would like them.

Your friend,
Alex.

P.S. L. Septimo has been a regular at the track. Your father is often in his company.

* * *

The news that Alex would be returning to New England was a relief to Herbie. Continuing his role as a racetrack prophet would have been a heavy burden without Alex around.

The postscript about Septimo and his father raised a question: why couldn't Whitey Roberts learn from past mistakes? The association with Septimo could lead to no good. Just where it would lead was a subject of speculation by Herbie in subsequent weeks.

CHAPTER 20

For Gino Alessi, Valentine's Day, 1937, was a day of hate. First, he hated himself for putting his livelihood, the Capricorn Restaurant, into hock with the loan shark, Fats Romano. Second, he hated Vincent Curcio for manipulating him into the jaws of a giant nutcracker from which there was no escape. None at all.

It would never have happened, he told himself, if he had listened to Margo, his wife of 19 years. She told him to open the Capricorn on the southwest edge of town where he would have been visible to traffic moving North and East through Barnfield. The Capricorn would have been just two blocks from one of Connecticut's largest insurance companies and its droves of hungry executives and secretaries. Instead, he had located in the built-up center of town where the marks of the depression showed least.

In three years of operation, the Capricorn lost its credit standing with all suppliers except M. Roberts & Company of Boston. It had seemed essential to stay tied to M. Roberts: how can you run a first-class steak restaurant without first-class steaks? When his debt to M. Roberts reached $22,000, Vincent Curcio suggested he see the "banker" Fats Romano and offer the Capricorn as security for a loan. A $30,000 loan for two weeks quickly swelled to a $95,000 loan in six weeks at five percent daily interest.

Curcio's valentine was short and sweet:

"The Capricorn is mine. Get out by six o'clock tonight.

V. C."

What wasn't spelled out, but was fully understood, was that Gino's brains would be spilled over the entrance to the Capricorn unless he did as he was told. The lesson of Renato Turco and the Hotel Napoli was fresh in Gino's mind. Turco had gone deep in the hole to Vincent Curcio's company. The Napoli was pledged as security for a $45,000 loan from Fats Romano. When interest swelled the debt to $90,000 in four weeks, Curcio not only took the Napoli, but severed the fingers of Turco's check-writing hand as a warning that dialing for the Feds would be still more costly.

It was five o'clock. Alessi looked out of the office window with its tiny panes that Margo had said was "Early American and just right for Barnfield." All the windows in the huge dining rooms had the Early American look, including the bow windows that leaned slightly into the path of foot traffic and showed the crystal vase of chrysanthemums gleaming brightly from each table.

A black sedan large enough to be a hearse sat across the street with two men in front. Now they looked in Gino's direction. He shivered. Then he dragged his heavy frame from his chair and walked slowly through the dining room. It was empty. The help had been dismissed the day before. A neat sign over the front entrance told patrons that the Capricorn was closed for repairs. The only living things were here and there a few yellow mums that he gathered into a bouquet.

The men in the black car watched closely as Gino got into his shabby green Buick and drove home.

Margo would be home at five-thirty from her job at the insurance company. He had three things to do: first, he penned a lengthy letter that required both sides of two sheets of paper. He wrote the address: Federal Bureau of Investigation, Washington, D.C., inserted Curcio's valentine note and sealed the envelope. Then he wrote a love letter to Margo and leaned it against the bouquet of mums. He turned on the jets in the stove and sat in a chair with his eyes fixed on the flowers until he was dead.

CHAPTER 21

Herbie would never have found out about the sneaky changes at M. Roberts and Company from his brother Larry. Although Larry, after nearly a year working there, should have known what was going on, he didn't. That was because he had the gift of walling himself off from unpleasant things happening under his nose. The more pressure he got from Whitey, the thicker his protective shell became, and the more it suited him not to know what went on.

So it was no wonder that Herbie had to learn from Freddy Carmine that Vincent Curcio had become the head bookkeeper, replacing gentlemanly Charles Pohler, a veteran of twelve years with Whitey's firm. Also that Curcio now signed the payroll checks. Also that Curcio was a stooge for Louie Septimo.

On Friday, February 23rd, a week before Whitey and Myrtle were due back from Miami, Freddy arrived at the Roberts home with the usual weekly basket of provisions, per order of Whitey. It was just before Delia's typical Friday night supper of baked haddock, potatoes au gratin and homemade apple pie. These were Freddy's favorite dishes and Freddy, being Delia's favorite Italian singer, had earned these and other favors from the Roberts housekeeper.

The Roberts kids welcomed Freddy's regular visits during the absence of Whitey and Myrtle from December to March. Not only because he brought food, but for his remarkable tenor voice. After supper, he would entertain for an hour with selections from Rigoletto, La Traviata and Il Trovatore. With his olive skin, marvelous white teeth, shock of black hair and beautiful smile, Freddy would have been irresistible to Delia Ryan if he had croaked like a frog. But when his voice soared to heights of pitch, vibrato and feeling that echoed Caruso and Pinza, Delia fell like a failed soufflé. The Roberts kids were almost as appreciative, Reggie more so because handsome unmarried young men never visited the Roberts house.

Tonight, however, there were no beautiful Carmine smiles, and no songs .He arrived unsmiling and sat unsmiling through dinner, his long, thin, meat cutter's fingers entwining restlessly. After apple pie, the Roberts kids looked at him expectantly.

"So, what's wrong, Freddy?" Herbie had an idea that Freddy's mood was connected to his last letter from Alex and the reference to Whitey Roberts often being in Septimo's company at the racetrack.

"Your father is working for the racketeer," said Freddy. "Septimo has control." Larry reacted first. "Whaddya mean? I work there, too. Why wouldn't I know about it?" He was as indignant as Larry could ever become.

"That's the way it is," said Freddy. "Pohler's out, we've got a ginny for a book-keeper who's got the upper hand on everything. He hires and fires, he pays us, he locks up. And this Vincent Curcio he works for Louie Septimo. That's it. And that's why I'm all through. I'm quitting." With that, Freddy wiped the crumbs from his mouth with the corner of his napkin, excused himself, pecked Delia goodnight and was gone.

A week later, Whitey and Myrtle returned from Miami. Myrtle, deeply tanned from mornings at the beach and afternoons at the racetrack, was her usual gushy self, oohing over "my darlings" and promising Delia "a nice surprise" when she unpacked her bags. Herbie saw nothing in his father's "I'm back-from-Florida" smile to indicate that a catastrophe had occurred. In fact, from Larry's reports all winter long, business was booming as never before.

When Herbie went out to the Chrysler to bring in the bags, the trunk was bulging with crates of oranges, cases of coconut patties, bags of coconuts, two new sets of golf clubs and half a dozen apparel boxes bearing the coats of arms of the exclusive stores along Millionaires Row.

Reggie and Larry had expected that on Whitey's return the family would be assembled in the living room to hear an announcement of the changes at M. Roberts and Company. Herbie thought otherwise. First, because his father would consider his setback only temporary, a move by Septimo he would finesse on the next cut of the cards. And second, because any such announcement might weaken his grip on his family.

There was no announcement. Nor was there a lengthy cross-examination such as might be expected after a gap of three and a half months. Herbie's expected inquisition was non-existent. "Everything all right at school?" That was the extent of it.

Larry suffered through a mild half-hour discussion of his progress at M. Roberts then skipped out to join his pals on their usual weekend tomcatting. Reggie retired to her room to try on a handsome outfit. Delia scurried to the attic to map a campaign with the half-dozen bottles of perfume received from Myrtle.

There were gifts of expensive sweaters, caps and ties for Larry and Herbie. Boxes loaded with goodies for the Satcor cronies and their wives were tucked into the hall closet for the grand presentation at the Saturday night pinochle session.

It would be almost a month before Narragansett Park opened the New England racing season. So the question was: where would Whitey get his betting action until then? Herbie didn't have to wait long to find out.

Early Saturday Myrtle drove down to the news dealer and returned with the Telly. It was business as usual, with Herbie asked to handicap "your four best races at Hialeah", and Myrtle was given a list of delicacies to fetch for the evening pinochle. Whitey got on the phone to talk with Nick Civitello and Vincent Curcio at M. Roberts.

Herbie worked out his choices in two hours. Myrtle returned from her shopping to find a surprise in the driveway. A brand new Buick convertible, lemon yellow, with a card on a red ribbon that read, "To my sweetie pie from her Daddy."

Herbie thought it a typical ploy to turn Myrtle's head while Whitey resumed his philandering ways, but made enough noises of congratulation to earn a promise that the Buick would be available for transportation to band dates and for engagements with very special young ladies at your college affairs."

Herbie said to himself that the wire wheels wouldn't last long in the neighborhood of Hibernian Manor. But the Buick would be useful on gigs at Monty's-on-the-Charles. And if he could manage a free night or two, it would make a suitable impression on his date, whomever that might be.

"Thanks, Mom," he said. "That's great."

It was barely daybreak the next morning when Herbie was awakened by a gentle tugging on the collar of his pajamas. It was his mother, motioning to keep quiet so as not to wake Larry. All the while her eyes asked him to get up and accompany her. She was smiling with a strange excitement, so Herbie's first thought that she needed his help in a quarrel with Whitey, was quickly banished.

"I had a dream," she said. "A wonderful dream about a song."

"O.K. So you had a dream," he replied kindly. Though he often felt put upon by her dependence on him, his resentment occasionally showing, this time what she was about to tell him seemed so important to her that he stifled his impatience.

"Tell me your dream. What did you see?"

"I didn't see, I heard my dream. I heard a song, a melody," she said, her eyes, green-blue like Herbie's, sparkling with anticipation.

"And you'd like me to play it for you, is that right?" His tone was patient, hiding annoyance. It was just after five o'clock, and she had cut his sleep short for some crazy whim. No one, it could be said, really understood Myrtle, because she never seemed to be wholly in command of her thoughts when she spoke. Herbie supposed that her uncertainty was caused by his father's brusqueness and impatience. Now he forced himself to wait for her thoughts to be voiced.

"Listen," she said, framing her words carefully. "I can't sing very loud." Myrtle Roberts was easy to listen to when she sang. Her small, mellow, alto voice had played a part in the Temple choir before she discovered horseracing to be a better palliative for her anger and regret than religious music. The melody that flowed gently from the depths of Myrtle Roberts was, like the singer herself, sweet and uncomplicated. It was also surprisingly catchy. Herbie found himself humming along with her after a few moments and several encores, exploring for a beat that suited. He hummed the tune in four-four and three-four time. Three-four seemed to fit. Of course—it had to be a waltz. Waltz time was a perfect fit for Myrtle's picture of life as-it-should-be—romantic and elegant.

Herbie now saw the notes in his head and quickly notated them on music script in the key of F major. There would be time after breakfast to add the chords giving the melody intrinsic truth. When he finished, he turned to his mother, kissed her on the cheek and said, "I like it—it's good."

Myrtle flushed with pleasure. "It wasn't me, dear. It was God who sent it, to be on the earth."

CHAPTER 22

When the blood that bonds two brothers is frequently brought to a boil during their growing up years, owing to one crisis or another, their sensitivity to each other's needs often remains extraordinarily high for the rest of their lives.

When Dan Roberts made his once-a-month call to Whitey on Sunday morning, May 9th, he sensed disaster behind his brother's too-casual remark that "M. Roberts & Company has seen better times." Four days later, having buttoned up his immediate obligations at his accounting offices, he climbed behind the wheel of his LaSalle with as much alacrity as can be expected from a man with two artificial legs. Destination 55 Green Street, Brookline, Massachusetts. Driving time: nine hours and twenty minutes, including three stops for Dan to get out and restore circulation to his stumps.

Usually at least one of his four sons accompanied Dan to share the driving and the intelligent banter that flowed freely among the members of Dan's family. But the urgency he sensed behind Whitey's inference of financial trouble would not wait for Erwin, Dave, Bob or Jay to conveniently detach himself from school routines.

As the LaSalle headed north, Dan thought back to other times when he had gone to his brother's aid. The previous June he had interceded in a bitter quarrel between Whitey and Myrtle. Myrtle said her husband was involved with another woman. Dan sequestered himself with Whitey at the latter's office.

"What's the matter with you? Don't you feel your duty to support your kids and see them through college? They need your support if they are going to get an education."

Dan had no illusions about Whitey's morals. Whitey was a neighborhood Casanova in New Brunswick. On one occasion, when Whitey taught part-time at Kayo Counihan's School for Popular Dance, Dan had to go bail for his brother. Whitey was jailed as the result of a fistfight with Counihan. Kayo had found Whitey in bed with his wife.

Dan inherited his mother's high ideals and intelligence. Before Whitey married Myrtle Nattelson, Carrie Roberts had warned Myrtle she'd be unhappy with her son. Dan agreed. Whitey, he told his mother, should have married a harridan with the guts to pin Whitey's ears back when he indulged in his frequent temper tantrums. Instead, Whitey married Miss Innocence herself, a pretty, spoiled girl who was content to bask in the undeniable radiance of Whitey's good moods, and was in helpless awe of his stormy outbreaks.

Dan had spoken harshly to Whitey.

"Dammit, why can't you keep yourself under control. Every .hot little bitch becomes your meat when you're on the road. Don't you understand you're ruining your marriage, and putting your kids' future in a lousy situation?"

Whitey was defensive. "Of course I want to make a go of it with Myrtle. But she's always on my tail, looking for reasons to stir up trouble. I'm willing to do my part if she'll stop this insane harassment"

"Goddammit, Whitey, you're already giving yourself an excuse to jump in bed with another broad. What do you see in that kind of a life? Don't you know that all broads are alike when you turn them upside down?" This coarse inference that Whitey's brains were in his groin was unlike Dan. He was gentle with his own family. but it was the only way he could reach his brother.

As the LaSalle reached the outskirts of New Haven, Dan's thoughts raced through the years, from one struggle after another with Whitey's problems. His thoughts arrived at the point where it all began. The day it happened. The memories were still terrifying. 37 years later, so he shut them out as he had always done. He fastened his attention on keeping the baby blue LaSalle unscratched in the mad scramble of trucks and pleasure cars on the way to Massachusetts.

He clicked on the radio.

"The explosion of the Hindenburg is being investigated by Federal authorities, who have set up a board of inquiry to find out the cause of the catastrophe that killed thirty-four persons when the Zeppelin mysteriously exploded at Lakehurst, New Jersey." The announcer's voice crackled with excitement.

Good, Dan said to himself. That's one weapon less for Hitler to use when he tries to conquer the world. The next news item raised Dan's fighting spirit.

"Jews in Poland are being targeted for extermination, according to informed sources. In New York, Rabbi Stephen Wise has warned that extermination of Polish Jews is a real possibility unless Hitler is stopped now."

Good for you, Rabbi. We Jews need leaders who will speak up. The announcer went on:

"Tomorrow is the twentieth anniversary of the World War. And today is the fourteenth day of the fishing season."

Good luck, Hitler, Dan thought grimly. You should only catch a bomb.

Dan sighed and turned off the radio. So much trouble in the world. And the worst is yet to come. He thought of his sons. Only Jay, now thirteen, was unlikely to go to war.

At Danbury, he stopped for lunch and a rest cure. His stumps would burn when the numbness wore off, but mild exercise had proven its worth in the years since he lost his lower limbs. He had a salad, apple pie and a stein of beer. The place was cozily decorated. He could see a nice lounge and stage for entertainment beyond the restaurant area. The cashier was pleasant. Her manner said she was an owner.

As he pulled away from the curb, he glanced at the sign. The Dunes Club. The land behind it was pretty and well grassed. It stretched into gentle rolling hills. Two horses frolicked within shouting distance of the highway. One was a huge bay, the other a gray, sway-backed horse. How nice, Dan said to himself. That's the life – out in the country with good land, horses and a thriving business.

After Myrtle's extra special baked chicken dinner – she really loved her brother-in-law—Dan and Whitey relaxed over cigarettes and brandy in the den off the living room. Herbie was busy at the piano on his arrangement of "My Dream Melody." He had two weeks to complete it for rehearsal by Sy Kasselman's orchestra, per order of Whitey Roberts. Whitey had invited his Satcor buddies and their wives to celebrate his 25th wedding anniversary at the Golden Bull on the 28th. As a courtesy to Whitey, who he knew as the club's meat supplier, Sy asked Herbie to play piano that night. Sy knew Herbie could handle the assignment – they had worked together at Monty's-on-the- Charles on half a dozen occasions. Sy accepted enthusiastically Herbie's suggestion that Myrtle be surprised with a special arrangement of her song. Sy was known for providing the best music in town for an anniversary party – playing the Myrtle Roberts number would enhance his good name.

The arranging went smoothly. Herbie had the harmony as well as the melody in his head. Notation for the various parts went down quickly on paper. The voices in the next room throbbed on, their owners evidently undisturbed by Herbie's work on the piano.

As he was completing notation of the saxophone parts, after which he intended to call it a night, rising intensity in Dan's voice shifted his attention to the brothers' talk.

"How in hell you got yourself into this mess is beyond me," said Dan.

No reply from Whitey. This was rare. He was always the needler, the protagonist, and the attacker.

Dan continued:

"You want fifty thousand from me? You must be crazy."

"Just for six months. I know I can pay you back in six months." Whitey's voice had become a weak whine.

"And how do you know these bastards won't put the squeeze on for another fifty thousand?"

"I've got a paper, signed and sealed." Whitey pleaded. "An option to buy them out if I come up with the money by June one."

Dan's tone turned kindly.

"Whitey, you're my little brother. You know I've always looked out for you. You're always sticking your neck out and I've always tried to save you."

Herbie was startled. What did Dan mean? The invincible Whitey Roberts having to be looked out for, watched over?

"You were always impetuous, from the day I jumped on that freight to bring you back home."

"Freight!" The word slammed into Herbie's brain. Dan must have lost his legs trying to stop Whitey from hopping a freight train!

Herbie strained to hear more. But the voices dropped off as though Dan had become aware that Herbie might overhear them.

He slid silently from the piano bench and went upstairs to his bedroom. He had to sort out the odds and ends of family history and see where this stunning discovery fitted in.

Herbie's earliest recollection about Dan's accident was when Whitey told his kids barely out of diapers that Uncle Dan, then eleven years old, had lost his legs under the wheels of a freight train. When Whitey's kids were older, Dan himself had talked about how Whitey had trundled Dan, legless for two years, in a child's wagon. The wagon went into the schoolroom with Whitey pulling and Dan riding then back home at the end of the day with the same arrangement of "horse" and rider. That was all Herbie had known. He knew nothing about the circumstances that led up to the accident. Herbie, Larry and Reggie had assumed Dan had either been on his own in the freight yard or in company with older kids.

Herbie was exhausted by the revelation. Lying on his back, staring at the ceiling, pictures jumped into his head: an eight-year-old boy scrambling onto a freight car, the train starting to move. Then another boy, older and bigger, trying to leap onto the moving car and falling between cars to the tracks below.

Other frightening images thrust themselves before him: a stricken boy, helpless on his bed at night, moaning piteously, because at that time there were no effective pain-killing drugs. The terrible cries heard by his younger brother, a brother who cried silently and tried to shut out the other's screams by putting his hands over his ears.

Now Herbie understood. Why Whitey couldn't stand hearing children cry – even infants in their cribs. Why Whitey was paranoid about obedience from his children –

Whitey, the impulsive one, who couldn't trust himself so couldn't trust his children to use self-control, to think about consequences.

Yes, now Herbie knew so much more. Melton Whitey Roberts, you are a strange, cruel father. Now I understand.

* * *

Uncle Dan stayed the one night and was gone before Herbie arose the next morning. Whitey was subdued over Delia's breakfast of kippers and eggs. He barely spoke to Herbie as Myrtle fluttered in the background, readying her usual popovers for her Daddy.

Herbie felt hopeless about the family's future. To the outside world, the Roberts family was riding high, with two new cars, a son at Harvard, a housekeeper, a lavishly furnished home. His mother, of course, was in the dark about the coming storm. So what's next, Whitey, Herbie asked himself—a fire, a flood, a bank robbery or some other cataclysm you'll contrive to get your business back?

Whitey caught his son's gaze, and then looked back at his newspaper.

Could he know that I was listening? Probably not, thought Herbie. He hoped he would not be asked to go to the track the next day.

On Saturday Herbie went with his parents to Narragansett Park as requested, but with no heart for it.

Myrtle bought a racing paper, but Herbie resolved not to handicap per Whitey's standing orders. Whatever would be would come at the pleasure of whoever, or whatever inhabited the huge structure that had come into Herbie's life on the wings of hope and now hung over him like a flesh-eating albatross.

A year ago it had seemed crucial to his survival that he succeed as the prophet of the odds board in order to earn the love and respect of his father. Events had shown how useless his struggle had been. The more money he earned for his father, the more his father poured down the rat hole provided by Louie Septimo. Herbie's idealistic nature, nurtured by religious training and the heroic books of his boyhood, had taught him that being good to others was bread cast upon the waters. It would come back to him tenfold. But his father had proven to be an empty vessel.

Alex stopped by to say hello. He read the cynicism in Herbie's mood.

"Something tells me you'd rather be on the tennis court today."

"You're right. I'm losing my taste for this sort of thing." Alex had made a timely suggestion. A match tomorrow afternoon would be just the change he needed. He'd be able to look at life from a fresh perspective. Of course he should be cracking the books instead, with finals ten days off, and damn near a whole semester's work to make up in three of his four courses. Only harmony was in good shape, thanks to the interaction with weekend piano jobs.

"Thanks," said Herbie. "You've given me an idea. Don Budge does need more competition than he's getting."

"Check me out anytime," smiled Alex and moved off.

I may take you up on that offer sooner than you expect, said Herbie to himself, depending on what crazy plan my old man comes up with.

Herbie look at his watch: ten minutes to two. He glanced indifferently at the odds board. He wasn't angry. Not even anxious. Just plain indifferent.

The 9-1 odds opposite Number Two blazed bright orange. That was it. No pleading. No yammering at Baal. Just plain flat out with it. Alex had been telling him, if not in so many words, that whatever good he was getting from consulting the odds board came from himself, not from any mystical outside agency. Was he right? Possible.

Just then Jake Michaels came over, hungry for a crumb.

"Number Two, Jake," Herbie said, without being asked.

"Groovy, kid."

Jake brought the word to the men of Satcor. Myrtle hustled to Scalplock Larson's window and laid three hundred to win on Number Two. Number Two, Dance King, won by three lengths. The $22.4o payoff put $3,360.00 in the kitty for the second race.

Herbie said to himself that whatever was going to happen to the Roberts family as a result of his father's stupidity was going to happen. You can't control the world, Herbie. In this mood of total acceptance, the 3-1 odds on Number Five, Avacola, showed bright orange. Again Jake showed to find out what was what. Once more Satcor went heavy for Herbie's choice: two thousand to win on Number Five. Avacola won. The $5.60 payoff pushed the kitty to almost six thousand.

In the third, Herbie's winner plaid $12.60 The kitty jumped another eight thousand. And so it went right through the seventh race: nothing but winners.

Satcor treasurer Frank Bannerman told the others that the kitty was now over $50,000. What was their wish: bet the eighth or call it a day?

They didn't have a say. Herbie's mood of neutrality vanished after the seventh when Septimo claimed Whitey for a drink in the Paddock Club upstairs. The specter of Septimo's squat frame sitting opposite his father and gloating over control of the Roberts family's future tipped the applecart. Herbie felt his whole body tense up, his breathing become short and pressured. When he looked at the odds board, the odds on all ten horses showed the same dull orange.

"Sorry, Jake," Herbie said to Michaels. Although Satcor had voted to bet five thousand on whatever Herbie came up with, their action was rendered defunct by Herbie's statement,

"This one is too tough." Whitey, Jake, Frank, Sam and Mitch each took home ten thousand for Herbie's work. Each put a hundred into a kitty that Myrtle presented to her son. It was more money than he had ever been offered.

"Next year's tuition. Isn't it wonderful?" Myrtle hardly expected her son's reply: "It's the worst thing that ever happened to me," he said.

* * *

You might say that Carlo Dannon was born with a mint julep in his mouth. Not that mint juleps were so popular in Danbury, Connecticut. But for as long as he could remember, Carlo had dreamed of being in the Kentucky Derby, first as a jockey and later as an owner.

Carlo and his sister Julia had lived in Danbury with Uncle Paolo since their parents were killed in an auto accident when Carlo was three and his sister barely two. Growing up, Carlo's only recollection of his father, Patrick Dannon, was of a tall, spare figure sitting ramrod-still on the spirited gray gelding with which he earned prizes in jumping competitions sponsored by the local hunt club.

Uncle Paolo saw to it that Carlo learned to ride a horse when he was five. When Carlo was twelve, Uncle Paolo presented him with his own horse, an elderly, mild-mannered retired thoroughbred.

Approaching adulthood, Carlo proved an adept horseman. The classically rhythmic gait of horse and rider became familiar to townspeople and sportsmen alike.

"My God, he rides like the Prince of Wales!"

"Did you ever see anything so beautiful?"

The admiration excited by his straight carriage and olive-skinned features turned heads even off the riding trail. In tight-fitting white breeches, white boots and scarlet coat, he was the focus of smitten clubwomen as well as teenagers.

At eighteen, it was only natural that he joined the pursuits of frightened foxes organized by the Danbury Foxhunters Club. Uncle Paolo died on Carlo's nineteenth birthday. Since he had never married, it was quite right that he left Paolo's Lunchroom to Carlo.

Brother and sister faced up to realities.

"Of course I'd like to go to college, sis. But it's more important that I carry on the Dannon heritage and honor Uncle Paolo's name." Carlo had no intention of abandoning his felt duty to take care of his sister.

"In a few years, I can still go on with my education. But it's first things first, Sis."

"We'll do fine, Carlo. I'm a pretty good cook, and you know I'm good with figures." Julia was more than sweet sixteen. She had solid Old World values that included respect for the male head of the family, now Carlo.

Dedicating himself to make the most of the opportunity left him by Uncle Paolo, he did so well that within a span of ten years, he upgraded the lunchroom into a first-class restaurant he renamed The Dunes Club. When liquor was legalized, he added a cocktail lounge. The Dunes Club was perfectly positioned on the road to Boston and included thirty acres of beautiful rolling countryside.

Carlo's next goal was to enter his colors in horseracing circles, which he did with purchase of several claiming platers. His colors, crossed red bars with red and white polka dots on the sleeves, were raced at Narragansett Park in Rhode Island.

His horses won enough purses to enable him to purchase a half interest in a promising colt at the annual Saratoga yearling sales. The total purchase price was $14,000, $7,500 more than he had accumulated in purses won at Narragansett. He phoned his cousin Louie, who had a family reputation for getting things done, even if there was a hint of illegality in his activities.

"Carlo, my cousin, who is this great horse you believe will win the Derby?" Louie was also involved in horseracing, although more on the bookkeeping side of the game.

"He has the conformation of a champion. That's all I can tell you."

"Good enough for me. Let's make this money a loan, and you can pay me back out of his winnings."

"That could be a couple of years down the road, Louie."

"Again, it's good enough for me. I don't mind waiting for big things to happen."

So the colt joined the Dannon Stable, headquartered near the Dunes Club. A half-mile dirt track, walking trails and clean, well-manicured stables became the training center for the new Saratoga purchase. The colt grew into a lusty eleven hundred pound yearling and was registered with the Jockey Club as Hoist The Blue.

The horse schooled well enough to earn a start at Atlantic Downs in May. He won the four and a half-furlong race by five lengths in time that was two-fifths of a second over the track record. Carlo immediately entered him into the Kentucky Derby for the following year. Three weeks later, he won by six lengths at Jamaica on Long Island. He beat some well-regarded two-year olds. Over the New York season, he won five of eight starts and became one of the choices in the Derby winter book.

Cousin Louie followed the history of Hoist The Blue, phoning Carlo once weekly to keep on top of the situation. When The Blue met adversity during Florida winter racing, developing a slight case of tendonitis, he was reassured by Carlo on the phone.

"Not to worry, Louie. My trainer says the problem will be corrected with a few weeks rest." But in February, Hoist The Blue finished last in an overnight allowance race at Hialeah Park. Examination showed the tendonitis had reoccurred.

"Louie, we may have a problem. I've entered him in two weeks against other Derby horses. I don't want to race him if there's any danger of permanent injury. What do you think?"

"I think we have to know where we stand. Race him. Find out. It's better to find out what's going on than wondering about it."

Louie's advice was followed. The Blue raced and finished last, pulling up lame.

"My trainer says the horse can't run in the Derby. I'm sorry, Louie."

"It's all right, Carlo. Business is business. Let's race him and get what you can out of him."

Over the next several months, The Blue raced half a dozen times, pulling up lame on each occasion. In July, he was entered in a claiming race for the first time. He ran last. Down the ladder went The Blue until on September 25; he was entered for $1,500 at Narragansett with no takers. Once more he ran last. With severely bowed tendons, Hoist The Blue would never race again.

Offered $500 for The Blue by a riding school, Carlo said no. He brought the animal back to Connecticut and called in a veterinarian. Leonard Shaddon had a reputation for doing well with unsound horses. He put The Blue's forelegs in plaster casts for six weeks and idled him completely. The next spring, he was jogging, apparently without pain. The Blue had Camel, companion of his yearling days, as his sidekick during recuperation. They were an odd couple: the magnificent bay colt and the old gray with dipped back and pitiful bones.

"Now what?"

Cousin Louie had to be brought up to date.

Carlo's tone was mildly encouraging.

"So far, so good. Now we're going to the shore for conditioning on the beach. I'll keep you advised, cousin Louie."

Two days a week, Carlo left The Dunes Club and vanned The Blue south to the Connecticut shore. Here The Blue galloped across the sands. The other days of the week, the horse breezed a quarter mile at near racing speed or jogged two and a half miles on the dirt track.

On April 27, Carlo called Louie to come down from Boston to take a look at the horse. . Louie was no horseman, but he was impressed with the development of the colt: the muscular masses of the hindquarters, the long, powerful back muscles, the straight, even foundation of legs and the strong, bulging muscles reaching from elbow joint to forearm. In a lively canter, the length and force of his stride forecast great power at a full gallop. Most important, The Blue pulled up as sound as any champion thoroughbred in top racing condition.

Carlo and Louie vanned The Blue to Narragansett the afternoon of Sunday, May 1, long after horses stabled there completed their exercising and retired to their stalls for the day. Nor were any of the usual horse-watching crowd present. The Blue's startling 1:11 clocking for the six-furlong test went unnoticed, except for his two sponsors and the 135-pound exercise boy, who was straight up in the saddle over the final sixteenth.

After the sensational time trial, The Blue's nostrils were as red as tomatoes, his veins bulging, his sides steaming. But he had no cuts or bruises. He had a drink, his bridle removed, his face sponged, the sweat wiped from his back legs. He walked around slowly, the tension gradually releasing. Soon his body was dry, his eyes quiet. He was taken home.

"No question, he's as good as new," said Carlo to Louie, back at The Dunes Club.

"You've done well, Carlo. What's our next move?"

"There's an allowance race at Atlantic Downs on Saturday, May 29. The conditions are just right: our horse carries 110 pounds, compared to 118 for the competition. He's ready."

Cousin Louie allowed himself a smile. "Sounds good to me. But you know me, Carlo. I don't like to take chances."

This mysterious comment required no explanation. Carlo understood that cousin Louie would take steps to see that the riders of the leading competitors on May 29 would pull back their horses during the running.

Cousin Louie, while admittedly in the gambling business, was a church deacon in his personal habits. He never gambled himself. The only times he would bet was if he were laying off bets on favorites in races in which he was a sure winner, or if the result were guaranteed.

Two weeks later, when Whitey Roberts arrived at The Dunes Club in late afternoon for the sweetest part of his business trip, Julia came right to the point.

"Whitey sweetie, I may be in Boston May 29, a Saturday. Would you excuse yourself from Myrtle for a few hours to be with me?"

"Julia honey, I would love to, but you know it's impossible. We have to be careful when I'm home. As much as I love you, I have to spend my time in Boston with my wife. But I'm curious. What might bring you to Boston on May 29?"

"I'd like to see my brother Carlo's horse win his comeback race."

"And who is that horse?"

"Hoist The Blue. Isn't that a nice name?"

"Very nice. Is that the horse your cousin Louie helped to purchase?"

"The very same."

"I don't believe I understand. Louie never bets. Is this an exception?"

"A very important exception. Carlos says the result is guaranteed by Louie."

With the details gleaned in the course of a delightful two hours spent in bed with the lissome Julia, Whitey began planning his participation in this most unusual race.

CHAPTER 23

Usually Whitey Roberts came home from Connecticut with a chest full of complaints against his family. Tuesday night, however, he was quiet and thoughtful.

Larry nudged Herbie and Herbie nudged Reggie. Myrtle smiled beautifully at Delia and Delia wrinkled her nose in delight. Peace, for any reason, was wonderful.

After dinner, Whitey ordinarily stretched out in his easy chair and called in the children for cross-examination. This was like walking the plank. So the Roberts kids welcomed the new Whitey Roberts who, following dinner, retired to the den off the living room and requested that no one disturb him.

Anyone strolling by the half-open door would have seen his pencil working industriously over a long sheet of paper. After an hour or so he asked Herbie to come in.

"Please close the door," he said, his eyes on his worksheet, rather than drilling right through Herbie as usual.

Herbie figured that whatever had calmed down Whitey was probably related to the ten thousand dollars Herbie's prophecies had put into his pocket three days earlier.

"Herbie, I may need your help a week from Saturday."

"Of course." Why was his father making a federal case out of something that was routine? Why pick out May 29? What was wrong with May 22?

"Herbie, do you know how much money is bet to win on a race at the track?"

"No, I don't." Damn, Whitey was being mysterious. And he was using what Herbie called his "metronome delivery", a style of speaking reserved for special occasions when he expected unusually close attention. Each word was held a second longer than usual on his lips before it was allowed to settle gratingly on the ears of the listener.

"Last Saturday, sixty thousand was bet to win in the feature." The blue eyes looked closely at Herbie over smoked glasses that had been allowed to slip down the straight-arrow nose.

"Uh, huh." Come on, stop dangling me, pleaded Herbie silently.

"What do you suppose would happen to 20-1 odds," the metronome paused, and then continued at an even slower pace, "If ten thousand were dropped on him to win?"

A glimmer of a smile nipped at the corners of the thin mouth.

"I suppose they'd drop a good deal, maybe to ten to one."

Whitey shook his head.

"Assuming the win pool was now seventy thousand, the odds would drop to six, maybe even five to one."

"I see." Herbie did not see, of course. What was he driving at? Herbie often met strangers whose words he knew before they were sounded. But communication] had been shut off so completely between father and son that he was never able to read his father's thoughts.

"Now if I were to bet ten thousand on a horse that paid off at five to one, I'd get fifty thousand. Right?"

"Sounds right to me." The puzzle was unraveling. Whitey was thinking about betting the ten thousand on a long shot a week from Saturday that he hoped would pay him fifty thousand, the amount he needed to pay off Septimo and get back his business.

"It's exactly right. That's what the money I won on your horses is going to do for us."

"You've said yourself there's no sure thing in racing. Why chance it?"

A triumphant gleam made Whitey's eyes still bluer, colder, and more penetrating.

"Because it's guaranteed. By Septimo himself."

Herbie couldn't believe it. Why should the gangster tell his father if a race had been fixed?

"Septimo doesn't know I know."

"What can I do?"

"I want you there and available as a runner to back me up. For this race, I can't afford to depend on your mother."

"Okay. What else do I have to know?"

"Just that it's the sixth race on the 29th and the name of the horse is Hoist The Blue."

It was a nice name. Hoist The Blue. Was it a ringer? A top class horse with markings close enough to a poor horse to pass the inspection of a friendly track vet? Or was it a needle job? Curiosity forced the question.

"Is it a ringer?"

Whitey shook his head. The triumphant gleam still lit up the steel-blue eyes.

"It's a class horse that's been brought back to top condition, and Septimo has bought insurance to guarantee the win.

"By fixing the other entries?"

"By fixing the jockeys of the only three horses in the race with a chance against Hoist The Blue."

There it was. The whole scheme. Or as much of it as Whitey knew. Herbie said to himself that it didn't make sense. Why should a bookie that made money by encouraging others to bet against the odds, suddenly put himself in the shoes of a bettor? From what Alex and Dennis had said, the only money ever bet on a horse by Septimo was layoff money, money on logical winners which insured a profit whether these horses won or not, simply because of the odds spread on other horses bet with Septimo on the same race.

But what if his father's story of a fixed race were true? Wouldn't a sudden drop in the odds cause Septimo enough concern so that he would react? He voiced his thought:

"I don't imagine Septimo will be very happy to collect a twelve dollar win instead of forty dollars?"

Whitey brushed him off. "Who can keep a good thing secret at a racetrack? It happens all the time."

You can't fight City Hall, Herbie. Whitey believes what he wants to believe.

And why was he so concerned anyway? Wasn't the tiny tremble of excitement he felt at the back of his neck because he was glad his father might die at Septimo's hands? Wasn't this the way out after nineteen miserable years? He blanked out the thought He always solved the love-hate thing by blanking out.

He shrugged: "You could be right" He studied the grim set of his father's jaw. Nothing was going to get in Whitey's way on the 29th. That is, unless Alex could think of something.

It was late, after ten, but a sense of foreboding had taken root that would not allow Herbie to let the matter rest. He told his mother he had to go to the drugstore for notepaper. At Levine's he called Alex Goodman.

Alex proved the interested listener Herbie expected. His father had warned him against even hinting at the "boat race" on the 29th to anyone. But Herbie didn't consider Alex "anyone."

When Herbie finished the story of Whitey's "sure thing", Alex said nothing for a long moment. Herbie visualized Alex chewing at the corners of his mustache, sifting the probables from the possibles, until he had narrowed down to "most likely".

"There's something missing," said Alex. "I've never known Septimo to bag a race. Why bother? The odds spread guarantees a profit. On the other hand," he paused, "I don't know of it happening here, but in other areas a bookie has occasionally sandbagged another bookie."

"To put him out of business?"

"Right," said Alex. "It's done very neatly. And if any blood is spilled, it's the enemy who's got to start it."

"Who's Septimo's enemy?"

"There are half a dozen gypsies making book at the track. If they were taking enough away from his action, Septimo has enough influence to have track management push them out." He paused again, then continued:

"But why start a war when you're not getting hurt? No, it's not the gypsies who'd worry him. It would be the Fenwick mob."

"Who's Fenwick?"

"Jack Fenwick is Septimo's counterpart in the southeast, only he's bigger. He's been operating a few betting parlors outside Boston. And operating his network at the Downs since the meeting started."

Alex said nothing for a minute. Herbie broke the silence.

"If my father bets, Septimo finds out. Is that right?"

"I'm afraid so. Especially if he bets with Larson."

Herbie found this interesting. Scalplock Larson in Septimo's network? The man had been feeding at Whitey's trough for years.

"Are you sure, Alex?"

"Dennis sees a lot in the restroom. It's a meeting place for business that can't stand the light of day. Larson and Septimo meet there often."

Herbie was alarmed. If Septimo intended to cripple Fenwick's operation, he'd watch every substantial bet registered on the odds board and the odds changes on Hoist The Blue. The more the odds dropped, the more vindictive he'd be against Whitey Roberts.

"But we don't really know that Septimo is out to get Fenwick."

"We've got to do two things," said Alex. "First we've got to know if Septimo is out to ruin Fenwick with this bet. Then you must convince your father that he will lose his life if he tries to bet the ten thousand."

"I'll try with my father," replied Herbie. "But how can we find out about Fenwick?" Even as he asked, he was thinking about Lenore Sarnow. She might furnish a clue.

It was Alex's turn to read Herbie's mind. "I think it's time you paid a call on Warner Sarnow's daughter"

"Agreed." Herbie would have to phone Lenore tonight and see her Wednesday or Thursday. Friday and Saturday he was booked at Hibernian Manor. Next came final exams.

"I'll see if she's available."

It was nearly eleven when he phoned Lenore. He would hang up if Warner or Nancy answered.

"H'lo, Sarnow residence." The girlish voice was a treat to his ears.

"Lenore, my dear. It's Herbie,"

"What a romantic time to call! I'm in my nightie, and it's a sheer shortie."

Dammit, why was she always trying to get him in bed, even on the phone! He hadn't seen Lenore since the Adams House dance in February. That had been a near thing for Lenore's virginity and Herbie's peace of mind.

"I'm sure you're very lovely," he said. "I'm calling about Thursday night. There's a new Chinese restaurant on the Parkway. I thought we might have supper and see Jean Harlow at the Strand."

"Marvy! But why Thursday?"

"I'm working Friday and Saturday."

"You poor darling." Her concern was all too genuine. "Thursday is fine. We'll have a marvelous time."

He made the date for six-thirty, absorbed a long "thought" kiss from Lenore and said goodnight.

Now for transportation. It would have to be his mother's new Buick. Whitey's Thursday night routine called for a meeting with Curcio and Septimo at the Golden Bull.

This would be Lenore's first look at the jazzy convertible. She'd go nuts over it.

Myrtle Roberts made it a practice to retire after he husband went to bed. In this way she made certain she would be the one to answer calls from Whitey's paramours. Herbie didn't know of any such call being intercepted. His mother had often hinted that this one or that one hung up when Myrtle's voice came on the phone.

Myra Brown's call taken by Herbie on the day of Whitey's accident was the lone exception. And Myrtle would never know about that.

Myrtle was reading her armchair next to the phone when Herbie returned and asked for the Buick.

"Of course. Lenore is such a sweet girl." Her delight in Herbie's infrequent dates with the daughter of her bookie was sincere. Although she voted Republican n every election on the grounds that voting for "those Dammocrats" would send the country to wrack and ruin, Myrtle played no favorites when it came to approving her boys' dates. She insisted on being thought of as "democratic in the pure sense, you know." If it ever came to that point, Herbie was sure she'd walk down the aisle at his wedding to the daughter of Louie Septimo's most productive bookmaker without a second's thought.

After dinner and the Harlow movie, Herbie drove to Beachtown and parked in a lovers' area abutting the ocean. The evening was warm, so Herbie re-started the engine to fold down the top. Lenore expressed pleasure at his thoughtfulness and nestled close. She took a long breath of the briny night air and sighed deeply.

"Gee, what a great car. This is the kind of car I've been telling my Daddy I've got to have."

"And what does he say?" Herbie offered his question out of politeness, not because he thought it might lead to anything useful.

Another long sigh. "He says business hasn't been so good." Then she brightened. "He said the funniest thing."

"And what did he say that was so funny?" For crying out loud, Lenore, get to the point.

"He said that after the cue ball was scratched, he'd be in a better position to talk about my car. And that's only a little over a week from now," she added delightedly.

That was a funny thing to say. Herbie sensed this cryptic statement may have referred to the fixed race. "A little over a week from now" was certainly a clue. What the reference to "cue ball" meant was altogether mysterious. Scratching a cue ball happened in a game of pool when a player lost points by knocking the cue ball into a pocket by mistake. Herbie wanted desperately to be rude and cut the evening short so he could phone Alex, but he'd have to play Romeo for a while longer. Lenore wasn't particularly bright, but she might get some sneaky ideas if he ended their date abruptly.

One hour and another close call later, Herbie deposited a frustrated but happy Lenore on her doorstep. Under the most extreme provocation, Herbie had declined to penetrate, "Because," he said, "you're just too dear a person to treat like a whore." Lenore was happy because the compliment seemed to promise much more in the future than a single act of intercourse.

It was two a.m. when Herbie pulled over to a roadside phone and called Alex at his hotel.

"I thought you'd call," said Alex. The sleepiness went out of his voice and he voiced intense interest when Herbie repeated what Sarnow said to his daughter.

"Have you ever seen Jack Fenwick? No, of course you haven't. Well, when his back is turned, some people refer to him as "Cueball" because he hasn't a hair on his head."

"I get it," said Herbie. "Scratching the cue ball means putting him out of business a week from Saturday."

Alex summed it up:

"Now we know the situation. Whether your father bets with Larson or at the fifty-dollar window in the grandstand, or whether someone bets for him, that ten thousand dollar bet will be traced to him as surely as if his picture was on every bill. It means the worst for your father if he bets. If you can't convince him to drop the idea, he's dead."

"I'll do my best."

After he slumped into bed, Herbie lay awake for a long while. There might be no opportunity to talk with his father until Tuesday night after his return from Connecticut. He wouldn't see him the next two nights because he had to work. Sunday morning would be a bad time. Whitey was always tense and irritable, impatient to hit the road after dinner. Moreover, Herbie had to use every minute available the next three days to cram for his finals starting Monday morning. Otherwise Herbie Roberts would be among the missing when the Class of 1940 arrived back in Cambridge for its sophomore year in September.

He had said to Alex that he would try to change his father's intended course of action. That would be like stopping an express train with a slingshot. And with Herbie's history of shaking in his socks whenever his father cast a look his way, anything remotely resembling a successful confrontation on Tuesday night would be a miracle.

CHAPTER 24

The weekend went by quickly. By the time Tuesday evening arrived, all that Herbie could recall about Friday and Saturday nights was pounding out "Peggy O'Neil" at least a dozen times to satisfy requests from the waltz-happy dancers gathered for "Old Timers Nights."

The words of the song, sung by Ken Riley, stuck in his brain:" If her eyes are blue as skies, that's Peggy O'Neil. If she's smiling all the while, that's Peggy O'Neill."

His own eyes were red-rimmed and bloodshot from cramming for final exams in all the hours not spent at Hibernian Manor. French and harmony, which would confront him Wednesday, were his first exams. Thursday morning would bring psychology, and English 51 would confront him Friday morning.

If only he hadn't cut so many classes, he wouldn't be putting himself through the wringer now. Having to cram was part of the price he paid for being absent from more than half his classes. For weeks after midyears, he had nightmares in which he walked aimlessly around the Yard with an exam schedule in his hands and a total inability to find the exam rooms. In his dream he'd go to Allen Litton's room to borrow Allen's notes. The door would be locked. Then, as his watch said the exam starts any minute, he'd search frantically for the exam room. But every time he opened the door, the room was empty and he'd race around the Yard looking for an exam room occupied by his fellow students. After these horrors subsided, he tried to find a great meaning in them. He concluded it was eternal damnation for all past wickedness—his lustful nature and his buried wish to do away with his father.

Now it was Judgment Day for Whitey Roberts. Supper had gone by without any titanic outbursts. And for the second Tuesday night in a row, the usual inquisitions didn't take place. Herbie found himself launching a drive to stop the inevitable from a position no worse than "frightened normal", yet a good deal better than "scared shitless."

"Dad, I want to talk with you, in the den." Herbie was surprised his voice didn't tremble.

"All right."

No bristling, no challenge. Whitey was comfortable with the new purpose of his existence. There was a grim set to his jaw He seated himself with the same grimness in his shoulders and the placement of elbows on the edge of the small table between them.

Herbie closed the door. The house was well built, with walls of sound-deadening thickness. Myrtle had furnished lavishly—floor-length draperies and thick rugs would smother any sparks flying between father and son.

Whitey's ice-blue searchlights were aimed right at Herbie. And for the first time in his life, Herbie did not look away.

"You can't make that bet Saturday."

The barest flicker of surprise darkened the milk-blond skin.

"Why not?"

"Because Septimo has a lot more riding on this race than simply an opportunity to win a bet."

"What are you driving at?"

"You know I dated Lenore last week. I found out why Septimo is putting on this boat race."

The corn silk brows lifted skeptically.

"It's another bookie," Herbie said. "Jack Fenwick. Septimo is using the race to put Fenwick out of business."

Herbie waited for a show of dismay, even anger. But Whitey put his head back and laughed.

"It's true," said Herbie, nettled at his own ineffectiveness. "Go ahead and laugh, but Septimo will be betting Hoist The Blue up and down the coast, wherever Fenwick has a book. And if you drop the odds down with your ten thousand dollar bet, Septimo will find out and kill you."

This broadside had some small effect. At least Whitey stopped laughing, and then leveled a curious look.

"Do you expect me to believe that Warner Sarnow would let the cat out of the bag to anyone outside the organization? He'd be dead."

Be careful, Herbie. Better not say anything about "scratching the cue ball." Whitey would think he'd gone off his rocker. Herbie replied coolly:

"Her father didn't exactly tell Lenore. She overheard a phone call."

"And she goes around repeating her father's phone calls to squirts like you?" The blue eyes narrowed incredulously. "What kind of a cock and bull story are you trying to put over?"

Herbie braved the insult. This was no time to call it quits.

"I'm telling you the truth. Septimo has too much riding on this race. He can't afford to have you or anyone else foul it up."

Whitey shook his head. "Did you think I'd fall for a story like this without some kind of solid proof?" He thrust his face close to Herbie and demanded loudly, "Have you got any proof?" Then, as Herbie remained silent, he lowered his tone and said with finality, "there isn't any proof because there isn't anything to your story."

The discussion was about to close, so Herbie brought up his big guns.

"If you think you're going to march up to Scalplock Larson's window on Saturday and put down a ten thousand dollar bet without Louie Septimo getting the information five minutes later, you're not as smart as I think you are."

His father studied him for a moment, and then leaned back on the sofa, folding his hands behind his head.

"Another story. So tell me."

"You're well acquainted with what goes on at a racetrack. You know all about Septimo's network." Herbie paused to see if there were any confirmation in his father's expression. There was none. His look was pure curiosity.

"There are twenty or thirty people at the track in Septimo's network. The spotters who find the big bettors—or spot the competition, like Fenwick. The runners who take the bets, the layoff men, the muscle men like Dimmy Garino. Then there are the people who owe Septimo. The Pinkertons, ticket sellers like Larson, even the people who work the refreshment stands. Septimo's business depends on knowing who, exactly, makes big bets." He hesitated, then as emphatically as he had ever spoken to anyone, said:

"As sure as my name is Herbie Roberts and your name is Melton Roberts, Louie Septimo will know about your big bet. And you know what he'll do about it."

Whitey unclasped his hands and hunched forward, his gaze fastened on Herbie, thin lips compressed into a narrow line.

"You mean well," he began, "but you haven't been through the mill. My guts are eaten out with this Septimo thing. Do you know how I feel when I walk into my office and this punk Curcio hands me my pay? Do you know what it's like to see your brother working his balls off at the cutting bench—for nothing? For no future at all? Do you think it's easy for me to visit an old friend who's been my customer for ten years and have him ask me if there's any truth to stories that say M. Roberts is involved in extortion? Yes, I've had my lesson. And it tells me that if I have to walk through hell, I'm going to place ten thousand dollars on that horse this Saturday."

So that's it, Herbie. No more words. You gave it your best. Let the sonofabitch die. Isn't this what you've wanted for all your life?

CHAPTER 25

It was nine o'clock Wednesday morning. In a little more than 72 hours, Whitey Roberts would be dead; the victim of a cycle of self-destruction started by himself and finished by triggerman Dimmy Garino. The examination papers for French 105 were a blur. Once Herbie had decided to warn his father that Septimo would find out about his planned ten thousand dollar bet on Hoist The Blue, he was committed to stop Whitey from going through with it.

Herbie had told Alex he would call him at his room at eleven if he were unsuccessful in persuading his father to drop his scheme. Not that Alex would have any more success. Whitey's inflexible rejection of Herbie's plea was evidence enough that even thunderbolts from Mount Sinai would not be a deterrent.

Herbie squinted desperately at the first question. He tried to impose his usual feeling of urgency in taking exams for a prickly sensation of dread rapidly approaching an unbearable climax. The problem of finding his customary exam focus was compounded by the necessity of completing the exam by five to eleven in order to reach Alex before the tout left for the track. Normally he used the full three hours to take an exam: an hour to work out the answers in his head, an hour and a half to write them down, the final half-hour to re-check and change if necessary.

With an effort, Herbie banished the image of Dimmy Garino delivering the coup de grace to Whitey in the clubhouse washroom. He confronted the first of three essay questions: "From your reading of Victor Hugo, give ten examples of the use of the abnormal and bizarre as aids to Hugo's dramatic purpose." Fortunately, Herbie had crammed most of Sunday night on Hugo. Had the question been on the poetry of Lamartine or Alfred de Musset, he would have been sunk. Blessing his good luck, Herbie jumped into the exam with a burst of energy, and was finished by five to eleven. The proctor, a string bean grad student in a faded seersucker jacket, looked over steel-rimmed glasses at the sight of Herbie turning in his exam while fifty others still had their heads buried in the test.

Herbie summoned up a look of confidence, nodded to the proctor and departed for the phone booth in the basement of Sever Hall.

"It was no good. He wouldn't listen," said Herbie, when Alex answered. Hearing the desperation in the youth's voice, Alex put as much reassurance as he could into his reply.

"That's too bad, but we'll think of something. Call me from outside your home at seven tonight." Alex didn't have a single concrete idea that might bail out Whitey. But he had long since committed himself to Herbie's cause, partly because the boy's loneliness had touched a common chord, partly because Alex had a genius for espousing unpopular causes, and still again because Angela would have wanted him to help Herbie.

"Many thanks, Alex," said Herbie and was about to hang up when Alex interrupted.

"Keep tonight open should it be necessary to get together."

"Right, Alex, count me in."

Over a hasty brown bag lunch of cold chicken from Delia, Herbie looked through his notes for the harmony exam at two o'clock. His last exam would be English on Friday morning. Friday night he was due to sit in for the regular pianist at the Golden Bull, where Satcor was celebrating the Roberts 25th wedding anniversary. The thought that his father might be dead less than 24 hours later sat heavily on his stomach, along with Delia's chicken. Even the prospect of working with Claire Strong again did nothing to lighten his mood. Claire was Garino's property, and the triggerman would certainly be present, if only to get final instructions from Septimo on security arrangements for Saturday's planned coup.

All in all, the prospects called for the dreariest weekend in Herbie's young life And even though he had been moved by Goodman's offer "to think of something", he had little hope that this would come to pass.

While Herbie sat in the harmony exam and stared at the head-breaking requirement to construct an original composition in the key of F sharp, Alex was doing a bit of staring on his own.

The object of his interest was the huge odds board in the infield. Studying the board was unusual for Goodman. He wasn't swayed by fluctuations of the odds. He stared at the board for another reason: it held the answer to the riddle of how to save Whitey Roberts from his own foolhardiness.

On the way to the track, Alex mentally ticked off the options that might be open.

One. Where Herbie had failed to dissuade Whitey, could Alex succeed? Unlikely. Whitey wanted "out" of Septimo's grasp so badly that he was going to place his ten grand on Hoist The Blue if President Roosevelt asked him not to.

Two. How about stopping Septimo by tipping off the FBI about the fix? No good. The FBI wouldn't move unless a Federal law had been broken. What Alex could relate would come across only as conjecture and biased conjecture at that. The tout telling the story might very well have a grudge against a former employer.

Three. What would happen if track management were told of the fix? Dangerous. Septimo doubtless had one or more stooges planted fairly high up in management. Without proof, Goodman's information would be suspect. The only likely result would be that the informant would himself be "fingered" for Septimo.

Four. Why not go to the State Racing Commission with the story of the fix? The Commission would certainly look askance at such crookedness. But when Alex asked himself if Septimo's network might reach into the Commission, the answer came up "yes."

Five. Why not give the story of the fix to the Boston newspapers? But would Septimo get word from a newspaper pal in time to cover his own tracks and put a trace on the informer that might lead to Whitey? To Herbie? To Alex? Once again, Alex had to admit the possibility—underworld informers had their newspaper connections, and reporters protect their pipelines.

Six. It now seemed that the best way to cancel the race would be to cause a mechanical breakdown. The starting gate could be sabotaged. But starting gates had been known to fail; so all racetracks had a gate in reserve for just this possibility. But if the tote board itself were to fail, preferably just after the post parade had cleared the clubhouse and before Whitey placed his bet and beat down the odds on Hoist The Blue, track management would have no recourse but to cancel racing for the rest of the day, perhaps even through Monday, Memorial Day.

Now Alex studied the huge odds board to figure how its operations might be interrupted. First, of course, the master switch might be sabotaged. But this was located in the nerve center of the track – in the strong room and was protected by a legion of Pinkertons. Next, the electric service might be interrupted where it crossed the racing strip underground from the clubhouse to the distribution center on the board itself. But how to locate the underground conduit without a blueprint? Even if the conduit were sabotaged, what if the track had a backup connection across still another unidentified section of the racing strip? In this event, the only thing that would result would be a delay in the start of the sixth race.

Alex tried to relax. He took a deep breath. It was cool and cloudy for late May. The scent of approaching summer was sweet and strong. The roar of the crowd watching the running of the first race diminished to a low hum, like that of bees swarming.

As he continued to stare at the odds board, its outline seemed to take the shape of a structure out of his past. He saw the bridge again at Chateau Thierry as it appeared 18 years ago. He was on a hillside, hip deep in grape vines, with Lieutenant Harvey Sargent, Dennis and the other six members of Squad B, third platoon, 181st Engineers. He heard Sargent's pleasant Boston voice:

"Tonight we'll reconnoiter and plant the charges. When the Jerries start across at dawn, we'll; blow them to kingdom come."

That was it, of course. Demolition. The tote board would have to come down. A cold tremor passed over him. He had felt this way on August 21, 1918 – shivery with excitement, full of baleful premonitions.

Yes, it was the same, only it was different. It was the same because there was no going back, either for the 181st engineers or for Alex Goodman. It was different because this time there was no Lieutenant Sargent to direct the operation. Sargent was dead, killed by Jerry artillery, along with four members of Squad B when the squad led the way for the 181st across the Marne three days after they had blown up the bridge. Only Alex, Dennis, Barney King and Lester Novarro survived.

So all right, Goodman, it's your show. First, size up the problem. That meant pace off a distance equal to the length of the odds board. He set off along the perimeter of the clubhouse, across to the grandstand, and along the perimeter until he came to the north end of the odds board. His figures showed the odds board to be 312 feet long; he estimated the height to be between 32 and 34 feet. This meant the face of the odds board was approximately 10,000 square feet, the key to estimating the quantity of explosives necessary for certain destruction.

He had often posted himself on the further rail across the track to clock morning trials. So he knew other important facts. The odds board was basically a raft tipped up on its side, built of two platforms of one by twelve planks with rows of cutouts for the batteries of orange-colored bulbs that signaled the changing totals of dollars bet straight, place and show, the odds on each horse, and the payoffs. There were two complete sets of bulb cutouts—one opposite the grandstand, the other opposite the clubhouse. On the other side of the odds board were narrow walkways and ladders giving maintenance workers access to the batteries of bulbs. Massive steel stanchions supported the board in the rear. The hollow space between the front and rear sides of the board was capped with a weather overhang. This space would be the way in for Alex Goodman, pyrotechnist.

But where, with no friendly gully to secret himself, could the firing position be located? If located in a hole dug in the infield, he would be out of touch with the movements of the rival gambling networks, to say nothing of tracking Whitey's movements. And if his relatively exposed position were prematurely discovered, that would be the end of Whitey Roberts. No, the firing position would have to be his command post, his CP as well. An involuntary smile creased his cheeks. He hadn't used the term CP since Chateau-Thierry, when Lieutenant Sargent had asked Alex Goodman to find the CP that would provide visibility, ground control and protection after the blast.

In 1918 he had spotted the CP on the lip of a slash in the hillside, on whose brow the beautiful village of Chateau-Thierry was perched. After Lieutenant Sargent twisted the plunger of the generator, they found cover by sliding down into the gully.

Now he made his way back to the clubhouse and stationed himself on the rail thirty yards beyond the finish line. This was Herbie's "spot" on numerous Saturdays over the past year when the tout observed the youth leveling his gaze at the odds board from which he drew his inspiration. Several clients eager for a tip aimed questioning appeals at Alex, but he shook them off with a shrug of his shoulders as if to say, "Sorry, nothing looks good to me."

Alex took close stock: There were advantages to this spot as the CP. From here, he could sweep the apron for network actions. He could also observe any sign that track stewards or security people noticed anything unusual. Most important, this was the nearest point to the southern end of the odds board, the place where fuse line would connect to priming charge. Yes, he decided: the command post would, in fact, be a post. The very same fence post on which he now leaned. He put his hand on top of the post and quickly figured its diameter as five and a half inches.

Alex checked the time: ten past three. He must contact the two men would make his plan feasible. Alex left the track immediately and caught a taxi for the Western Union office in Beachtown. From this office he had often sent money orders to Angela. Now he sent a straight wire to Barney King, 1001 Weybosset Street, Riverdale, L.I., and to Lester Novarro, 36 Hanniford Street, Hartford, Ct. The message:

> SQUAD B MEETS HERE MAY 24-25-26-27. STOP PHONE TONIGHT IF YOU CAN CROSS MARNE AGAIN.
> ALEX GOODMAN, SHAMROCK HOTEL, 1424 WASHINGTON STREET, BOSTON. TEL: 647-423-7137

When Alex re-entered the clubhouse, it was four-fifteen, time to bring Corporal Dennis Larkin into the picture.

Like Alex, Dennis was a voluntary exile from the world of paychecks and time clocks, family picnics at Coney Island and visits to the Bronx Zoo. Before the war, he was a struggling apprentice rider on New York racetracks. The blow that separated Dennis from his goal of becoming a top class jockey was struck three years after being mustered out of the Army. On an unannounced inspection of jockey quarters at Aqueduct, a battery-powered device that spurred slow-footed horses into episodes of great speed was found in the locker of Dennis Larkin. Another rider or a groom, identity unknown had planted the device there. But despite a spotless record, both as a jockey and a soldier in the 181st, Dennis was ruled off New York tracks for life. Florida, Illinois and California also refused to issue him a license, deferring to the superior wisdom of America's oldest racing commission.

What did he do? After five unhappy years riding at Mexican tracks, Dennis chucked it and exercised thoroughbreds for Eastern trainers who believed him innocent. When the marriage of Alex and Angela broke up, the reunion of the two war buddies became permanent.

"This is the time, Alex. We're both ready for the big change. I want to do the job. Tell me how we're going to keep out of trouble."

This question, voiced quietly, reinforced by the seriousness of Dennis Larkin's expression, drew a frown from Alex.

"You mean how do we avoid being tied to the purchase of the juice?" "Juice" meant explosives.

Dennis nodded. "When they're asking how it happened, they'll check out everyone who bought dynamite within a thousand miles of Boston, how much dynamite, on what date and where they bought it."

Alex paused. A smile crinkled the corners of his large brown eyes.

"When we visited my cousin Reuben Glass, do you remember that he wanted me to take a week off to clean out the stumps where he's building a chicken ranch?"

"Uh huh. And of course he'll need to buy some juice?"

"I'll tell him to get enough for his stumps, and another lot for a road-building job I'm going to do for a contractor."

Alex shrugged. "If he buys the story, well and good. If he doesn't, at least he won't be bothered by anyone looking for suspicious purchases."

Dennis smiled in relief. "We're all clear, Alex. I'm satisfied. Let's get back on the job."

"Pray for dry weather," added Alex. "A soaking rain anytime in the next 72 hours could affect the reliability of the firing train."

They shook hands, something men who live together don't ordinarily do unless they're getting ready for an undertaking that can change the course of their lives.

CHAPTER 26

Whitey Roberts awoke Wednesday morning with buzzing in his head. He had chain-smoked two packs of cigarettes and downed a pint of scotch while going over his plans for Saturday. The cause of his insomnia was his confrontation with Herbie the night before. He kept thinking of what Herbie had said.

"Septimo has too much riding on the sixth race. He can't afford to have you or anyone else get in the way"

Herbie's story about Septimo's intent to use the race to ruin a rival syndicate's campaign to take over the New England gambling action was pure fancy, of course. When he had asked Herbie for proof, Herbie had nothing more than a theory made up of bits and pieces. Still, however remote the possibility that Herbie's story was true, it bothered him enough so that he left the office early Wednesday afternoon to see Warner Sarnow. He intended to bring up the subject of competition as a topic of general interest between businessmen. This would give Warner a chance to make comments about Septimo's competitors. Warner would know if any crazy business were afoot.

"How're things, Whitey?" Warner's query was unnecessary. He knew how things were at M. Roberts & Company since Septimo took over.

"Business is holding up, but we're getting some rough competition from the packers. They're going direct to our best customers." Whitey's business had never been better, but for the sake of his mission to find out how much Sarnow knew about the coming Saturday's scheme, he had to play the game.

Warner's perpetually troubled expression creased unto a still deeper frown.

"So what — you've got a good partner," he said, bluntly. This was the first indication to his friend that he knew Whitey had lost control of his company.

Whitey brushed off this body blow and forged ahead.

"The competition is still here," he insisted. "Every business, particularly if it's good business, has competition. Don't you feel pressured by competition now and then?

Warner shook his head and laughed.

"You have got to be kidding. And even if we had competition, we wouldn't admit it. Does Macy's tell Gimbel's?"

Whitey was satisfied. There was nothing to Herbie's story about the Fenwick mob.

As Whitey was about to leave, Warner repeated what Whitey had been told by Septimo two weeks earlier:

"The sixth at Atlantic on Saturday is one for us. Stay out of it and save your money."

""Thanks for the tip. I don't get many that are as reliable." replied Whitey.

On the way home, he reflected on the money hunger of the mobsters. Although he was kept on the fringe of the operation, Whitey was aware of the mob's interests in bookmaking, prostitution, the policy racket, loan-sharking and last, but not least, extortion from such protected bases as M. Roberts & Company. There was no limit to the gangsters' capability for satisfying their insatiable greed. No, it wasn't enough to make the huge bookmaking profits; controlling the results of horse races was simply an offshoot of that greed.

So, he argued to himself: what's wrong with maximizing profits? Isn't that what democracy and capitalism are all about? Wasn't that the goal of M. Roberts when he began his company? By telling Whitey to stay out of the betting on the sixth race Saturday, wasn't Septimo simply following a principle of sound business?

On the other hand, he said to himself, it's absolutely true that there is no such thing as keeping a secret in horseracing. There is always a trainer, a groom, a jockey, and an owner who spills the beans to a few close friends about the likely winner of a fixed race. Those few close friends tell a few more friends and so on. If Whitey and his buddies in Satcor were lucky enough to tune in to such a golden grapevine, the result could conceivably be a payoff on Hoist The Blue far below the original expectations of the mastermind of the fix.

Sure, it was risky. But nothing ventured, nothing gained – didn't he live or die by this maxim? However, he told himself, there was one thing Herbie said that stuck in his gut: the possibility that Scalplock Larson was a Septimo informant. If Whitey, Myrtle or even Herbie appeared at Larson's fifty-dollar window in the clubhouse and bet ten thousand on Hoist The Blue, Whitey's goose would be cooked. He'd die all right. So Whitey stopped at a roadside phone booth and called Don Hennessey in St. Johnsbury, Vermont.

Don Hennessey and Whitey Roberts had comprised Boynton Harrison's sales force fifteen years previously when the Harrison Margarine Company was pioneering the sale of the product in New England. The butter-eating natives had scalped the pioneers, but Don and Whitey had made a friendship pact that was renewed every year or so with a drinking bout spiced with the company of compliant maidens who were always willing to buy what Don and Whitey were selling.

On the phone, Don, who managed a dairy farm, was sympathetic to Whitey's story that Myrtle was down on him for heavy betting." She keeps so close to me at the racetrack that I can't stand it. She gets in the way when I'm in a position to make a killing on a real good thing. I'm calling you today, Don, because on Saturday I've got a real good thing going and I need your help in order to make it happen. What do you say – can you come down for the weekend and place this bet for me? Of course I'll make it worth your time and trouble."

"You can depend on Don," said Hennessey, "For old times' sake and a fast two hundred, I'm your man."

"Good boy, Don! Plan to meet me on Brighton Avenue at Sam's Deli at ten o'clock and I'll give you the whole story."

"Okay, Whitey. It'll be good to see you."

Even though the arrangement with Hennessey gave assurance of success at Atlantic Downs on Saturday, the realization that he was going against the sinister might of Louie Septimo kept Whitey Roberts awake a long time Wednesday night He was snuffing out his twentieth cigarette in the first floor den when Herbie came in at one o'clock.

"Up all night cramming again? What's going on with you and your exams? Why in hell can't you keep up your work so you don't have to go through this cramming shit?" Whitey's red-rimmed eyes fastened on Herbie with a vengeance.

Herbie didn't answer for a moment. He took in the pile of cigarette butts and the nearly empty bottle of whiskey and figured that his father was having a hard time planning how to make his ten thousand dollar bet and come away with a whole skin. He wished there were some way he could reassure Whitey that Alex's army was on the march and stood a fair chance of keeping Whitey alive. Keep your mouth shut about Saturday, he told himself. Instead, give the old man a report on Harvard College and exam procedure

"Things are going well for me on the exams so far. Hard to tell what grades I'm earning, because in most exams we're graded on a curve, which means that a certain percent of those taking the exam will be failed, most will pass, even though the exam may be a real bitch."

Better tell more, Herbie – the old man is footing most of the bill, after all: "So far I feel good about French and harmony. I think I'll do okay on the psych exam Thursday and English Friday, especially since I tuned up for psych tonight with Allen Litton. I'll be going back to the Yard tomorrow night to study for English with Allen."

"What about your mother's song? What are you doing about it?" Whitey's tone relaxed. Father and son were having an almost-normal conversation.

"I finished the arrangement for Kasselman at the Golden Bull and delivered it before I cane home, two hours ago. Sy told me they'd be all set to surprise Mom Friday night."

Whitey managed a faint smile and trudged heavily upstairs to bed. He had considered telling Herbie there was now no risk involved in the betting scheme for Saturday's sixth race, but thought better of it and said nothing.

When Whitey was finishing Myrtle's popovers Thursday morning, Don Hennessey was on the phone to his cousin, Harold Kelly, in Everett, Massachusetts. Harold was glad to hear that Don would be in town over the weekend and yes; he and Joan insist that Don stay over with them Saturday night. And if Don could break away in the afternoon from whatever business brought him to Boston, he would like Don to say hello at his place of work, the fifty-dollar window in the grandstand at Atlantic Downs.

CHAPTER 27

When Alex left Dennis after their meeting in the restaurant, he already knew the likely answer to the most pressing problem in their plan to disrupt Septimo's operation: how to bring to the track the explosives, tools and camouflage materials needed. It seemed clear that the only route that could be trusted was to transport the materials on the persons of Alex, Herbie, Barney and Lester. Numerous round trips would be required between the inside storage point, which would be the men's restroom supervised by Dennis on the ground floor of the clubhouse, and a central unloading point, a rented van in the track parking lot. There the van and the movements of those using it would be screened by other vehicles from the uniformed parking attendants and security men who hovered constantly on the perimeter of grandstand and clubhouse.

To better understand the problem, he made a test round trip after the sixth race. The trip took eleven minutes. Add three minutes for careful load-up, another minute for crowd delays. Each round trip would take fifteen minutes by way of the clubhouse, two minutes longer by way of the grandstand entrance, twenty minutes the longest way around—through the north entrance o the grandstand. All entrances would have to be used equally to lessen the likelihood of arousing curiosity by an entrance employee that might ripen into disastrous interference.

After the eighth and last race, Dennis killed an extra half-hour cleaning up in the restroom. Alex stayed glued to the clubhouse apron from where he could observe maintenance activity at the odds board. Sure enough. The casual observations he had made on other evenings waiting for Dennis were confirmed. At six o'clock two denim-clad workers busied themselves at the odds board, changing light bulbs and vacuuming the bulb cutout areas.

When Alex and Dennis arrived at their room at the Shamrock Hotel on Washington Street, it was six forty-five. Reuben's wife Rose would be annoyed at him for calling during the supper hour, but it was more important to have the question of obtaining explosives settled before Herbie called at seven than to worry about niceties.

Reuben's brassy Bronx tones spilled over the earpiece into Dennis's hearing, eliciting a broad smile on the face of the ex-jockey.

"Godammit, Alex, it's good to hear from you!" The warmth of his greeting was genuine .As his only link to the family that he had separated from years earlier, Reuben Glass was life itself to Alex. Reuben had insisted on bringing Angela, Max and Dinah to the Glass farm every August for the past nine years. Every July 4th, for added support, Alex spent three days with Max and Dinah at Reuben's place. Reuben and Nancy Glass made what could have been a strained, uncomfortable time for father and children a joyous reunion, filled with the excitement of re-discovery. The highlight for the children came on the evening of the 4th, when their father marked the occasion with a brilliant display of fireworks he made himself. Parting always arrived too soon, but Alex savored the sweetness for months afterward. Yes, Reuben and Nancy were pure gold.

"Reuben, I'd like to come down to Attleboro for a few days and clean up those tree stumps, unless you've already pulled them out." It would be more difficult to get his story accepted if Reuben's stumps weren't in the deal, but he had to prepare himself. Reuben didn't disappoint, replying, "Fantastic! Now, that's settled. Tell me what to do to get ready. You're coming on Saturday?"

"I'm coming Saturday and we'll start work on the stumps Monday if that's okay. But I'll also be at your place tomorrow morning for another reason." He explained that he was accepting a demolition assignment with a highway contractor that might turn out to be a career. Would Reuben be good enough to buy enough stumping grade dynamite sticks for both jobs? Alex would pay in the morning for his highway job dynamite and for the safety fuse, blasting caps and drills that would be necessary.

Reuben was enthused over the possibility that Alex might leave his racetrack habitat for the life of an engineer. He refused to consider payment for the materials destined for the highway work. "You'll earn it next week on my land," he said, "or my name isn't Reuben Glass!"

"There's better than an even chance," Alex continued," that Dennis will be unemployed at least a few days next week. Reuben said, "Dennis is invited, of course. We'll need all the help we can get."

"Okay, then. Reuben, can I ask you to pick up two hundred and fifty half-pound cartridges of stumping grade dynamite?" "Consider it done," replied Reuben, glowing with anticipation of a renewed Alex Goodman.

. Alex itemized the quantities of safety fuse, blasting caps and blasting drills needed and said goodbye to Reuben. He turned to Dennis, a rare grin nipping at his mustache: "Reuben has a two-year old colt that needs breaking and wants to enter him in the Preakness if you think he's got the class."

"Better a work farm than a prison farm," quipped Dennis, as the phone rang, with Herbie on the calling end.

Herbie had little hope that he'd hear anything positive when he called Alex. Alex had meant to be encouraging when he'd said, earlier that day, "We'll think of something." But when the tout said, "Come as soon as you can—we've got a plan," Herbie was speechless. He muttered, "Gee, Alex, great." He immediately phoned home, leaving word with Reggie that he was on his way to Harvard Yard where he was going to study for the next day's exam with Allen Litton. "Don't expect me till late," warned Herbie, as he hung up.

Before Herbie arrived, Alex phoned a rental agency to reserve a light van with particular specifications to be available at seven in the morning. An early start was essential in order to make the pickup from Reuben and return to the track before two o'clock. He also made a list of purchases for Dennis to make the next morning—items that would have unnecessarily piqued Reuben's curiosity. This list included four folding dirt spades, two wood chisels, two flashlights, a bottle of wood glue, bow saw, twine, two pints of quick-drying paint, a hundred pounds of beach sand, one hundred reseal able rubber bags and a paint brush.

To say that Herbie was overwhelmed by the daring plan to cancel Saturday's sixth race at Atlantic Downs was putting it mildly. As Alex unfolded Herbie's danger-laden role, tendrils of excitement rippled across his shoulders and up to his scalp. He was part of something important.

Even as the glow in Herbie's eyes told Alex that the youth would be a fit partner in the perilous enterprise, the clenching of muscles around Herbie's mouth said he was aware of the dangers.

"Why should you and Dennis risk everything for me and for my father?" The question reflected Herbie's concern for Alex and Dennis. Still more, it asked for sincerity in the reply, which Alex delivered in his gravest tones:

"Your need happens to coincide with our need to take a different direction at this time in our lives. And a successful result will not be without financial rewards. I intend that Squad B will appropriate the Fenwick layoff money—which should be a considerable sum." He looked at Dennis who nodded agreement.

"But why can't you just stop doing what you're doing and go on to something else? Why risk your lives?"

Herbie's persistence told Alex what he had long felt about him—an unsatisfactory relationship with Whitey Roberts had conditioned Herbie to walk around all sides of an offer for signs of a booby trap.

"I'll answer by asking you a question: how many real friends will you have in your lifetime?"

"Not many, I guess" Herbie couldn't say, outside of the pair seated across the table, that he had one real, honest-to-goodness, good as gold, real friend to this point in his life.

"If you have as many as the fingers on both hands, you will have a lot of friends," said Alex. He reflected a moment, then continued:

"People fight and risk for different reasons at different times. In my time, I've gone out on a limb for my country, for printers who went out on strike in New York in 1919, and for William Zebulon Foster."

Herbie's attention sharpened. Foster was a communist who had helped to create strikes in the steel industry after the war that nearly paralyzed the country. If Alex was Foster's friend, perhaps it was this association that had forced Alex out of teaching.

Alex read his thought. "No, I didn't share Bill Foster's political views. I admired his personal courage. I left Richmond Banks High for my own reasons." His gaze shifted momentarily to a picture of Angela, Max and Dinah Goodman on the bureau across the room, and then came back to Herbie.

"You are my friend, Herbie. I consider your cause as important to me, personally, as fighting for my country. I risked my life then, and I have no reservations about risking it now .How about you, Dennis?"

The horseman's blue eyes twinkled. "You're my friend, too, Herbie. He went on, half seriously, "I've made up my mind that if I'm going to work around a shithouse, it might as well be one for horses." He grinned, "Yes, I'm going into training horses, and I'd like to leave what I've been doing with a bang. Is that good enough for you?"

Herbie brushed the wetness from his eyes. "Good enough," he said.

Alex checked his watch. Barney and Lester should call any minute if they're going to call at all. "It's eight-thirty, which leaves you, Dennis, just enough time to step over to the five and dime for this list of small items we'll need. Oh yes," he continued, as Dennis rose to leave, "While you're gone, I'll brief Herbie."

Alex pulled a battered metal trunk from the closet with the initials "A.R.G. 181st Reg., C.E." on the lid. Alex translated. :

"Alex Raymond Goodman, 181st Regiment, Corps of Engineers." Then added, self-consciously, "staff sergeant."

Alex dug through several layers of musty-smelling, olive drab garments before finding what he wanted. He pulled out two strange garments that resembled vests, except that they were made of a canvas-like material and were ribbed front and back.

"Let's check the fit," he said, motioning Herbie to hold out his arms. Herbie removed his jacket and held out his arms. The garment went around his torso neatly. He put his thumbs in two oft the ribbed cavities. "For the dynamite?"

"For ten sticks," said Alex, "five in front, five in back." He checked Herbie's vest for tears that might allow a cartridge to fall through, then inspected the other vest.

"Pretty neat," said Herbie.

"My own creation," said Alex. "They came in handy on a few occasions."

The phone rang. It was Barney King.

"You bet Dennis is with me. How about you?" The tension lines around his mouth softened. He smiled. Whatever the caller was saying was good news. That much was evident to Herbie.

"You and Lester check in with Dennis in the clubhouse men's room, first level. Yes, it's a crossing." His tone got serious. "Tell you all about it when you arrive. Important. . . ." he paused, reaching for words that would camouflage from Herbie the ominous nature of the task for which Barney and Lester were being summoned. "Bring your dynamite vest, if you've still got it. And whatever else will help you make the crossing." Alex listened to Barney's recapitulation of his instructions, and then smiled. "That's right, you've got it right. See you at one-thirty tomorrow."

"Two war buddies are going to help us out," said Alex, after he hung up.

"You asked them to bring their guns, didn't you?" Herbie's question caught Alex by surprise.

"How could you know?" No mention had been made to Herbie of the part to be played by Barney and Lester. And Herbie knew nothing about the telegrams sent earlier.

"Don't forget I'm psychic," smiled Herbie, "with a little aid from 'whatever else will help you make the crossing'"

Just then Dennis returned with the items Alex had requested.

"Barney and Lester are both coming. Barney's leaving at five in the morning. He'll pick up Lester and check in at the washroom at one-thirty. They'll help out with transport and we'll introduce them around."

Alex was still being mysterious, so Herbie had to speak up.

"You mean you want them to be able to identify the people in the two networks?"

Alex pretended a groan. "What am I going to do with you, Herbie? Is nothing sacred?"

"Put me to work," Herbie replied. "I can spot the people for Barney and Lester. "

"We'll see." Alex had no intention of allowing Herbie to get involved in action where bullets might fly. "I'll go over the plan," he continued. "Stop me if you think I'm leaving something out."

His mustache twitched and a look of high intelligence illumined his sunken features. Alex was in charge.

"The way I see it, we've got two afternoons to bring in the trenching supplies and the dynamite, two nights to trench and wire the odds board. Herbie, Barney and Lester will meet me at the van in section 31-E of the parking lot at two-fifteen. Maintenance isn't out of here until nine p.m., so we don't come out of our holes until nine-thirty. Exercising and time trials begin at 4:30 a.m., so we've got to knock off by 3:30 at the latest. That's less than six work hours a night, maybe eleven net hours to do a job that should take thirty hours."

Alex paused to quickly sketch the salient areas and dimensions of the demolition job on a sheet of white cardboard purchased by Dennis.

"Manpower-wise, we're all right. Four of us will work on transport the next two afternoons. Dennis will be lookout each night. Friday night, Herbie is worth more to us playing piano at the Golden Bull. Septimo and his people will be there, and we'll need to keep an eye on them." He looked at Herbie, who nodded.

"If Herbie can stand up after working most of Thursday night and taking his exam Friday morning, we can use you Friday afternoon as well. That's when we move the juice."

"I'll make it," Herbie said. This was his whole life. He wasn't going to back away, no sir. Truth to tell, he was uneasy about the plan to transport the explosives on the persons of Alex, Barney, Lester and himself in some forty round trips between the parking lot and clubhouse men's room where Dennis would take charge. The plan seemed unnecessarily complicated.

Herbie asked, "Why couldn't the explosives be carried by vehicle through the stable area where Dennis has connections? Or why couldn't it be brought directly to the men's room camouflaged as restroom supplies?"

The logic of Alex's answer was irrefutable. "Because we don't know the extent of Septimo's network."

The implication that trainers, stable hands and track suppliers might be in Septimo's network was clear.

Alex continued, pointing to the diagram.

"Tomorrow night we trench and lay the fuse. Trench depth will be three feet to give us clearance from the grading machines and plenty of cushioning from vibrations set up by the pounding of hooves." He paused, waiting for signs of understanding from Dennis and Herbie before going on.

"We'll carry the fuse from this point at the south end of the odds board, across this ninety foot stretch of turf, under the far rail at this point, eighty feet across the track to this rail post. This is our CP, our command post. It's the third post south of the post parade path from the paddock." Again he paused to see that the others were following him. Herbie seemed about to interrupt, so Alex held up his hand for him to hold his question.

"You're going to ask how we set this whole thing in motion. We call this the firing train. We'll carry the fuse, as I said, across the track in the trench to the CP, then up into the CP itself right to the top. The post will be chiseled out to accommodate the fuse. The fuse end will be taped in place. I'll split the fuse down three inches from the end and put the head of a match in the elbow. When I squeeze the match head, at approximately 4:30 Saturday afternoon, it will fire the fuse, which will fire the priming charge, which will fire the blasting caps and explode the sticks by direct contact and propagation." Alex again held up his hand to forestall Herbie, who had plenty of questions.

"The reason why we're doing the earthwork tomorrow night and setting the explosives in place Friday night is because the people who maintain the odds board replace the bad bulbs after the last race. If we set the explosives into the board tomorrow night, there's a 50-50 chance they'd see our work inside the board." He looked at Herbie, who nodded, his question answered.

"Frankly," said Alex, "we'd be better off the other way around. Because even though it's water-resistant and impact-proof, the safety fuse gets less reliable every hour it's exposed to dampness and aging. As it is, if I don't get ignition from the match head on Saturday, I may have to re-cut the fuse and reset the match head. And if I do that, someone may see me." He continued grimly, "Even then, if they do see me, the train will be fired."

"As you can see, we live or die with the security we maintain at the CP. Herbie. Part of your job will be to stand guard at the CP without being conspicuous about it. You don't leave it unless one of us relieves you. No, you don't run bets for Satcor, you don't fetch drinks for Whitey, you don't follow the triggermen for Septimo or Fenwick." He glared at Herbie to make his point.

Herbie grinned back. This was an action to be part of.

Alex continued:

"Now we come to the fall-back moves. What we do if something goes wrong. Dennis has to remain in the restroom, to maintain his cover and keep an eye on the network people and the

Pinkertons who go in and out. If I should be waylaid by a dowager with long hooks who insists that I give her the winner of the sixth race, you've got to be prepared, Herbie, to fire the train yourself. Now let's go over the procedure,"

Herbie checked off the steps to take if worst came to worst and he had to substitute for Alex, starting with removing the CP cover, up to the resetting of a fresh match head and squeezing the match until ignition.

Alex had taken some unexpected developments into consideration. What to do if Whitey should bolt for the 50-dollar window to lay down his ten thousand on Hoist The Blue before instead of after the post parade. If the attempt to stop Whitey should fail, how quickly to fire the train before the outriders came onto the track for the post parade. What to do if Herbie were dislodged from his station at the CP

"You've left out something important. What about the timing on the hijack and the double hijack?" This from Dennis. Herbie's puzzled look had to be answered.

"Okay," said Alex, "But Herbie, you're not part of what Dennis is talking about. I hope you really understand," he said softly.

Herbie nodded. Yes, he understood and would comply.

Alex went on to describe the moves of Barney and Lester and the rival gangster networks before the sixth race on Saturday. How Fenwick's two layoff men, already identified, would appear at the fifty-dollar windows in the grandstand and clubhouse in the first five minutes after the windows opened, in order to bet up to a hundred fifty thousand on Hoist The Blue. How Septimo's muscle men would intercept them, steer them to the men's room in the far corner of the grandstand, disarm them and hijack the betting money. How Barney and Lester would then disarm and hijack Septimo's muscle men. Then return to the CP to shelter the firing of the explosives train. How after the explosion Alex, Dennis and Herbie would board the van and drive to the Glass farm in Attleboro. Barney and Lester would pick up Barney's car and return to their homes. Dennis would return the van to the rental agency on Wednesday. Alex, Dennis and Herbie would remain on the Glass farm for several days until the removal of the tree stumps, as promised, was completed.

"And, very important," said Alex, "Fenwick's layoff money pays Squad B for its trouble." The barest glimmer of a smile from Alex. The same from Dennis.

"It's a good plan Alex," said Dennis. "But what if Fenwick and Septimo don't stand still for this scenario? What if the muscle starts throwing lead?"

"That's a risk we're exposed to. I don't have an answer, except that we'll do our best to see that it doesn't happen." His grimness wasn't lost on Herbie. The training and experience of the engineers of Squad B also included a chapter on fighting that might have to be reopened.

The unknowns bothered Alex. No question that the two gang leaders would battle for the success of their operations, just as Alex intended to fight for the success of his plan. Just now, he felt very tired. He saw that Dennis and Herbie were dropping off their feet. Before putting a cap on the day's activities, he had a warning for Herbie that he had thus far omitted.

"So far, Herbie, we've been talking about handling a hundred and fifty sticks of dynamite as though they were sticks of baloney. And about blasting caps as though they were as harmless as mushrooms." He went on to say that although each stick of dynamite weighed only half a pound, it had the power, under compression, to move a thousand pounds of rock twenty feet .He explained how any impact might explode the dynamite. How important it was to avoid contact with anything solid when transporting the explosives, especially when moving through the iron turnstiles at the track entrances. He emphasized how much more sensitive than dynamite were the blasting caps, especially under the influence of stray electrical currents that might be encountered in the electrified odds board.

Herbie accepted the warnings soberly. He knew that the key ingredient in dynamite was nitro glycerin. Even in the modest 30 percent concentration he would be handling, the dynamite deserved the utmost respect. However, the potential hazards stirred a question:

"Is there a danger that the explosion will throw fragments across the track into people along the rail?"

"Yes," said Alex, "there is some danger. But our explosion pattern calls for shearing the odds board in four sections and directing the flow towards the infield, away from the people. This is not to say, however," and he grinned, "that there won't be something to see. Not exactly Tercentenary fireworks, but exciting."

Dennis sighed, filled with admiration for his sergeant.

"I think we should call it a night, but first, let's hear the weather and see if we're going to be blessed with thunderstorms. If we are, then we can cancel this show right now."

Alex switched on the radio. Catching the announcer in the middle of his news report: "In Tarrytown, New York, the body of John D. Rockefeller, Senior, lies in state . . . in Detroit, Mickey Cochrane's skull was fractured in a game between the Tigers and the Yankees . . . the official newspaper of Italian Premier Benito Mussolini said today that Italian Jews must give up Zionism or surrender Italian citizenship . . . "

Alex looked soberly at Dennis. "Doesn't sound good. You and I may be too old to fight, but I worry about Herbie. Mussolini and Hitler seem to have the inside track on the next war."

The news gave way to the weather report, which drew silent cheers from the listening trio:

"The Boston area can look forward to good weather through Sunday, perhaps through Memorial Day. Winds will be westerly, 10 to 15 miles an hour, temperatures in the city will be 65 to 70 degrees during the day tomorrow and Friday, a little warmer Saturday and Sunday, with some cloudiness developing. The chances of rain are 10 percent tomorrow and Friday, 20 percent Saturday and Sunday."

The goodnights were warmer than those usually displayed by three men of reserved temperament. The prospects were grim, anxious, promising for the next three days. But Herbie, as he left the room and said goodnight, was quite certain when passing the picture of Alex's family, that he caught a smile on Angela's face. She appeared to be looking directly at Herbie.

CHAPTER 28

They had been digging for an hour. Sweat coursed randomly down his forehead and his cheeks and under his shirt. Herbie rested a moment and was thankful that his fatigue was hidden from the others by friendly cloud layers that blocked the light of the moon.

The steady crunch of metal biting into soil said that Alex, Barney and Lester were wielding tireless shovels. Herbie told himself he shouldn't be tired, even though he had only four hours sleep the night before. He had risen at five, studied for two hours, taken a three-hour final exam and then had run hard between train and trolley changes to meet the others in the Atlantic Downs parking lot at two-fifteen.

Following the long, anxious afternoon spent covertly transporting supplies for the night's work, Herbie, like the others, had hidden in a toilet stall for three hours until nine-thirty, when Dennis signaled all clear. The respite should have restored his energy, but now he drooped as though he had just played five sets of hard tennis.

Maybe he was feeling the strain of the approaching showdown. He shook off the thought. If there were grounds for believing that Alex's plan might fail, there had been no evidence of it from the tout. On the contrary, the confident gleam in his eyes when he had introduced Herbie as "Harvard's best dynamite man" buoyed Herbie's hopes while getting him off to a good start with his new friends.

When Herbie met Barney King and Lester Novarro in the parking lot, Alex had already briefed them. This was evident in the comments when handshakes were exchanged.

"Welcome to Squad B, kid," said Barney, a gaunt-faced giant with luminous dark eyes that bored into Herbie, measuring his potential under fire. "You look like you'll do all right by your pa," he said, unsmiling.

"Herbie, you're okay with me," said Lester, a chunky fireplug with a friendly glint in his gray eyes that banished Herbie's customary wariness. "And the deal looks okay. We could all come out big winners."

Herbie's grin said everything for him. Gratitude for the support these men were giving his personal cause. Pleasure for their acceptance of him as a partner in a dangerous game. Yes, they stood to take home a lot of money. But only if they got out with a whole skin.

The real answer to why they would risk their lives, careers and the security of their families had to lie in their dedication to Alex. Herbie could wonder about this only momentarily, as Alex interrupted his thoughts:

"Let's get started," he said with cool authority. "Herbie, you'll bring in the trenching tools. Barney, Lester and I will handle the fuse."

The wisdom of choosing the rather seedy looking rental van was evident as they boarded the vehicle. Originally a bakery delivery truck, its high-roofed, walk-in proportions were ideal for the conspirators' purposes. A faintly acrid odor came from neatly cradled rows cartons of dynamite in the rear. This was tomorrow's work. Today they would transport shovels, shielded safety fuse, flashlights, chisels, saws, painting supplies and other necessaries for tonight's trenching labors. Two toilet cubicles in the men's washroom of the clubhouse would serve as hiding places for the supplies, protected by "out of order' signs posted by Dennis. Larkin.

Herbie and the others wore sweaters under suit jackets. When Alex positioned the first of four fold-up trenching spades on Herbie's torso, the sweater provided adequate concealment. The discomfort of steel and hardwood biting into his flesh was forgotten under the stress of passing through entrance turnstiles under the surveillance of Pinkertons.

The conspirators varied their routes in and out of the racetrack, in order to attract the least possible attention. After the first few round trips, Herbie felt "natural" in his assignment. The excitement of one trip toward the close of the afternoon with a coiled eight-foot length of fuse around his middle was reward enough for his adventurous spirit. Alex arranged this tidbit for Herbie so he would get the "feel" of carrying explosives in preparation for Friday's work. Technically a "safety" fuse, it was capable of being exploded if carelessly handled. The importance of this lesson was not lost on Herbie, who moved through the turnstile with the grace of a ballet dancer.

The slight figure of the tout, partly submerged in the trench, straightened up beside Herbie. He gestured toward the clubhouse upper level. A light winked briefly out of the blackness. The signal from Dennis said that the watchman was making his rounds and the trenching must stop for ten minutes. Two hours later, at one-thirty, there would be another tour of the mezzanine by the watchman, Sam Coleman. Over two racing season as custodian of the clubhouse washroom, which called for a good deal of cleanup drudgery after hours, Dennis had become familiar with Coleman's routine.

Soon Dennis flashed the all clear, and the trenching resumed. The others followed the careful digging of Alex, slowing when steel edges encountered rocks that must be silently repositioned by hand. The soil was loose and dry from an extended period without rainfall, and was easy to handle.

An hour later, the trenching was done. Now the fuse was laid across the track, and the lean, strong, electrician's fingers of Barney King spliced the eight-foot sections together. Alex inspected each splice. There was no room for error: the powder train must be unbroken. Turf broken between the inside rail and the odds board was replaced by Lester. In the darkness, Herbie could see no telltale signs that the lush grass between the rail and the odds board had been disturbed. Alex studied Lester's work closely and called for some reworking of turf matches before turning attention to the post itself from which Saturday's explosive train would be ignited.

"Time to deliver the baby," whispered Alex, with a smothered chuckle.

Once more the long, powerful fingers of Barney King were called upon. With bow saw, Barney cut a circular wood cap, constantly altering the angle of the blade so that the saw was never positioned where it might twist and break the blade. Moving horizontally and vertically, he kept the saw square with the wood, his skill drawing low grunts of appreciation from the others. With a chisel, Barney cut a neat channel for the fuse the full height of the post above ground and two feet below the track surface. With the chisel, he hollowed out a space at the top of the post for the ignition pit. After the fuse was snaked the length of the post, Barney cemented the channeled strip back into place. Under a flashlight held by Herbie, he examined every inch of the restored section for imperfections that were sealed with cement then masked by repainting the post. Alex cut an elbow at the end of the fuse and placed a match head in the seat of the elbow. Barney repositioned the cap over the ignition pit, spot-cementing so that a casual bump could not dislodge it. Finger pressure in the right place would remove it instantly when it came time to fire the train the next afternoon.

The last event of the night called for Alex and Barney to survey the interior of the odds board in preparation for Friday night's work. As they climbed the catwalk, Herbie mentally climbed with them, fearful that at any moment a false step would result in a terrible accident and discovery of their presence. Herbie looked down the stretch toward the stables as he had done many times during the evening. But there was only silence, with now and then a distant whinny to remind that horses dream, too. Herbie looked up into the clubhouse mezzanine and could see only blackness. No alarms from Dennis, that was good. Except for the muffled whispers of Alex and Barney as they pried up the overhang atop the odds board and aimed flashlights into the cavities below, there were no human sounds at all. Crickets went at it in the infield and there was an occasional shriek from a night bird making its rounds.

Lester's friendly hand on his shoulder reminded Herbie that he was shivering.

"Another ten minutes and we'll be on our way," whispered Lester. "It's been a good job all around."

Herbie was relieved; everything *was* going well. And he had done his part. His critical effort would come tomorrow, when he helped carry in the dynamite, and then play piano at the Golden Bull. Just now Herbie was aware that Alex and Barney were mapping the placement of every stick of dynamite, every blasting cap, every priming cartridge, every inch of detonating fuse. Even the placement of bags of sand that would be tamped into the columns of explosives to improve compression and shear patterns.

The two figures that had been poking into every corner of the odds board were suddenly alongside. Startled, Herbie realized he had been imagining himself in the role of explosives engineer.

"Hey, Herbie," whispered Alex. "I'm glad you're back. Let's go home."

His low chuckle warmed Herbie. This was really living – doing a dangerous thing with men who trusted each other. And cared for each other.

CHAPTER 29

For the most part, the walk-in with the dynamite during Friday's racing was uneventful. Carrying past performance newspapers in order to blend with the racing fans, the men of Squad B plus one Harvard freshman made a total of thirty-four round trips between the faded blue van in the parking lot and the clubhouse men's room. There were, of course some differences between the conspirators and those out for fun and profit. Layered with ten sticks of dynamite under sweaters and jackets, Alex, Barney, Lester and Herbie couldn't afford the casual distraction of a glance at the Telegraph while strolling through the turnstiles. Navigation became super-critical at this stage – the slightest bump, dynamite against steel, could have wiped out the carrier of dynamite as well as the whole mission.

Dennis Larkin had the most suspenseful assignment. Once through the turnstiles, the dynamiters unloaded in two toilet cubicles protected by the ex-jockey. Usual courtesies for restroom visitors had to be curtailed: personal escort to a comfortable seat, for example, brushing and straightening of garments, supplying fresh towels and, most of all, confidential chats about the winner of the next race. Dennis had to subordinate all these duties to the maintenance of security of the dynamite cache accumulating behind two doors hung with "out of order" signs.

A dozen times during the long afternoon, Dennis had to confront a harried patron and convince him that he really wouldn't find what he needed behind the forbidden doors. On one occasion, while Herbie waited for the sign from Dennis that it was all right to enter an "off limits" stall, a well-dressed, dark-skinned visitor wearing a red fez almost fingered the enterprise.

"Sir, you can't do that, the stall is out of order," said Dennis courteously but firmly, as the gentleman who appeared to be Middle Eastern, tried to wrest the doorknob from Dennis.

"Me, mayor, Algiers!" These three words, repeated several times, were all the English voiced by the would-be intruder. A stream of Arabic from the gentleman, whose countenance reflected terror at being denied his natural rights, failed to shake Dennis, one hand on the doorknob, the other holding off the other's push to enter the forbidden zone.

After a tense moment that could have turned into real trouble if the Algerian had complained to track management, a stall became available; Dennis ushered the man to his seat and winked in Herbie's direction.

Herbie looked around to make certain no one was observing his apparent breach of restroom etiquette, then left his perilous cargo in the cubicle indicated by Dennis.

Alex took several "breaks" from ferrying dynamite during the afternoon to practice his profession. A known racetrack tout must be seen doing his thing. His absence from the ferrying routine required the others to make extra round trips, but there was never a question from Barney and Lester about the fairness of their leader.

Herbie felt he would drop with weariness. He had only two hours' sleep on a couch in Alex's hotel room before he hopped the train to Harvard Square at seven-thirty that morning. The psych exam proved a killer. Herbie knew his stuff, but he was really hung over with fatigue and struggled to complete the exam. He had some consolation when Allen Litton gritted his teeth and said the exam was a "bitch." If Litton thought so, maybe the curve would be low enough so that he would pass.

There was time after the exam for a hurried call to his mother before boarding the first train on the long trip from the Square to Atlantic Downs.

"Right in the middle of the exams, Mom. I'll be in touch later. Gotta study for English."

"I wasn't really worried, dear. I know you're studying with Allen."

"Ready for the party tonight?" The Golden Bull anniversary party would make still more demands on Herbie's dwindling energies.

"I'm really excited, dear. Please be sure to change your shirt and tie."

"I'm all set, Mom," He had stopped in Filene's Basement for a shirt. He had to look fresh on the bandstand.

Sure, he was tired, Herbie told himself, returning to the parking lot for another ten sticks of "juice." But if anyone had a right to feel exhausted, it was Alex. Before leaving for the Downs at noon, Alex had to purchase and re-pack a hundred pounds of tamping sand in one-pound bags and carry it to the van. The conspirators would transport the sand in their dynamite vests before the end of the afternoon. But despite the depleting labors of Thursday, the tout continued to move briskly and have a ready smile for every inquiring look coming from Barney, Lester and Herbie as the day wore on.

It was Lester who told Herbie about Sergeant Alex Goodman.

In bits of time snatched from their perilous camaraderie Thursday and Friday, Herbie learned why Lester Novarro and Barney King had bolted businesses and families after receiving telegrams from the tout.

Recruit camp at Fort Belvoir in 1917 was a melting pot. The military draft dumped men of all callings and colors into one cauldron. In the space of twelve weeks, they were spewed out in a single malleable form recognizable as dogface engineers. It was an uncomfortable hot spot for the brainy Jew from Brooklyn, Alex Goodman.

On the way to establishing proficiency in laying mines, building roads and bridges and shouldering a rifle, Alex encountered many booby traps.

Top sergeant Furman Yancy, a trigger-tempered regular army sour face from Tennessee assigned to recruit training, was the first hurdle for Alex. Yancy greeted the skinny college kid like a long-lost punching bag. During the first four weeks, Alex suffered through a non-stop diet of latrine cleanup, kitchen mess duty and "dirty Yid" epithets. The second month, he slogged through marsh and woodland on twenty-mile marches that concluded with bridge-building exercises one which he distinguished himself.

"The tougher the training, the more we learned about the real Alex Goodman," said Lester, smiling with his reflection. "In the last three weeks of our basic training, Alex showed what he was made of. First, he devised a new bivouac cluster pattern."

"What's that?"

"When we got to France and were strafed by the Jerries almost every day, the pattern that Alex designed made it much tougher for the Jerries to wipe us out." This Goodman idea, suggested through Platoon Leader Harvey Sargent, earned stripes for Alex.

"How good was the idea? The Lieutenant said it reduced our vulnerability to strafing attacks fifty percent."

"How did Alex get wounded? You know – he covers it with his mustache. And how about his limp? Is that from the war?" Herbie's questions came rapid-fire.

"Right on both counts, Herbie." Lester described the last week of field exercises in Maryland,

"We belly-crawled under fixed-height, live machine gun fire through a cornfield cratered like a battlefield. I got myself snared on barbed wire. I thought I was done for, really. But Alex, who had already finished his run, or rather, crawl, came back and cut me free. Not without pain." Lester grimaced at the thought. "He was badly gashed and lost so much blood I thought he'd never make it." He brightened. "Imagine—he made darn sure he'd recover in time to make the boat to France with all of us in Squad B."

"So that's how he got the scar over his lip?"

"Right you are, young fella."

In France, the first months were spent building docks and warehouses at the port of LeHavre in preparation for the arrival of the A.E.F. Then the 181st went on special assignment to help the French stop the German drive on Paris.

"One day," said Lester, "we blew up a bridge on the Marne near Chateau Thierry. The Germans were about to cross over on the bridge. A few days later, after we built a pontoon bridge for the French to use, we got ourselves pinned down under German artillery fire on the wrong side of the river." Lester shook his head. "Four of my buddies and Lieutenant Sargent were killed by a direct shell burst."

"Alex took shrapnel in one leg, but he still had it together. What did he do? Just ferried Dennis, Barney and myself back to the safety of covering fire."

Alex received the Silver Cross for the rescue and a ride back home to heal his wounds. After being mustered out, the quartet of Dennis, Lester, Barney and Alex saw each other at weddings, the birth of a baby or the start of a business. Every few years, on the anniversary of the events on the Marne, they had a reunion as well.

"We've been with his kids. Max and Dinah. On the 4th of July a few years ago on the farm owned by Reuben Glass. He's Alex's cousin, down in Attleboro. The kids go there every 4th of July."

"You know, Herbie—divorce from Angela broke up Alex. He's been recovering ever since. But it's damn tough. Some day, he'll get back together with her and his kids. He just has to work it out," was the way Lester put it, late Friday afternoon, as the pair loaded up at the van for a final carry to the dynamite cache.

CHAPTER 30

Years later, Herbie would see the picture often in his mind's eye. Nothing but beauty and grace – Melton and Myrtle Roberts dancing to the strains of "My Dream Melody" on that fateful Friday night at the Golden Bull.

Now, as Sy Kasselman coaxed a little more schmaltz from the muted trumpet of Harvey Slamin, Herbie saw another side of the man who had carved a reputation with his family as tyrant, bully, and yes, enemy. In the softly rotating lights and shadows of the dance floor, the hulking figure of Whitey Roberts was transformed. He was in complete control of himself and his partner While others made work of the dancing, Whitey and Myrtle made it look easy, whirling round and round in an ever-widening circle, drawing ripples of applause from dancers who made room for them and stopped to watch.

After two choruses of "My Dream Melody," featuring different soloists, Herbie made an eight-bar modulation from the key of B flat, in which he had arranged the song for the orchestra, to the key of B major to suit Claire. With a sly wink in Herbie's direction, Claire stepped to the mike and sang a surprisingly soft, sweet chorus in the words that Myrtle had written: My Dream Melody.

> Come back to me my love. Come back in the dream melody we love; I love to dance with you. Holding me in your arms. So true, so true. Come every night to me. In my dreams, you bring sweet liberty. Gently on the west wind before moonlight is dimmed, come in my dream melody.

Herbie grinned his thanks to Claire who tossed a finger kiss in return. Then Sy called on all twelve musicians to unite in a richly woven final chorus of the song that was actually spawned in Myrtle's dream.

The velvet movements of Whitey and Myrtle, perfectly synchronized; had a hypnotic quality that captured all seated around the dance floor, and brought tears to Herbie's eyes .He wished his parents could go on dancing forever.

While the dancers were returning to their tables, Sy called for a flourish on the snare drums from Rogo Benton. Then he came to the mike and told the fantastic story of the conception of "My Dream Melody." He asked Myrtle to rise and accept the applause that came from all corners. Jake Michaels thrust his forefingers in the corners of his mouth and whistled loudly, which encouraged whistling and foot stamping from others. Myrtle showed her beautiful teeth in a wide smile, giggled and leaned over to kiss Whitey. Whitey pretended to wipe the kiss away, but he was pleased with the attention paid to Myrtle. Of that Herbie was certain.

The Satcor group embraced just five couples, but Herbie thought they did a good job of setting the pace for the other guests. Binnie Michaels, a generously proportioned lady with a belly-shaking laugh, seemed taken with little Sam Dana, a head shorter and, it seemed to Herbie, a good hundred pounds lighter. She towed Sam to the dance floor for a swinging version of "Little White Lies." Binnie commanded plenty of room from the other dancers, showing a nice expanse of bared thighs as she twirled about. While Binnie drew the attention of the crowd, Herbie reminded himself of his instruction from Alex to take note of Septimo's visitors.

When the Satcor group sat down for dinner at eight o'clock, Septimo was nowhere in sight. This meant he was closeted in the club office, phoning up and down the East coast to his straws that would bet on Hoist The Blue the next day with Jack Fenwick's books. According to Alex, Septimo's other responsibility would be the imparting of final instructions to the people who would monitor the betting windows at the track – Dimmy Garino, Monk

Coozman and one or more as yet unknowns imported to backup the operation to crush Jack Fenwick.

It was eleven o'clock, time for the orchestra to take a break. Perhaps now Septimo would show. Claire sat alongside Herbie on the piano bench and prattled on how handsome Whitey was and what a superb dancer and how Herbie looked like his father. Herbie allowed himself a small smile. He had always hated being told he looked like his father. While he listened to Claire, he kept his eyes on Septimo's usual table near the exit.

Just as Kasselman tapped his music stand to bring back the musicians, a light shone from the office entrance. The squat figure of the gangster chieftain appeared, accompanied by Garino, Coozman, and a solidly built, curly-haired man with a red carnation in his lapel. They seated themselves and a waiter hastened to take their orders.

Then Herbie had to concentrate on the music and lost track of Septimo for a while, as Kasselman whipped his band through an extra-long set, pleading with every man to go all out. They played every popular mode: syrupy, soothing music, then groovy music that brought out the Lindy Hoppers and, when Harvey Slamin led the trumpets in a hot, slick rendition of "The Music Goes Down And Around", jitterbugs in pageboy hairdos and peg leg zoo suits came out of the woodworks to do their stuff. Claire did her thing, too. She poured herself into brassy solos of "I Cried For You" and "The Very Thought Of You." Occasionally Herbie glimpsed his parents gliding expertly around the floor, Whitey with a set smile and Myrtle shining with happiness as though she'd never known anything else.

There was another break, then another long set and it was "Good Night, Sweetheart" with the rich, live sound of twelve musicians playing with power, and Herbie thumping big, fat chords, until the last few bars when Kasselman slowed the tempo to draw all the guests into joining Claire in the final "Sweetheart, Good Night."

The musicians wrapped up their instruments quickly as the guests vanished into the night, all but Whitey and Myrtle, who waited for Herbie. Claire gave Herbie a peck that glanced off his mouth and was off to wherever Dimmy would take her.

No, it would never be the same again with Claire. But that wasn't important, said Herbie to himself. What was important was that his parents be given another opportunity to dance. And that, he concluded, was up to Alex Goodman.

CHAPTER 31

He hadn't intended to play the role of Herbie Roberts, dandy gardener, on the most important day of his life, but his father had said, quite in character, "If you expect to go with us today, I expect the lawn mowed and the hedge clipped before you set foot in this car."

Whitey then went off to keep his secret date with Don Hennessey. To Myrtle, he said he was going to pick up cigarettes.

As the neat rows of grass cuttings fell into place, Herbie conceded that he was glad to have this distraction, The monotony of the work helped him sort out a fresh batch of fears that had attacked since awakening.

Visions of Alex, Dennis, Barney and Lester being blown to bits kept him awake. With difficulty he was able to summon up a picture of Claire's caress able body to curtain over his fears and finally allow sleep to take over.

Several hours later, Herbie crept downstairs to listen to the six-thirty news He caught his breath when the announcer reported that a trainer at Atlantic Downs had been suspended for drugging a horse. But outside of n avalanche in Mexico that killed 500 people, a threat from Goebbels to expel Catholic priests from Germany, and a crash that killed two drivers in a test run at Indianapolis Speedway, the outside world received no other shocks of special note on this verdant, sweet -smelling May morning. The morning newspaper arrived a few moments later. Herbie scoured it for any other scary developments, like the arrest of prowlers at Atlantic Downs. Besides the charts of Friday's races and the entries for Saturday, the only reference to the racetrack was an item of interest to war veterans:

"SIXTH AT ATLANTIC DOWNS WILL SALUTE AMERICAN LEGION POST"

The management of Atlantic Downs has named the 6th race today in honor of Darrington American Legion Post No. 2416. The William W. Darrington Stakes at six furlongs for three year olds and up is named for the World War hero who earned the Congressional Medal Of Honor posthumously. Adjutant Wellington Gates of the Watertown post has announced that post members will present the Darrington Cup to the owner of the winning horse, and will provide a color guard for the occasion. Two other races, on Monday, Memorial Day, will also honor the nation's war dead."

Herbie's first thought was that it was too bad the legionnaires would not get to see the race that honored them. His next thought was more disquieting: what if Alex, Dennis, Barney and Lester were recognized as war buddies by any of the celebrants? Such an unwanted reunion could delay ignition of the explosion train past the start of the sixth race and cost Whitey Roberts his life. At the very least, it would draw attention to the firing team just when they needed anonymity.

Wurrp, bang! A pebble suddenly jammed the mower blades and interrupted Herbie's thoughts. He shut off the mower and fished out the pebble, thinking how unexpectedly trouble can appear. Anticipating them, he reasoned, could lessen the shock of surprise happenings. Even his father's ostensibly innocent trip for cigarettes could harbor an unknown danger to today's plan. Certainly there were grounds for suspecting Whitey's action—wasn't it usual for Whitey to ask one of his slaves to run such an errand? Could Whitey's "cigarettes" be an excuse to hide a special arrangement for today's planned big bet on Hoist The Blue? Alex thought it likely that Herbie's warning about Scalplock Larson's ties to Louie Septimo would deter Whitey from making the bet personally or risk undercutting his opportunity by betting at a ten-dollar window. This would take so long that someone in the Septimo network would likely become suspicious and investigate the identity of the bettor and the horse being backed.

Alex had asked Herbie to watch his father closely for any sign of contact with strangers. There had been no such indication through the week past, either at home or at the Golden Bull.

By the time Herbie finished wiping the green scum from the mower, Whitey's Chrysler appeared. Whitey pretended to inspect Herbie's work briefly, then went into the house, brandishing his carton of Kools. He had been gone, Herbie figured, an hour and a half on an errand that should have taken twenty minutes. Yes, Whitey was up to something that could conceivably upset Alex's plans.

At the track, Herbie excused himself as Whitey and Myrtle went to the restaurant to meet the Satcor buddies. In the washroom, Herbie's questioning look drew a smile from Dennis Larkin. Herbie felt a delicious soaring in his chest—all was in readiness!

It was one-thirty, time for Herbie to take his position at the command post. But half a dozen middle-aged men in olive drab campaign caps were there before him.

Patches sewed on their caps said "A.L. Post 4216." They were talking loudly and the smell of whiskey suggested that the veterans were determined to make this Memorial Day weekend unforgettable. Herbie picked a spot on the rail nearby, stared impatiently at the opening odds, and wished the legionnaires would disappear.

A tap on his shoulder startled him. It was Alex. "Easy." A gleam of excitement lit his eyes. "What did you find out last night?"

Herbie told him about the curly-haired man who wore a flower in his buttonhole.

"Could be new muscle. I'll tell Barney and Lester. What about your father?"

"He went out for ninety minutes this morning. He said it was to get cigarettes. I think it was to line up a runner to place his bet."

"Probably it was. If you see a possible runner with your father, hold up your program as a signal to me."

Alex left for his "office" at the top of the clubhouse apron. He did not look at the legionnaires, or they at him. Herbie sighed with relief.

One of the legionnaires said he'd like to get close to the post parade, so the group moved off, leaving the space before the command post free for Herbie.

Herbie looked at Barney's "artwork" several times to assure himself that the top of the rail post designated the CP was undisturbed. But would the fuse ignite when the time came? Herbie saw his father in his usual spot, with Myrtle and Satcor buddies. At five minutes to two, Frank Bannerman appeared and asked for a selection. The request caught Herbie unprepared. He had been preoccupied trying to pinpoint the identities and positions of the members of both the Septimo and Fenwick gangs.

"Really, it's too tough a race," he said. Bannerman sighed and mentally forgave Herbie. "We're asking a lot from Herbie—nobody's perfect."

When the race started and the horses rounded the stretch turn, Herbie worried about an explosion being started by the pounding of horses' hooves coupled with the roar of the huge holiday crowd. He saw Barney and Lester near the finish line—they looked worried. There were several dozen legionnaires near them but there was no sign that Barney or Lester had been recognized.

The horses got closer; the thundering hooves grew louder, drowning out Herbie's throbbing pulses. This was the first test of the immunity to reverberation built into the explosion train. The only thing of note that happened was that Alex Goodman's pick, Vindicator, won and paid eight dollars. There were pleased looks from Satcor, except for Whitey, who was subdued and thoughtful.

The day's racing wore on, with Herbie keeping the lowest possible profile with Satcor. Only in the fourth race did he proffer a selection, courtesy of Baal. It won, at short odds. Most of his attention was directed at layoff men, "muscle", spotters and the "senators" of the rival gangs.

Herbie saw Louie Septimo on half a dozen occasions, each time in the company of the curly-haired man who was with Septimo at the Golden Bull the previous night. The soft-hatted, black-browed Jack Fenwick showed several times, alone or with the lean gray shadow Alex had called "Blue Eyes" Pisano, or with the heavily built hood known to Dennis as Carson Scott. But not until just before the fifth race did Whitey provide any clue to the identity of his runner.

At this time Alex took his place at the CP—this freed Herbie to visit the clubhouse men's room. On his way to Dennis Larkin's headquarters, Herbie noticed that Whitey had left his perch. Where had he gone? To give last minute instructions to his mystery runner? Something told Herbie to scan the alcove under the stairs to the Paddock Club. Whitey was there, with a very tall, thin man with a red, pockmarked face and prominent nose. They were talking animatedly—the feeling that Herbie knew this man crystallized into a name: Don Hennessey, his father's friend from the margarine days. Don had showed up for weekend visits at the Roberts home several times in the past ten years. Whitey tried to get him to take over the Vermont territory for M. Roberts, but Don had begged off, saying, "My ticker couldn't stand the pace." Instead, he had chosen comparative tranquility—managing the Hennessey Dairy Farm.

Herbie stayed out of sight—it would not do to alarm Whitey. Herbie backed away slowly, keeping a concrete column between him and the pair. Then he visited Dennis in the restroom. Dennis signaled "no news."

Returned to the CP, Herbie briefed Alex on Don Hennessey. Alex then left for a final survey of the 50-dollar windows to make certain that Barney and Lester were in position and got a description of Hennessey. Hennessey would not be permitted to place Whitey's bet.

The ticket seller in the 50-dollar window of the grandstand had a visitor. The lean, olive-skinned features of the hood Harold Kelly knew from past encounters as Dimmy Garino, direct representative of Louie Septimo, to whom Kelly owed special allegiance the past several racing meetings, showed at the window as Kelly was leaving on his "break."

"What is it?" Kelly was accustomed to inquiries from Septimo's people. Kelly was a "spotter" — he put the finger on big bettors for Septimo. And was well rewarded for his diligence.

"This is special, Kelly. If someone shows with big money on the sixth race, we have to put the finger on him or her ten minutes before the race goes off. The boss will have his eye on you. Understand?"

"You bet I understand." The short, blocky, black-haired cashier shook his head as Garino disappeared into the crowd. What was up? Kelly shrugged off the shiver he experienced in such encounters and headed for the coffee bar downstairs.

4:05 p.m.
The buzzer sounded to open betting for the sixth race Barney King waited and watched from the shadows of a stairway near the 50-dollar window in the grandstand. Since Alex's visit, he had three assignments: one, observe a well-armed villain named Dimmy Garino relieve another villain named Carson Scott of a large sun of money just before Scott was about to bet; two, follow the pair to the expected destination, the men's room in the northwest corner of the grandstand. Here, Alex's scenario called for Garino to slug Scott unconscious. Then it would be up to Barney to relieve Garino of the money and immobilize him. Barney was then to return to the 50-dollar window in time to stop Hennessey from betting, before making his rendezvous with Alex at the CP.

In the clubhouse, Lester Novarro inched his chunky figure into a recess next to the snack stand. From here he could watch a hood named Mack Coozman take a sum of money from Blue Eyes Pisano before he could bet with Scalplock Larson. Lester was to wait until this action was completed, then follow the pair to the nearest restroom. There, after Pisano was disabled by Coozman, he was to take the money from Coozman and immobilize the gangster. Then he was to stop Hennessey from betting and return to the CP.

4:10 p.m.
Alex had correctly surmised Septimo's intent to put Fenwick out of business. But he had not anticipated the bloodletting that was part of Septimo's plan. Underestimating the Mafia fondness for eliminating rival "muscle" stretched Barney and Lester to the limit and propelled Herbie into an unexpected role.

Instead of steering Fenwick's layoff men to restrooms, Garino and Coozman directed them with snub-nosed revolvers concealed in their pockets to a large black Cadillac in the parking lot. A thug named Joe Fermone waited at the wheel. Barney and Lester followed closely, slithering between cars, occasionally belly-crawling. When the car doors shut on the hijackers and their victims, Barney and Lester had to improvise. While Fermone, Garino and Coozman were absorbed in the task of shooting Scott and Pisano, Barney and Lester quickly and silently slashed their tires. Puzzled at the poor ride from the Caddy, Fermone, Garino and Coozman got out to see what was wrong. Influenced by a display of weapons, the gangsters were herded back into the vehicle. They were relieved of Jack Fenwick's stash, struck unconscious by well—placed blows, bound, tied, gagged and left for later salvage.

4:18 p.m.
When the bugle sounded for the post parade, Don Hennessey was fully alerted to his responsibilities. As Herbie had thought, he had met Whitey that morning. He was instructed to wager Whitey's ten thousand five minutes before the sixth race, at the fifty-dollar window in the grandstand. But between the second and fifth races, Whitey had second thoughts. He instructed Don to bet ten minutes before post time, and at the ten-dollar window rather than

the fifty-dollar window. Hennessey was unaware that Whitey had observed no less than three meetings between Septimo and Garino during the afternoon. He had not heard any of the conversations, but such public meetings were rare. Whitey figured there might be some truth to Herbie's story about Septimo out to bankrupt Fenwick. If so, it would be safer to bet at the ten-dollar window. Though this wager, made ten minutes before post time, would lower the odds on Hoist The Blue that much faster, it was still safer. Septimo's men would be on guard at the fifty-dollar windows, not at windows for small bettors.

It was break-time for Michael Kelly, senior grandstand cashier at Atlantic Downs. Kelly was mindful of two unusual events that added tension to his usual hectic Saturday in the fifty-dollar window of the grandstand. One was the phone call from his cousin Don, and the possibility that Don would seek him out at the track. The other was the visit from Dimmy Garino. ; Kelly knew from hearsay that the Septimo organization brooked no rebellion from its network associates .Now, as Kelly headed to the first level of the grandstand for a quick smoke and java, he caught sight of his cousin, Don Hennessey, his carrot top and great height marking him from a distance. Kelly smiled to himself. He'd tap Don on the shoulder and surprise him.

His pulses heating up with the excitement of a man charged with a heavy obligation, Don started across the pass-through, waved to come through by the attendant watching for the lead rider's approach from the paddock. Don's six foot-six height and beet-red face made him an easy target for Herbie and Alex following his movements.

Alex instantly divined the purpose of Hennessey's early move towards the grandstand. "Stop Hennessey", he said to Herbie with quiet urgency. "Delay him until Barney and Lester are free to help you."

As Herbie started toward the pass-through, Hennessey clapped a hand to his chest and collapsed on the grandstand side of the pass-through. The bulky figure of Whitey Roberts, moving with incredible swiftness between two outriders, vaulted the low gates and bent over the fallen Hennessey. Herbie, equipped with his own wings, was ten steps behind, dodging between mounts and their startled riders. He vaulted the gate in time to see his father wrest a money belt from the stricken Hennessey, punch out a stumpy, black-haired man who fought him for the money belt, then shoulder his way through startled onlookers.

As his father disappeared in the tightly packed crowds, Herbie felt panic. Whitey Roberts would seal his own fate if he put his bet down now, ten minutes before post time. It wouldn't take Septimo's network more than a few minutes to get the word to the 'senator'—Whitey would be fingered before the horses broke from the gate.

To Herbie, overtaking his father through the milling thousands seemed impossible. For the span of less than a minute, he remained frozen, thinking that retribution for nineteen years of hell was at hand. Then the luminous brown eyes of Alex Goodman as he said, "stop Hennessey", flashed through his mind. That look said, "I trust you and depend on you."

"Alex believes in me," he muttered to himself, working his shoulders, elbows and hands to make a path towards the betting windows two hundred feet distant. Good manners were forgotten as he fought to untangle himself from the cross-tides of bettors headed for vantage points along the rail or towards the ticket sellers.

"It is now seven minutes to post time!" The announcer's call stirred dread in his chest. What had gone wrong? Why hadn't Alex fired the train? When the towering figure of Don Hennessey toppled and Whitey, followed by Herbie, sped to his side, Alex Goodman scanned the clubhouse for Louie Septimo. Any happening out of the ordinary would attract the gangster's attention and shift the odds against the success of Goodman's plan to dynamite the odds board while sheltering Whitey from certain death.

Septimo was at the cigar stand. Alongside was a well-built, curly-haired man. Their backs were turned away from the commotion at the pass-through. But Septimo's people were everywhere.

Ushers, ticket sellers, even the cigar stand attendant might have seen the sudden dash of Whitey Roberts toward the grandstand and alerted Septimo.

So, as the eight horses filed onto the racing oval for the post parade before the start of the sixth race, Alex left the CP for an unscheduled mission He gave himself four minutes to find out if Septimo suspected what Whitey was doing If Septimo did know what Whitey was doing, Alex would take planned countermeasures. These involved the interception by Barney and Lester of Septimo's reserve triggerman, the curly-haired individual with the carnation in his lapel. Barney and Lester should have done their job and been on the way back to the CP.

As he approached Septimo and his companion, the "senator" turned to face him, heavy features struggling to be pleasant.

"The meeting's been on for three weeks, Alex. I wondered if you were going to say hello." He offered his hand and introduced his companion.

"Gus Wales, this is Alex Goodman. We were associated for a short time on the Big A."

"It was Jamaica, Senator, not the big A."

"A sign of age, forgive me." His small eyes glittered beneath heavy lids, taking in the tout's shabby dress and sunken cheeks.

"You were always a good handicapper, Alex. If I ask who you like in this race, I hope you won't send me a bill." He allowed himself a short laugh.

Alex swung his binoculars into position and turned to look at the post parade, now rounding the turn into the backstretch. He focused on Hoist the Blue, number eight. The deep-chested bay was the biggest horse in the race and judging by the tight hold of the jockey, he was full of run. He wore no bandages. There was little question,—from all appearances, that Hoist the Blue was back in the form that had made him one of the choices in the Kentucky Derby future book as a two-year old.

Lowering the binoculars, Alex decided to toss a dart at the "senator", who was smugger than smug.

"This one's on the house, Senator. The best-looking horse is the eight, Hoist The Blue." He looked directly at Septimo.

The coarse olive features blanched. He winced as though he had been slapped.

His eyes narrowed and a single furrow channeled his forehead.

Septimo seemed about to unleash an ugly retort, then thought better of it. He could afford to play it cool. In a few minutes Hoist the Blue would bring him two million dollars and Jack Fenwick's scalp. He pulled out his wallet and peeled off a ten-spot.

"There's time to back your guess, Alex. Here's ten. Go ahead and bet it for yourself on the eight." He couldn't resist showing his scorn. "At twenty to one, this could be your best score in years."

"I don't bet myself, as you know, thanks just the same." Alex nodded at Wales and limped off to the CP. He was drawing it close. The horses were turning back towards the starting gate in the backstretch. But the delay had been worth it. He had not only learned that Septimo was unaware of Whitey's dash for the betting window, but the shocked expression at the mention of Hoist The Blue confirmed his commitment to this horse. Septimo was on the verge of the biggest coup in the history of horseracing. Only a clear working space at the CP and a live fuse could stop him.

The legionnaires, in a belligerent mood, were huddled around the CP. Barney and Lester, back from their brush with Septimo's muscle boys, were joking with the legionnaires, trying to clear the way for Alex.

"It is now three minutes to post time!" The announcement spurred Alex. He sensed the veterans were getting ugly as Barney and Lester tried to steer them from the CP. Alex got his partners' attention and shook his head "no." He glanced at the odds board, still showing 20-1 on Hoist the Blue. Herbie's try to restrain Whitey from betting was a long chance. At any second the odds could drop to 5-1 or less when Whitey shoved his wad through a ticket window. Alex straightened his thin frame. It was now or never.

"Fall in!" The barked command drew smiles from fans that had completed their betting and congregated at the rail. Alex nodded at Barney and Lester, who got his idea. Clicking their heels at attention, they marched several paces toward the clubhouse.

"Legionnaires, fall in!" The command caused the veterans, none the sharper for heavy drinking, to stumble into the line anchored by Barney and Lester.

"Forward, march, column left, march, to the rear march!" The brisk commands cleared the area. Alex arrowed to the CP. Barney and Lester shouldered Alex on either side to form an impenetrable phalanx.

"It is two minutes to post time—the horses are nearing the gate!"

This was it. While Barney and Lester leaned over the rail to shield his movements from railbirds, Alex removed the CP cover to reveal the firing pit. He quickly grasped the split fuse and squeezed the match head. The match flared, but the fuse did not catch. It was dead.

Alex glanced at the stewards' stand. Their binoculars were trained on the starting gate across the infield. The horses were about to be led into their stalls.

It required less than eight seconds for Alex to draw a razor blade from his pocket, cut off the dead section of the fuse, re-cut a fresh elbow, place another match head in the elbow, and squeeze the match into flame.

While Alex was dealing with the interference of the legionnaires, Herbie had his troubles tracking his father's dash to a ticket window. When the two-minute warning sounded, Herbie was locked between walls of people. He dropped to his hands and knees and scrambled through the forest of legs in the direction of Whitey's flight. For a moment, Herbie felt that the blond head of his father was receding, getting away. Whitey Roberts, striking with elbows and fists, beat a path toward a ticket seller's window. Old men, servicemen on a holiday, dowagers, clerks and sailors' girls were all grist for Whitey's manic obsession as he hurled himself toward his goal. Once he fell and angry blows struck his glasses to the pavement. Whitey got up and brushed three bettors aside at once in a final surge to the ten-dollar window.

As Whitey fished a thick stack of currency from his pocket, he was ridden to the pavement by a whirlwind attack from the rear. Whitey staggered to his feet and looked into the tear-stained face of his son.

"Why you dirty sonofabitch!" A heavy fist thrown at Herbie glanced off his shoulder, freeing Whitey from Herbie's grasp long enough so that he could reappear before the startled ticket seller.

"Ten thousand to win on number eight," shrieked Whitey.

Just as the ticket seller was about to punch out the tickets, a shudder shook the concrete canyons, followed by a series of ear-splitting blasts that echoed from wall to wall. Everyone but Whitey Roberts was stopped in his tracks.

"I said ten thousand on number eight," hollered Whitey.

"The machine is locked. I don't know what's happened," gasped the ticket seller," a balding scarecrow of a man, become gray with fright as powerful hands reached through the window and circled his throat. Herbie's fists pounding on Whitey's shoulders finally hammered a message through the red haze of anger. Whitey released the man who quickly vanished from view.

The big bang had always been the least interesting part of a fireworks display for Alex. His powers of concentration on the visual details were so great that even the most violent detonations reached his ears as the distant roar of breakers on a rocky shore. All about the men of Squad B, people screamed and placed their hands over their ears to block out the tremendous shock wave set off by the blast. But to Alex, Barney, Lester and Dennis, what was happening was a thing of beauty. The huge odds board, half the length of a city block, was transformed into four air-borne theater stages, rimmed with tongues of white fire, that lazily spiraled upward and briefly east toward the Atlantic, then settled to the emerald carpet of the infield, the life torn out of it by a man who had earned his livelihood from the huge board for years—Alex Goodman.

The grid work of suddenly useless steel girders that had anchored the odds board, now bent and twisted, slowly crumpled earthward, clawing feebly at the board's entrails.

Hordes of racing fans, pushing and yelling, struggled to the exits. Others seemed paralyzed, staring into the debris. In a corner of the clubhouse, a slim, dark-skinned man dressed in a red riding coat and black boots in the manner of an English country gentleman, drew a revolver and blew his brains out. His name was Carlo Dannon.

Dazed, Whitey Roberts looked around at the incredible scene of panic. A thick blanket of grayish yellow smoke hung twenty feet below the ceiling. The acrid stench of gunpowder stung Whitey's nostrils and forced a fit of coughing. He saw Herbie, catching his breath, young eyes fastened on him.

"What did you do to me, you dirty sonofabitch! What did you do to me?" Whitey continued to scream abuse. But Herbie hardly heard him. The odds board was down. The sixth race never happened. And he, Herbie Roberts, had helped bring the board down. All his life he had tried to use magic to will the impossible. Now he knew that no matter how high the mountain, it could be climbed. With preparation. With planning. With the help of others. Yes, there were costs. Physical pain. Giant fatigue. Great anxieties that accompany the taking of great risks. But these were all transient. A feeling of indescribable triumph swept over him.

Herbie looked at his father. The hard cobalt eyes that had ruled his waking existence and tortured his dreams were watery with tears. Whitey Roberts was weeping for the big one that got away.

"My God," Herbie thought, "I almost let it happen. I almost let you die. You're alive, thanks to me. Yes, I've settled the score between us."

Aloud, he said," "let's go find mother and see that she's all right."

Uncaring whether or not his father went with him, Herbie set off for the clubhouse. His father followed him.

As Don Hennessey's mission came to an untimely end, due to

a fatal coronary occlusion, Jack Fenwick decided to end the career of Louis Septimo. Jack was a patient man. He always gave those in debt to his loan-sharking business one more day to come up with the scratch—for another five percent interest. So, when fifteen minutes went by after the betting opened for the sixth race, and the odds still showed 20-1 on Hoist the Blue, Jack told himself to wait for one more minute. But at 4:19 there was still no change in the odds on the horse on which he had accepted $150,000 in win money at his bookmaking offices up and down the East Coast. By now the layoff money wagered by Pisano and Scott should have lowered the odds to less than even money. So, where were his layoff men? They should have reported back to Fenwick ten minutes ago. The thick neck reddened above his hulking shoulders as the truth sank in. What had looked like a sweetheart deal on a broken- down horse now loomed as a Septimo coup that would take two million dollars from the Fenwick coffers .It would wipe out his New England action.

It took Fenwick a good ten minutes of persistent shoving to reach the clubhouse pass-through from his position on the grandstand apron across from the finish line. Fenwick started through the pass-through, murder in his heart, just as a tremendous explosion shook the racetrack and demolished the odds board. Momentarily dazed, he quickly recovered, staring first with disbelief, then joy to see the wreckage of the board strewn over the infield. The voice of the track announcer blared through the smoky haze:

"Ladies and gentlemen, we're sorry to announce the cancellation of the rest of the day's racing. Please exit slowly and calmly and follow the directions of the track security people."

Fenwick's bloody intentions vanished. His broad, sensual features framed a beatific smile that would have amazed those in the fleeing throngs who looked at him. Unfortunately for Fenwick, his smile was caught and noted by Louis Septimo.

Right up until the odds board was blasted from its foundations, Louie Septimo was having the time of his life. Five minutes after betting opened for the sixth race, the odds still showed 20-1 on Hoist the Blue. This meant that Dimmy and Cooz had made their strike and were on their way to the Cadillac with their pigeons. Twenty minutes later, after the visit by Alex Goodman, the odds were still 20-1. It was then that he stepped up to the cigar stand to purchase a victory cheroot. It was time to relax. There was no way Goodman could know about the fix. He was simply a horseman commenting on a fit—looking animal when he remarked that Hoist The Blue was the best-looking horse in the post parade.

As Hoist The Blue was being led into his stall at the starting gate, Septimo's small, pig—like eyes remained transfixed by the 20-1 odds on Number Eight. Suddenly, the glorious numerals dissolved before his eyes, went black and disappeared in a huge pall of smoke. He was only dimly aware of the massive explosion and shock waves that followed.

With his house of cards collapsing on the floor of the infield, the sleeping volcano inside Septimo's squat trunk erupted. Sweeping the whole scene, he caught the smile of relief on the face of Jack Fenwick and interpreted it, quite naturally, as the smile of a gambling man who has warded off a wipeout by surprising his foe with a full house.

"Fenwick!" The guttural roar burst through the shouts and cries of the departing crowds and speared Fenwick in his tracks. Jubilance quickly gave way to wisdom. Fenwick properly read murder in the menacing, advancing Septimo. He rapidly backed off in the only route open to him—down the paddock path between grandstand and clubhouse, onto the surface of the track itself. Fenwick's neat gray fedora tumbled to the ground, revealing his huge, polished skull.

Septimo followed, brandishing his snub-nosed revolver to melt his way through the dispersing throngs. Among the several thousand witnesses to this scene were Herbie, Whitey, Alex and the partners of Squad B, Myrtle, the Satcor cronies and several dozen tipsy legionnaires become hoarse from cheering the downfall of the odds board.

"They're off!" The cry came from a legionnaire at rail side, his gaze aimed across the infield. Sure enough, Herbie, Alex and the rest of Squad B could see a riderless horse moving swiftly along the backstretch toward the far turn.

"A runaway," said Alex, tugging Herbie to his knees as the others also crouched for safety. The two gangster chieftains had squared off thirty feet in front of the CP.

Weapons in hand, Fenwick and Septimo stared at each other for a long moment reading bottomless hate in the other's eyes. Then flame spit from Septimo's weapon and Fenwick's massive frame slumped slowly to the ground.

Sirens wailed as a fleet of police cars entered the track from the stable area at the head of the stretch. Septimo did not hear them. He advanced over the prostrate form of his enemy and raised his weapon to insure the kill. Just then, the fear-maddened hooves of a bolt of horse lightning flashed across the finish line and found their mark. Septimo crumpled in the dust, his skull crushed by a champion thoroughbred with the number 8 on his saddlecloth.

CHAPTER 32

The stunning end to Whitey's hopes for a cleanup on Hoist The Blue, followed by the demise of Louie Septimo, left him shaken. He was aware that Septimo's organization was a many-headed hydra. It would be no easier with Vincent Curcio on top than it had been with Septimo. Whitey plodded slowly to where Myrtle stood with the Satcor group. Whitey said nothing. Whitey's expression is funereal, thought Frank Bannerman. Frank consulted with the others. They had no idea why Whitey was so despondent, but whatever the reasons, they weren't going to desert their leader in an obvious hour of need.

"Are we going to let a little thing like this disruption derail us? I say we reclaim the high ground with a grand assault on Wonderland." Jake Michaels, like the others, sensed that Whitey had suffered a loss of some kind. What kind of loss was not disclosed by Whitey; that was unimportant. What was important was the maintenance of the high plane of good fellowship to which every member of Satcor subscribed.

"Sounds like the right approach to me," chimed in Bannerman. Sam Dana and Mitch Weller nodded approval. Just then, Alex and Herbie caught up with them, in company with a well dressed, curly-haired man sporting a pink carnation in his lapel. The newcomer, flashing an I.D. from an inside pocket, addressed Whitey:

"Melton Roberts, I'm George Walsh, Federal Bureau of Investigation. I'd like to talk with you about a complaint I have been investigating from Mrs. Margo Alessi."

Whitey promptly came out of the shell to which he had retreated after the violent end of his dream of reclaiming M. Roberts & Company from the mob.

"Yes, I know Mrs. Alessi. Her husband was a friend and customer. Can we talk about this in private?" Whitey's manner was sober and deferential.

"Of course. Alex Goodman has been helpful to your position in this case."

Not a word from Alex, who nodded, confirming a prior discussion with the F.B.I. agent, who had been introduced to him as "Gus Wales" by Septimo an hour earlier.

"See me in my office Monday morning, about 9 o'clock," said Walsh, handing his card to Whitey. He tipped his hat to Myrtle and disappeared in the throng of police and security people flocking to the scene of the encounter between the gangster chieftains.

Whitey said nothing for a moment, then, rousing himself to the realization that the F.B.I. entrance into the situation would likely require a complete shift in his own business future, pulled himself together.

"I think it would be more appropriate, guys, if we did our thing at 55 Green Street rather than at Wonderland. Okay?" The faces of his cronies relaxed. The somber mood dictated by the intrusion of the F.B.I. agent was quickly dissipated. Whitey had reclaimed leadership of Satcor.

The part that his son may have played in the cancellation of the sixth race required further exploration, but in the meantime, Whitey experienced a feeling of relief that the F.B.I. was interested in the present legal owner of M. Roberts & Company, and his name was Vincent Curcio.

Alex suggested that since Herbie was finished with his exams, that he was free to accept an invitation for the next few days at his cousin's farm in Attleboro. Myrtle, recovering from the uncertainty raised by the visit of the F.B.I. agent, said, ""That's wonderful, and you be sure to brush your teeth, dear."

Whitey, unable to look at his son, glanced the other way and grunted his assent.

Herbie concluded that Whitey's buddies knew nothing about the intended wager on Hoist The Blue, since they themselves had made no such wager. Their sympathies were for a friend who they suspected had been in trouble with an underworld organization.

His father's avoidance of him now, when departure from the racetrack was usually accompanied by crossfire of instructions, gave Herbie cause to think for a moment. Was it possible that Whitey thought his son had a hand in dynamiting the odds board? After all, Herbie had registered the strongest possible protest against the wager on Hoist The Blue. First by word, then by physical action. No, concluded Herbie to himself, the afternoon's doings had come off as a power play by two underworld mobs that had washed their dirty linen in public. His father, Herbie figured, was simply adjusting to the shock of a son behaving like a man rather than the timid boy he had always controlled.

Herbie kissed his mother, gave a half-salute to his father. "See you Tuesday night," he said, adding "don't worry, everything will be all right."

As most of the fans continued to file out, some lingered. They stood mute at the rail or tried to get onto the track itself as fire engines, police and ambulance vehicles put on their show. Sirens screamed. Huge columns of water were hurled on the smoldering remains of the odds board. The police held back the rubbernecks as stretchers took away the bodies of Fenwick, Septimo, Hennessey, and Carlo Dannon. Some persons wept. Herbie told himself that their tears were inspired by the death of the odds board rather than the deaths of four strangers.

Herbie felt tremendous exaltation, a feeling that must be shared. He realized how much he had changed over the past year. How differently he felt about himself. And about his father. He wondered at his own calmness. And at the conviction he had felt when he told his father everything would be all right.

The jubilation that surged beneath the surface of his calmness exploded finally, in the van on its way to Attleboro. Herbie sat squeezed between Alex and Dennis on the front seat of the van. However uncomfortable the seating, nothing could affect his jubilation. "Wowee! Holy mackerel!" Joy burst forth unbounded for ten minutes. The trio bombarded each other with exclamations, questions and compliments. In the rear view mirror, Herbie saw Barney and Lester having their own celebration in the Buick trailing them through the Sumner Tunnel.

Once through the Tunnel, Barney and Lester waved goodbye, on their way to Connecticut. Alex stopped at a gas station near the exit. There he made two phone calls while the van was refueled. Headed south towards Attleboro, Herbie and Dennis looked questioningly at Alex "I called the FBI, told them if they checked out a certain black Cadillac in the parking lot at Atlantic Downs, they would make an interesting discovery." Alex smiled: "Barney told me that the guns which shot Fenwick's men were in the right hands when he and Lester left the Caddy." Alex smiled and continued, "in the hands of the murderers, Garino and Coozman. Unloaded, of course."

Herbie was puzzled. "You mean their hands were left free? They won't be in the car when the FBI gets there."

Dennis chuckled. "When Barney ties his electrician's knots, a gorilla could have a bunch of bananas in his hands and starve to death."

When the van cleared Dedham traffic and straightened away down Route 1, Herbie thought it was time to ask questions.

"Alex, you said you had to make two phone calls. Want to tell us about the second call?"

"I called Reuben at the farm. I believe he's going to have a special welcome for us." Alex smiled, but there was tension in his voice and about his eyes when he spoke.

"We certainly had the wrong slant on the F.B.I. agent, Walsh," said Herbie. "Here we thought all along he was muscle for Septimo."

"My guess is that he sold himself to Septimo, under the name of Gus Wales, as a former F.B.I. agent looking for work either as muscle or syndicate spotter. And all the while he was getting closer to the extortion racket going on under the cover of M. Roberts & Company." Alex got serious.

""From what we know, M. Roberts is in Curcio's name. And Curcio has taken over half a dozen hotels and restaurants in the past five months, all of who were in debt to M. Roberts. Does that sound about right?"

"I guess so," replied Herbie.

"Curcio was getting away with these takeovers, evidently, until the widow of one of the owners who killed himself, went to the F.B.I. What was his name—Alessi?"

"That's correct," said Herbie.

"I'd say that Vincent Curcio and M. Roberts are in big trouble. And your father, frankly, lucked out, when he signed his company over to Curcio."

"So you think he can reopen his beef business?" Herbie showed some anxiety in his expression.

"Not likely. At least not under his own name."

Herbie brightened. "In that case, all my father has to worry about is what business to get going again, with his ten thousand."

"Wrong," said Alex.

Dennis butted in. "What Alex means is that your father could have more than ten thousand to invest."

"As a member of this dynamiting team, you get a full share of the layoff money that Barney and Lester recovered. It came to one hundred fifty thousand dollars, so your share is thirty thousand. You can do what you want with it."

As Herbie started to speak, Alex continued: "Just remember that any money you give your father has to be explained. I can't give you any help on this except to suggest that you disobeyed his instructions not to bet."

"Well," said Herbie, thinking how resilient Whitey had proven in other crises, "It might be a good thing that he has to start over again."

"That's what Dennis and I are doing," said Alex.

"Amen," said Dennis.

At age 37, Angela Goodman was beautiful, divorced, employed as personnel manager for a New York department store. She was also the mother of Max and Dinah Goodman, ages twelve and fourteen. For ten years, Angela had suffered the pain of separation from the one man she had ever loved, Alex Goodman. Severed from her marriage by societal pressures, Angela had bridged the gulf between herself and Alex with yearly visits to Alex's kin, Reuben and Nancy Glass, believing that some day the gulf would be eliminated. Alex's voice on the phone had been warm, encouraging, and full of anxiety. The call he made from Boston had brought back the pain, embarrassment and anger surrounding their separation ten years earlier. It had also reminded her of the wonderful promise of their coming together, student and teacher, the ripening of that classroom meeting into joyful love and marriage.

Now, Reuben and Nancy shared hope and anxiety about the coming encounter. What if they had made a mistake calling Angela to come to Attleboro at once because Alex needed her? No question—Alex did need Angela, had always needed her. But the resolve Alex had expressed about changing his life's direction had finalized their determination to play God.

"It's now or never, Rose," Reuben had said, after conveying to her the fact that Alex was interested in saying goodbye to the precarious existence of the racetrack in favor of a solid engineering career.

When the van turned off the highway onto the long, narrow dirt road connecting the Glass farm to the outside world, Herbie could feel the tension in Alex hunched over the wheel next to him. Why was Alex so tense, so anxious about what should be a happy visit to his cousin? The answer came swiftly: of course, Angela was the "special welcome" Alex had mentioned in reporting the phone call to Reuben.

Herbie smiled; his smile was caught by Dennis and interpreted as another roof of Herbie's psychic abilities.

The five people waiting on the porch were the first solid evidence of the new life of Alex Goodman.

As Alex leaped from the cab and flew up the stairs to Angela, Herbie said to Dennis: "In the language used by Alex that brought

Barney and Lester to Atlantic Downs this past week, the destruction of the odds board was a "crossing", as the crossing of the Marne was in 1918. Right?"

"That's right, Herbie. But as tough as those two crossings were—and believe me, they were tough, what Alex is doing right now, this very minute, is the toughest 'crossing' of them all."

Watching Alex embrace Angela and seeing her fiercely warm response, elicited a crisp response from Herbie.

"Looks like a piece of cake to me."

9 780738 828091

90000